CRASH
AND BURN

Books by Fern Michaels:

No Safe Secret
Wishes for Christmas
Fancy Dancer
About Face
Perfect Match
A Family Affair
Forget Me Not
The Blossom Sisters
Balancing Act
Tuesday's Child
Betrayal
Southern Comfort
To Taste the Wine
Sins of the Flesh
Sins of Omission
Return to Sender
Mr. and Miss Anonymous
Up Close and Personal
Fool Me Once
Picture Perfect
The Future Scrolls
Kentucky Sunrise
Kentucky Heat
Kentucky Rich
Plain Jane
Charming Lily
What You Wish For
The Guest List
Listen to Your Heart
Celebration
Yesterday
Finders Keepers
Annie's Rainbow
Sara's Song

Vegas Sunrise
Vegas Heat
Vegas Rich
Whitefire
Wish List
Dear Emily
Christmas at Timberwoods

The Sisterhood Novels:

Crash and Burn
Point Blank
In Plain Sight
Eyes Only
Kiss and Tell
Blindsided
Gotcha!
Home Free
Déjà Vu
Cross Roads
Game Over
Deadly Deals
Vanishing Act
Razor Sharp
Under the Radar
Final Justice
Collateral Damage
Fast Track
Hokus Pokus
Hide and Seek
Free Fall
Lethal Justice
Sweet Revenge

Books by Fern Michaels (Continued):

The Jury
Vendetta
Payback
Weekend Warriors

The Men of the Sisterhood
  Novels:

Fast and Loose
Double Down

The Godmothers Series:

Classified
Breaking News
Deadline
Late Edition
Exclusive
The Scoop

E-Book Exclusives:

Desperate Measures
Seasons of Her Life
To Have and to Hold
Serendipity
Captive Innocence

Captive Embraces
Captive Passions
Captive Secrets
Captive Splendors
Cinders to Satin
For All Their Lives
Texas Heat
Texas Rich
Texas Fury
Texas Sunrise

Anthologies:

When the Snow Falls
Secret Santa
A Winter Wonderland
I'll Be Home for Christmas
Making Spirits Bright
Holiday Magic
Snow Angels
Silver Bells
Comfort and Joy
Sugar and Spice
Let It Snow
A Gift of Joy
Five Golden Rings
Deck the Halls
Jingle All the Way

FERN MICHAELS

CRASH AND BURN

KENSINGTON PUBLISHING CORP.
http://www.kensingtonbooks.com

KENSINGTON BOOKS are published by

Kensington Publishing Corp.
119 West 40th Street
New York, NY 10018

All Kensington titles, imprints, and distributed lines are available at special quantity discounts for bulk purchases for sales promotion, premiums, fund-raising, educational, or institutional use.

Special book excerpts or customized printings can also be created to fit specific needs. For details, write or phone the office of the Kensington Special Sales Manager: Kensington Publishing Corp., 119 West 40th Street, New York, NY, 10018. Attn. Special Sales Department. Phone: 1-800-221-2647.

Kensington and the K logo Reg. U.S. Pat. & TM Off.

Library of Congress Control Number: 2016933901

ISBN-13: 978-1-4967-0313-2
ISBN-10: 1-4967-0313-8
First Kensington Hardcover Edition: September 2016

10 9 8 7 6 5 4 3 2 1

Printed in the United States of America

CRASH AND BURN

Prologue

The young woman walked down the familiar path that she alone had created. It was bordered on both sides by wild, fragrant ferns. She loved the scent of them, of the wet earth, the brush, and even the smell that the trees gave off. This was her place, her secret place. She came here in the spring, summer, autumn, and winter. Sometimes just to be here, other times to sit and think; and sometimes, like now, to take a dip in the little crystal pool, which was all her own, before going to bed.

This secret place, which she considered all her own, was usually quiet and peaceful, but in the summer months, especially now that it was late in August, she could hear the going-away parties a mile or so down the road. The summer educational camps were closing for the season. All the students had left this morning. She'd seen and heard the buses as they trundled up the hills to take the students back to their families.

That night was the going-away party for all the counselors. She'd lived through the sounds of them for twenty years, not that she knew what the noise was all about until she was twelve or so. From that day on, her mother and the others in the little community made sure that all the young girls were inside, safely hidden away from the revelers, who too often tried to make their way to gawk at the strange hippies who lived here in the little community. But she was twenty now and not exactly a young girl who needed her mother's protection to keep her safe.

As she walked along the path, a nymph in a free-flowing white-muslin gown, her feet bare, flowers in her hair, she knew she shouldn't be out here tonight—the night of the counselors' going-away party. But she had spent the entire day with her dying mother—combing her hair, crying, singing to her, crying, reading to her, crying some more. Feeding her or trying to feed her, but her mother said it hurt too much to swallow. She'd asked for more pills, and the girl had given them to her, knowing it couldn't hurt. Not now. It wouldn't be long now, another day or so, the doctor from the small town had said. She didn't want to think about that. Not now, not tonight. Tomorrow, she would think about it. Tonight, all she wanted to do was dip into her little pond and let her thoughts be washed away.

She took off her gown, folded it neatly, and slid into the cool, bubbling springwater. It felt delicious. She closed her eyes, but the blessed peace that she always felt here in her secret place eluded her. She could hear the partying counselors laughing and bellowing to one another. College boys. Mostly *rich* college boys having a good time before they went back to their studies. She opened her eyes and looked up at the sky. It had turned orange from the bonfire that always signaled the closing of the camps. She hated the intrusion in the quiet life of the small community she and her mother were a part of.

The stars seemed to be incredibly bright tonight, she thought—so many sparkling diamonds winking down on her. There was a full moon, too. Her mother said bad things happened when the moon was full. She wasn't really sure if she believed that or not. Her mother said a lot of things she wasn't sure about. When she was younger, she had believed everything. But as she got older, she had started to ask questions. Her mother always answered, but the answers weren't always to her liking. Her thoughts turned sad. In a few days, her mother would be gone, and she would never hear her opinions again. She would miss her mother. The woman had always been in her life, her rock. She'd had a father for only five days. At least he had lived to see her born before he passed away from some sickness whose name she couldn't even pronounce. Her mother said that he was a good man, a wonderful man, because he had provided for them and all hundred friends who still lived in the little community in the hills.

It would be her responsibility to take over the community once her mother was gone. She dreaded the day she had to put on her mother's robes. Life was not going to give her any alternatives, so she had to step up and run the community. There was enough money in the bank, her mother had told her, because her father had been very, very rich. The property alone, she said, was worth many millions of dollars.

The girl blinked. She'd been so lost in her thoughts she hadn't noticed that the bonfire was already dying down; the sky was now black, but it was still filled with blinking diamonds. The full moon was the only light in the dark night. It was also quiet. Too quiet. She could hear the trees rustling, but not the crickets. And yet there was very little wind—actually, none at all, so how could the trees rustle? She felt her body go tense in the cool water. There must be someone nearby; otherwise, the crickets would still be singing their evening song. She paddled to the edge of her private pond and got out. She stood still for a moment, a silhouette frozen in the moonlight as she listened for the sounds she'd heard earlier. Hearing nothing, she bent over to pick up her white-muslin gown, which was as soft as a baby's cheeks from so many launderings.

That's when she heard the voices. She wasn't sure exactly what a drunken voice sounded like, since there was no drinking alcohol in the community, but she assumed that was what she was hearing. The remarks were crude and ugly. She wanted to run home, but her private path back to the house she shared with her mother was blocked by five men, who looked very young. They were obviously departing camp counselors.

Four of them came at her then, all at once. Even in her panic, she could clearly see one young man back away. He was shouting something to his friends, but she couldn't hear what he was saying because the others were grabbing at her, touching her in places she wasn't supposed to be touched. She cried out, asking them to stop. They just laughed at her feeble efforts to avoid them. She turned to the one young man standing alone, and cried out for him to help her. He disappeared into the darkness, and she was left alone with the drunk men, who kept shouting gibberish as they threw her to the ground and attacked her, one after the other. Her last conscious thought before she slipped into a black void was that she had to remember the gibberish. She had to remember—"qg4+qg6" and "bf7 bxf3."

The girl woke slowly, remembering very clearly every single detail of what had happened to her. The moon was low in the sky, which had to mean that several hours had passed since the attack. Her body hurt. She felt like she was bruised from head to toe. She wasn't sure if she could even stand, so she rolled her way down to her little private pool and into the cool water. She almost fainted at the shock to her body. She closed her eyes.

She wanted to die. Just die. But she couldn't die. It was her mother who was dying. She had to take care of her mother in her last hours. How, she wondered, was she going to do that in her condition? *By sheer willpower,* she answered herself.

The girl stayed in the pool for a long time, time to gather her strength and to repeat over and over the gibberish she'd heard as the men pummeled her. Gibberish she would never forget as long as she lived.

It was an hour before dawn when the girl finally felt she was strong enough to climb out of the water and make her way down the fern-bordered path to her mother's cabin. The soft white-muslin gown felt like sandpaper against her bruised body.

The girl crept quietly up the different paths that led to the wide array of cabins in which her mother's friends lived. She quietly let herself into the house and down the hall to her mother's room, which smelled of sickness and over-ripe fruit. She tried to be quiet, but her mother heard her.

"Where have you been, honey? I've been calling you. Please, can I have a pill?"

"Of course, Mama. It was hot. I went down by the little pond. I lost . . . track of time."

She shook two pills into the palm of her hand and helped her mother sit up so she could swallow them.

"What's wrong?" her mother said. "Did something happen? I can feel your tenseness. You've been crying, I can hear it in your voice, and it has nothing to do with me. Tell me what happened."

Because never in the whole of her life had she lied to her mother—she, in fact, did not even know how to lie—she told her what had happened down at her little pond. She told her about the gibberish she'd stored in her memory. Her mother stopped her and told her to immediately write down what she remembered. "In the morning, our friends will help you. You will have to file a police report. Can you describe them?" The girl nodded. Like she would ever forget their ugly, leering faces? "The day will come, my darling girl, when those words will be important. Do not ever forget them. I don't know when that will happen, but it most definitely will happen. Can I please have a pill, honey?"

Even though she'd just given her mother two of the pain pills, she gave her another one. No one should have to suffer the way her mother was suffering. Unless it was the four men who attacked her.

As the sun began its climb to the horizon, the woman in the bed slipped into eternal sleep, the weeping girl's hand in her own.

Chapter 1

It was early. Just barely past seven in the morning, when Alexis Thorne carried her cup of steaming coffee, the first of the many she would consume on this blustery early-October day, over to the huge, plate-glass window and stared down at the nearly empty parking lot. Her BMW was the only car in the lot so far that day. She sipped at the hot coffee just as another vehicle, Nikki's bright red Jeep Cherokee, swerved off the street and into the parking lot and came to rest next to hers. She smiled to herself. As was always the case, she and Nikki were the first ones into the office, beating each other out by a bare minute or two. She laughed out loud when she saw Nikki look up at the window and snap off a salute. Alexis did the same, unsure if Nikki could actually see her past the glare of the bright, early-morning sun on the window.

Alexis continued to watch her boss as Nikki sprinted across the lot like a gazelle. Alexis was holding out a matching mug of coffee when Nikki blew into the firm's kitchen. "Beat you by seven minutes, boss."

"Traffic was a bear this morning. Bumper to bumper two lights back, and I even left ten minutes early this morning. Hmmm, this is good."

"New coffeepot," Alexis said, giggling. "What's on the agenda today? Anything earth-shattering?"

"Not on my part. I have a ten o'clock appointment this morning. I don't even know what it's about. Mitzi said the woman refused, yes, absolutely refused to discuss with her why she wanted the appointment. Very mysterious. My new girl is due at eight-thirty to finalize her divorce. I plan to leave at noon if nothing else comes up.

"Listen, Alexis, we need to talk here. I really want to make you a partner in the firm. Why do you keep fighting me?"

"Because you have already done enough for me. You pay me way more than I'm worth, and we both know it. I'm happy with the health benefits. This is *your* firm, Nik. Yours and yours alone. I know what you had to do to get to this point, and I'm not going to take any of that away from you. If the day ever comes when I think I deserve a partnership, I'll let you know. Another thing—I really, really do not want to be perceived as the firm's token black partner. I know full well that you and the other associates don't look at it that way, but there are lots of other people who will."

"If anyone ever deserved to be a partner, Alexis, it's certainly you. Without you at my side, we never could have handled those two class-action suits. You did more than I did, and you know it. You need to be rewarded for all your hard work. Because of those two big wins, we suddenly became the go-to firm for class-action suits. That's the reason I'm hiring this new girl. And I have two more I'm considering."

"One more time, Nik. You did reward me with that super-duper end-of-the-year bonus that made my eyeballs pop out of my head and let me buy that monster sitting in the parking lot. I don't need or want anything more. Can we stop talking about this now?"

"Sure. For now. Doesn't mean I won't keep trying,

though. By the way, you are coming out to the farm tonight, right? With all the guys in New York on some secret gig, you can leave your car here, hitch a ride with me, and come in with me in the morning. Does that work for you?"

"Absolutely. A hen party and not a rooster in sight. My kind of party. Did you call everyone?"

"Everyone other than Maggie, since this meeting is about her. Don't look at me like that, Alexis. You know as well as I do that we all need to talk this through. The others agree."

"It's not that I disagree, Nik. It's more like . . . oh, I don't know . . . maybe I'm feeling disloyal or something. Uh-oh, you'd better check this out. There's some drama going on down there in the parking lot. I think it's your new associate. And is that her husband? The one she's divorcing? She's got a lip-lock on him like you wouldn't believe. Or . . . is that guy someone she had waiting in the wings?"

Nikki ran over to the window to look down at the parking lot. "That's the soon-to-be ex-husband. I have to say, this is, without a doubt, the strangest case of divorce I've ever handled. You know who he is, right?"

"No, actually, I have no idea. Should I?"

"He's Jeffrey Lambert, son of the current Speaker of the House, Wilson 'Buzz' Lambert. Jeffrey Lambert started up that software company called Lobo, the one that just went on the stock exchange at the beginning of the year. If you believe the hype and the media, the guy has money blowing out his ears.

"He wants to give Amy half, and she won't take it. She settled for a set of assorted bedding, some dishes, a Crock-Pot, and a few other odds and ends. It got a little contentious at our last meeting. She doesn't want anything. It's weird. They actually love each other, but they are not *in* love. They're both agreeable to the divorce and want to remain friends. Will that work? Who knows? If I had to guess, I'd say *probably,* but only because he will be on the West Coast and she'll be in the D.C. area.

"Actually, Myra said she could stay in our safe house. You remember, the one that belonged to Marie Llewellyn, the woman who got the Sisterhood off the ground in the first place when we defended her. We keep it up and use it when needed. Amy is all set. She's going to be a great addition to the firm. I can feel it in my gut."

Alexis nodded. "Looks to me like they're both crying. I'm not getting this."

"Me neither. This is how Amy explained it to me. She said they were like an old comfortable shoe and a warm sock. They found each other in college, at a time when they each needed someone. She said there was never any passion, just contentment. She wanted more, and so did he, but for five years, neither one wanted to rock the boat. Once Amy passed the bar exam, and Jeffrey got his company off the ground, they became a little more vocal about their needs, wants, and expectations, and, for better or worse, this is the outcome."

Alexis nodded. "I think they're coming in now, and they're holding hands. Why is he even here?"

"Because he has to sign off on the divorce. He absolutely insisted on setting up a trust fund for Amy. Margie is handling all of that. He needs to sign off on that, too. Amy balked, but he shut her down and said he wouldn't agree to the divorce unless she agreed to the trust. He finally wore her down."

"Is there a lot of money involved?" Alexis asked.

"Oh, yeah," Nikki drawled. "The number of zeros is enough to make you dizzy. Amy no more needs to work than Annie does. Not that she is likely to touch any of the money in that trust. That guy is right up there, nipping at Mark Zuckerberg's heels. You know, the Facebook guy."

"Just when I thought nothing else could surprise me, I

hear something like this. You'd better get moving. By the way, I just realized that since you're leaving at noon, I'll have to drive myself out to the farm. I have two late-afternoon appointments back-to-back. And the more I think about it, I might even be late, depending on traffic. Don't start without me."

"No problem. You want to meet the new associate?"

"It can wait. I need another cup of coffee before I'm ready to face strangers. Good luck with the Bobbsey Twins."

Nikki found herself giggling all the way back to her office. Before she did anything else, she turned on the gas fireplace in the casual seating area, which she preferred to use rather than dealing with clients, at least the ones she cared about, over her massive, shiny, cold desk. She knew that Mitzi Doyle, her office manager and notary public, would have a pot of coffee on the coffee table before her clients made their way to the office. Before that thought could leave her mind, Mitzi, a motherly gray-haired woman, appeared, tray in hand. "Anything else, Nikki?"

"Nope, I'm good, Mitzi. Thanks. By the way, hold my calls, and I'm planning on leaving at noon. You can reach me at home, if you need me. You can show the Lamberts in now."

They were such a nice-looking couple, Nikki thought, as they all shook hands and seated themselves. Amy was petite, a ball of fire with blond hair and eyes that were laser blue. Jeffrey was tall, ripped, with dark, untamed, curly hair, and puppy-dog-brown eyes. Both of them had killer smiles, which they didn't show often enough, at least to her knowledge. "Coffee?"

"I think I have already had my quota for the day," Jeffrey Lambert said. Amy nodded as she kept trying to shred her fingers, which refused to remain still in her lap.

Nikki poured herself a cup of coffee and leaned back. "You both look so nervous. Why is that? You ironed everything out weeks ago. We spoke on the phone, and you both assured me that things were on track. It's okay if you have changed your minds. It happens more often than you know."

"It's just that . . . neither one of us has ever been divorced. I guess it finally hit us that this is the end of . . . of . . . our being together. We won't be cooking any more meals together or meeting up to eat something on the run at the end of the day. No more movie nights. No more sharing our day's experiences. Togetherness will be just a memory, and I find it sad, but, no, I haven't changed my mind, and neither has Jeff. We are going to go through with the divorce. Just tell us where to sign, so Jeff can catch his flight back to California." Nikki cringed at the jitteriness she was hearing in Amy's voice.

Nikki made a big production out of leafing through the folder on the coffee table in the hopes that she was covering up what she was suddenly feeling. She didn't know why, but she didn't have a good feeling about this divorce. Finally, when she realized she couldn't stall any longer, she placed the papers in front of the young couple. "My notary is on the way in, so it will be just another minute."

Amy Lambert went back to shredding her fingers, while her husband, for the moment, stared at the Jackson Pollock paintings on the wall. Nikki thought he looked more nervous than his wife. She felt her sudden uneasiness ramp up a notch. She let loose with a soft sigh the moment Mitzi and her notary stamp appeared. Seven minutes later, everything was in order, and the Lamberts were on their feet, waiting to shake Nikki's hand.

"Amy, I'll see you on the first of November, when you report for work. I was going to have you meet up with Alexis Thorne this morning, but her calendar is full. So when you get here for your first day of work, ask for Mitzi Doyle, the woman who just notarized your divorce papers.

She's also our office manager, and she'll take you down to HR so you can get all of that out of the way. That's when you'll meet with Alexis.

"Everything at the house is ready for you. You'll have to do some grocery shopping, but that's about it. Is there anything else I can do for you before you leave?"

The Lamberts shook their heads and tried for smiles, which never quite made it to their faces, much less their eyes.

"Well, then, I guess this is good-bye, Mr. Lambert. Don't worry about Amy. We'll take good care of her."

Out in the hall, Nikki leaned up against the wall as she struggled to take a long, deep breath. *Something's out of kilter* was all she could think of to explain her sudden attack of nervousness. Long ago, she'd learned to pay attention to such feelings. She pushed away from the wall and headed straight for the door whose plaque said the office belonged to Alexis Thorne. She rapped softly, turned the knob, and peeked into the room. "Good, you're alone. I have to say that was one stressful meeting. And yet nothing happened. We were up to speed on everything. Smooth as silk, as they say. I had this crazy set of feelings, almost a panic attack. I don't know why. Some days, and this is one of them, I hate being a lawyer."

"What's happening?" Alexis asked.

What was happening was that Amy Lambert was licking at her lips. There was so much she wanted to say to this fine young man who was still her husband until a judge stamped her divorce papers. But the words wouldn't come, and even if she had known what to say, she seriously doubted that she would have been able to give voice to them. And to her eye, it looked like Jeffrey was having the same problem.

"Amy, if you . . . if you ever need anything, anything at

all, promise you'll call. You know I'm not just saying the words. I mean it. I think you know me better than anyone on earth, even better than my mother knows me."

Amy's head bobbed up and down. When Jeffrey walked out of Nikki's office to go to Margie Baylor's to sign the trust agreement, he was also walking out of Amy's life. At that moment, she had at least a two-minute window of time to change her mind. If she wanted. The door opened. Scratch the two minutes. This was it. She clenched her teeth so hard, she thought she might have cracked a tooth. *Don't cry. Crying is a sign of weakness. You can do this. You're a big girl now. Right now, Amy Jones, you are on your own. I should have told Jeff I was taking back my maiden name. Why didn't I do that? Why? Probably because I thought it would be like pouring salt on an open wound. How could I tell him that I don't want to be associated any longer with the name* Lambert—*not because of Jeff, but because of his father and those around him?*

Damn, she should have left when Nikki left. There was no reason for her still to be standing there, and yet, there she was. She whirled around to search for her purse, found it, and slung it over her shoulder. From somewhere deep inside, she managed to drag out the words. "Let's not say good-bye, Jeff. Let's just go with 'I'll see ya.' If I find the law isn't for me, I might hit you up for a job at some point. Don't forget to send me a Christmas card." She was stunned at how blasé her tone was. Mind over matter. She almost faltered at the strange look she was seeing on Jeff's face. *Move! Just get the hell out of here. Move. Don't think. Go, for God's sake.* Earlier, on their way into the building, Jeffrey had warned her that the office might be bugged and to be careful with what she said.

How she got to the lobby, she didn't know. And then she was outside, with the fierce October wind bent on attacking her as her hair blew in every direction. She walked around the building to the employee parking lot and her sad little gray Honda Accord, which had 140,000 miles on it. She'd insisted on driving it cross-country because she knew she would need a car to get around once she reached her final destination. Jeff had insisted on driving with her and refused to take no for an answer, saying he would fly back. Jeff had wanted to buy her a new car, a fancy high-end Mercedes, but she had declined his generous offer. How noble she was, how proud. She'd gone into the marriage with nothing, and that's how she was leaving it. She had no intention of touching the money in the trust fund. She had her pride.

Amy wrestled with her wild mane of hair as she tried to pull it back into a ponytail. Finally satisfied that she could see, she started the engine. It purred to life like a contented cat. As she was typing in the address to her new, albeit temporary, home on the portable dashboard GPS, a gift from Jeff, she saw a shiny black Lincoln Town Car drive past her and park next to a bright red Jeep Cherokee. As she waited for traffic to slow, she watched the car in her side mirror, saw a man in a dark suit wearing a chauffeur's cap get out and open the passenger door in the back. She gasped as a tall, handsome man with snow-white hair, despite his relatively young age, got out and strode forward. "Damn!" Amy fumbled with her cell phone and pressed the number one on her speed dial.

"Pick up, Jeff! C'mon, pick up." And then she heard his voice, and she calmed down.

"What? You're missing me already?" The words were lame sounding, but still music to her ears.

"Listen to me. I was leaving the parking lot, and your father was just arriving. He's entering the building now, Jeff. *Now.*"

"Are you sure?"

"Of course I'm sure. I even recognized his driver. Your

father, the Speaker of the House, is now in the building. Okay, I'm outta here. Have a good flight, Jeff. Send me a text when you land, so I know you arrived safe and sound."

"Okay, *Mother*." It was meant to sound funny, and it might have come across that way if the tone hadn't been so brittle and brusque. Amy didn't bother to respond. Wilson "Buzz" Lambert, the Speaker of the House of Representatives, was not her problem. Not any longer. He was Jeffrey's problem. She would never forget the day Buzz, of all people, called her a gold digger, among even other less-than-flattering names. Never.

Amy cracked her window, then slid a CD into the portable player that Jeffrey had installed for her. She smiled. She loved Bon Jovi. So did Jeff. Scratch Jeff. She had to stop including Jeff in her thoughts. It was just her now. *Amy Jones*. She felt a momentary thrill of excitement at her maiden name. *Amy Jones. Look out, world, here I come—a little late to the game I intend to be playing, but I'm here now. And when the game is over, the whole world will know about who I am and how I won.*

Jeffrey Lambert, CEO and principal shareholder of Lobo, son of the Speaker of the House, Wilson "Buzz" Lambert, was thinking almost the same thing as his now ex-wife. *I'm here now, inside the building, and what do I do?* Such a stupid question he thought as he ended his call with Amy and scrawled his signature to finalize the trust fund he'd set up for her. Sweat beaded on his forehead. He suddenly felt stupid to have thought he could get in and out of Washington without meeting up with good old Buzz.

"Is there any way I can leave here beside through the door I just came through, Ms. Baylor?"

Margie Baylor banged down on the stapler, looked up, and pointed to a door to the left of her office. "That door will take you to the outside corridor that leads straight out to the parking lot."

Jeff's mind raced. He wished he could take the time to explain to this nice lawyer, with the panicky look, why he was acting like he was, but he simply did not have the time. "I don't want to go to the parking lot. Is there another way?"

"I'm sorry, but that's it. You could take the steps or the elevator to the basement, walk up one flight, which will bring you inches from the revolving door at the entrance. There's usually a line of cabs waiting. Well, maybe not a line of cabs, but at least one or two. Is everything all right, Mr. Lambert?"

"No, everything is not all right. I understand my father is in the building, and I want to avoid him. He's a pretty forceful kind of individual and is probably right now trying to intimidate your receptionist and your office manager with his bluster. Look, I just need to get out of here!"

Margie laughed. "Our people do not know or recognize the word *intimidate*. We're women! I assure you that if anyone is going to be intimidated, it will be your father. Nikki trained us well. Like I said, we're women!" She pointed to the side door, and said, "Go!" Jeffrey didn't need to be told twice. He literally flew through the doorway.

"Never a dull moment at the Quinn Law Firm," Margie mumbled under her breath. She pressed a button on the console and spoke quietly. "I need you to take these papers over to the courthouse and have them filed. I'd like you to do it *now*, Judy."

"Yes, ma'am, I can do that. There is someone here to see you. He doesn't have an appointment."

Margie's mind raced. She knew who it was. "And what is our rule here at the Quinn Law Firm, Judy?"

"The attorneys only see clients with appointments. Mr.

Lambert is insistent, Ms. Baylor. He asked me to tell you he is the Speaker of the House."

"All our clients are treated equally. One more time, what is our rule here at the Quinn Law Firm, Judy? Tell the Speaker to make an appointment." That said, Margie hightailed it out the same doorway Jeffrey Lambert had just gone through. She did exactly what she told Jeffrey to do. She rode the elevator to the basement and walked up a flight of steps to the lobby and was through the revolving door in minutes. Outside, a cab was at the curb. She climbed in, and said, "Take me to the courthouse." She leaned back against the cracked leather seat. Sometimes, you just had to do things yourself. It was important to Jeffrey Lambert to have the trust documents filed today. As his attorney, it was her job to make sure it happened.

This whole thing—the ever-so-friendly divorce, the unwanted trust, and the Speaker of the House showing up at the eleventh hour—was enough to boggle her mind, and yet people said the law was boring. She sniffed. Those people didn't know anything about the all-female Quinn Law Firm. Not a damn thing. Nikki's mantra, to which they all subscribed, was "Take no prisoners."

While Margie's cab crawled through traffic, Buzz Lambert was railing at her secretary, demanding to see the head of the firm.

"I'm sorry, *Mister* Speaker, but rules are rules. I have a job here that I love, and I want and intend to keep this job. I will, however, call Ms. Quinn to see if she has time to meet with you. Take a seat, please," said Judy.

"Don't you dare to tell me what to do, young lady. It works the other way around—I tell you what to do. Is it necessary for me to remind you who I am? I need to get back to the Hill."

"No, sir, you have already told me four times who you

are. But it just doesn't matter. You are not my employer, and you do not set policy for the Quinn Law Firm. Now, either you sit down or you leave, or I will be forced to call security. How do you think that is going to look on the evening news? I can just hear the news anchor: 'And now a story about the Speaker of the House, Buzz Lambert, being escorted by security out of the building housing the Quinn Law Firm. Calls to the Speaker's office asking for comment on the incident have not been returned.' I am calling Ms. Quinn now."

Buzz couldn't believe that this slip of a girl was telling him, the man two heartbeats away from becoming the president of the United States, what to do. And yet, here he was, sitting down. He seethed like a fire-breathing dragon as he waited.

"Ms. Quinn instructed me to escort you to her office. She said she can give you five minutes, not one minute longer, as she has a client who is due to arrive momentarily. Here at the Quinn Law Firm, we do our best not to keep our clients waiting. Follow me, sir."

Nikki was standing in the open doorway to her office. She nodded to Judy that she should return to her own office, that she could and would handle things from here on in. "Mr. Speaker, I'm Nikki Quinn. This is my firm. I don't care who you are or why you're here, but do not ever try to bluster your way in here and try to intimidate my employees. We do not tolerate that kind of behavior. You have five minutes, so talk fast. I have a client who is due to arrive any minute."

"Where's my son? Where's that gold digger he married? Jeffrey's mother told me they were getting divorced and that you were handling the divorce."

"I have not the slightest clue as to the current whereabouts of your son. I assume that he has finished what he came here to do and has departed. Likewise for his wife.

"And as a lawyer yourself, you should know that I cannot discuss my clients' business with you. This might sound trite, but I would bet dollars to donuts that you have your son's phone number and access to a telephone. Perhaps you should try calling him to find out where he is, instead of coming here and disrupting my law firm. I think we're done here, Mr. Speaker."

"This isn't the end of it, lady," Buzz blustered. He couldn't remember the last time anyone had talked to him like this blond floozy. Even men didn't dare talk to him like she had.

His face red and mottled like the old bricks on the building, Wilson "Buzz" Lambert turned on his heel and marched down the hall, his back ramrod stiff.

The fine hairs on the back of Nikki's neck moved. So her gut was right, and right now her gut was telling her that the Speaker's words were true. This wasn't the end of the Lambert divorce, not by a long shot.

Chapter 2

The dowdy-looking woman in the stretched-out sweater, ankle-length skirt, and shoes with run-down heels spotted the Speaker of the House a second too late. She'd stepped into the revolving door just as the Speaker gave it a hard slam that forced the woman to do a full circle before she stumbled out into the lobby of the Quinn Law Firm, where a buxom blonde reached out just in time to catch her before she fell to the floor.

"Are you all right, ma'am?"

Of course she wasn't all right. Why would anyone think that she was? But, being polite, she nodded, and said, "Thank you, young lady."

"Are you sure? You look a little shaky. Can I get someone to help you?"

Of course she was shaky, the dowdy woman thought, but not for all the tea in China would she admit to it. "Really, I'm fine, thank you very much for your help." On less-than-shaky legs, the dowdy woman made her way over to the receptionist's desk, and said, "I have an appointment with Ms. Quinn. My name is Selma Roland."

The receptionist, a fashion plate in her own right, tried not to stare at the woman and couldn't help but wonder how she could afford the hourly rate the firm charged.

"Yes, you do, Ms. Roland. It will be just a moment until someone gets here to take you up to Ms. Quinn's office. Please have a seat."

The dowdy woman shuffled her way across the small lobby and took a seat. Thank God her breathing was back to normal. Of all the people in the world, Wilson Lambert was the last person she had expected to run into. Here at this office. At this hour of the day. Her mind started to race. She asked herself why she was surprised, since Wilson Lambert seemed to know whatever was going on before anyone else did. Thanks to the network of flunkies who kept him apprised of everything that went on in the District and genuflected in front of him for the privilege of doing his bidding. It was sick. Sick, sick, sick.

A door behind the receptionist's desk opened. "Ms. Roland. I'm Mitzi Doyle. Ms. Quinn asked me to fetch you up to her office. She's waiting for you. Just follow me." If the woman's shabby attire puzzled Ms. Doyle, she gave off no outward sign.

Nor did Nikki give off any signs that the woman's shabbiness bothered her when she held out her hand for a handshake. "Please"—Nikki motioned to the casual seating area—"take a seat. Would you like some coffee or tea?"

"No thanks. I . . . appreciate your seeing me on such short notice. I have this really bad habit of waiting till the last minute to . . . to make appointments. I'm working on trying to do better. Should we discuss your retainer fee first?"

"I like to wait on that until I hear what it is you want my firm to do for you. That way, I can gauge how much time I'll need to work on your case. Tell me why you're here and how I can help."

I know I've seen this woman before, but she didn't look anything like she looks now, Nikki thought. *Did she fall on hard times, or is this a disguise of some sort?*

"I've heard really good things about your firm. So I feel like I'm in good hands."

"That's nice of you to say that. We try very hard here at the firm to do what is best for all our clients. Now, how can I help you?"

"First things first. I have a confession to make. I came here under a false name. I had . . . have my reasons for that. I just want to apologize right up front for deceiving you. I never . . . I never do things like that. This . . . this time, I am afraid, I had no other choice. My real name is Livinia Roland Lambert. My friends call me Liv. Selma is my middle name, and Roland is my maiden name. So I didn't exactly lie. I detest liars. Yes, I am the wife of the Speaker of the House, Wilson, or Buzz, as he likes to be called, Lambert. And I am also the mother of Jeffrey Lambert, who was here to see you earlier. I look . . . like this . . . because I didn't want anyone to recognize me. Case in point . . ." She went on to describe the revolving-door incident and could not keep herself from laughing about it. Nikki found it impossible not to smile as she visualized the outraged, and thoroughly objectionable, Speaker of the House slamming through the door, having no idea that he was spinning his very own wife in a full circle.

"I want to file for divorce. I talked to my son, and he helped me reach my decision. By *helping me,* I mean we talked for hours, and he helped me wade through all the years of my marriage and how I arrived at this point in time. Jeffrey found the courage, as did Amy, to come to terms with the end of their marriage, and may I say I adore that young woman, but even so, they were not right for each other. They owned up to what each of them wants, and it wasn't marriage. So they took steps to rectify that. Jeffrey said I had to look it all in the face and ask myself if I wanted to spend the rest of my years like all the years that have gone by, or did I want to live. As in *live*. When put that way, it was not a hard choice at all.

"Actually, to me, it was a no-brainer. What really startled me, however, was that my son is smarter than I am. If Jeffrey and Amy hadn't filed for divorce, I do believe I would have just stayed in the unhappy rut my marriage had become a long time ago.

"There will be problems. I can guarantee that. I am very wealthy. Please don't think I'm bragging, because I am not. The money in our marriage came from me, and it is all mine. I have some very good old family lawyers who have been with me since I became of age. Of course, I will give you their names and permission to talk to them.

"Wilson earns something around $223,500 a year as Speaker of the House. He will earn that amount every year until the day he dies. He spends that much during the first quarter of the year. He loves to live high.

"My . . . ah . . . game plan is to get up one morning and walk out of the house and not actually disappear but depart the East Coast and head to California, to be closer to my son. On that day, I want my husband served with divorce papers, preferably at his office. But I want to be airborne when that happens.

"I also want to ask you if the firm can handle the sale of my family home. Again, only after I am gone. To facilitate that, I am going to give you power of attorney so that you can sign anything that needs to be signed.

"Moreover, I want Wilson evicted as soon as possible. I fervently hope that he ends up living in a tent and peeing in a bucket. I think I know how that must sound to you, but I have finally reached the end of my rope. The only thing other than my son that man ever gave me was the flu, and even then, he didn't take care of me. I'm sorry if I sound bitter, because I am bitter. No point in lying about it at this stage of my life.

"You need to know that we will have a fight on our hands, I can absolutely guarantee that. Wilson will go immediately to the Chessmen, as he calls them. The law firm of Queen, King, Bishop, and Rook. I'm sure you know of them. I think Wilson is responsible for that firm's success."

Nikki childishly crossed her fingers that Livinia Lambert wasn't picking up on what she was feeling. *As Jack was fond of saying, I certainly didn't see this coming.* Of course she knew of the firm—everyone in Washington, D.C., knew who the Chessmen, the firm's founders and only partners, as they liked to be called, were. Nikki opted for silence and simply nodded, pretending that she was not letting on about how that reference to the Chessmen rattled her.

"Wilson has no idea I know this, but I tapped into his personal e-mail account, and there are those out there who want him to make a bid for the presidency. I think the Chessmen are the driving force behind the plan. That buffoon, meaning my husband, actually thinks he can win. And perhaps he can. Stranger things have happened in Washington, D.C.

"I've heard him whispering on the phone from time to time. Wilson would make a terrible president. Even the thought that he is now second in the line of succession scares the wits out of me.

"That's another reason I'm doing this. I do not want to be attached to him in any way, should he make a run for the presidency. Assuming he can even get out of the gate. If I can successfully remove myself, my money, and my friends, then I think they will very quickly lose interest in him as a presidential candidate. As it stands now, he needs me. He might, I say *might,* try to hit up Jeffrey, what with his newfound software wealth, but I can assure you that Jeffrey wants no part of his father. Wilson was an absentee father during Jeffrey's most crucial years."

Livinia threw her hands in the air, and said, "That's pretty much the condensed version of things, Ms. Quinn. Will you represent me? Should we talk about the retainer now?"

Every nerve in Nikki's body was screaming, *No, no, no, a thousand times no!* What she said was, "Of course the firm will represent you. I don't want you to worry about the Chessmen if you think that's who your husband will have representing him. We're all big girls here at the firm. We can handle them."

Livinia let loose with a mighty sigh. "I was so hoping that you would say yes. Thank you. What's my next step? Aside from paying you the retainer. What kind of paperwork do you need from me other than that power of attorney? Oh, one other thing. Jeffrey and I have what Jeffrey calls burner phones. And that means Wilson doesn't know about them. And we also have our own private e-mail accounts. Jeff, as I am sure you know, is very high tech, and he took care of all that. I even have separate sets of identity papers so when the day comes, and I walk out of the house, no one will know where I am. Not the Selma Roland name, that's too obvious. I know that part is illegal, but I really don't care at this point."

Nikki struggled to process all she was hearing. "Ah . . . it sounds like you and your son pretty much thought of everything. You do realize, don't you, Livinia, that this is not going to be a walk in the park, especially if the Chessmen are involved."

"My dear, I didn't just fall off the turnip truck. I know more than you think I know about those scoundrels at that firm. They're all about dirty tricks and intimidation. I lost count of the number of times the four of them came out to the house, ostensibly to play cards, but all they did was talk about how they *shafted,* that's the word they actually used, their clients' spouses in divorce settlements. When I finally realized what those meetings were all about, I hired someone to come in and bug Wilson's office. It was someone I trusted, so don't you worry about that end of it. I have a shoe box full of tapes I can hand over to you."

Good Lord, this woman is chock-full of surprises! "Really! That's good to know. Yes, of course we'll want to listen to those tapes. Is there anything else you want to tell me?" *God, I hope not,* Nikki prayed.

"No. That's pretty much it. I imagine you want to know if Wilson ever cheated on me or not. I don't know. I never cared enough to look into it. We haven't been man and wife in that sense for more years than I can remember. Now about that retainer. Will fifty thousand dollars work for now? I know all about billable hours, and I also know that, as you say, this is not going to be a 'walk in the park.' Just tell me what to sign, so I can get back home and out of this . . . this bag-lady outfit.

"My son said something I thought was very profound yesterday. He said the choices we make in life define who we are. He also said that fate is what happens to you. Free will is how you respond. I raised a very smart young man, and, yes, I take one hundred percent credit for that." Livinia shrugged. "I don't know why I felt the need to tell you that. I guess because I am going to do my best to make the right choices from here on in and let my free will rise to the surface. We're done, right, Ms. Quinn?"

"For now, yes. How do we get in touch with you?"

Livinia squinted, then completely closed one eye as she homed in on a picture on the wall. "I think it might be best if I get in touch with you. Don't send me any mail at my home. Wilson has the help on his side. What that means is they report to him on my comings and goings, although why he wants to know what I'm doing is beyond me. Jeffrey says he worries that either he or I will damage his reputation somehow, someway. Can we just leave it at that for now?"

"Yes, for now."

"How long before you are in a position to serve the papers on him? I don't mean to rush you, but now that I've made my decision, I want to walk out of that house and get on with my life as soon as possible. But you're the lawyer, take as much time as you need so we get it done right. I'll find a way to get all those tapes to you."

"A week from today should do it. Call me two days before, and I'll let you know if we are ready to act as soon as you are on that airplane to California."

And then they were at the door. "Is this where you say something to me like, 'If you change your mind, it won't be a problem'? A week will give me time to make my plane reservation. I thought I would book a flight to Kansas City. No one I know goes to Kansas. Then I will book another flight from there, a few days later, for San Diego, where I will stay another few days. The next step will be to buy an old car of some sort to finish off the trip. This way, I won't be leaving any footprints for Wilson to follow. Once I leave, I will only use cash to pay for everything, so he cannot trace any credit-card use."

Nikki laughed out loud. "You really did think this through, didn't you? Actually, I usually do say something like that, but in your case, I don't think it's at all necessary. Perhaps I should hire you to work on my investigative team.

"Good luck, Livinia. You know how to reach me, if you need me. Oh, wait, I do have one other question. What about your household help?"

This time, it was Livinia's turn to laugh out loud. "The way I see it, those people are Wilson's problem. He hired them all. Let him deal with whatever crops up. Have a nice day, Ms. Quinn."

"You too, Livinia. And please call me Nikki. Ah, here

comes Mitzi. She'll show you out and make sure no one is . . . ah . . . observing you."

Nikki smiled as she watched the spring in the dowdy woman's step. Even from where she was standing, she could tell that Mitzi, who took Livinia into her office to write the retainer and sign a standard power of attorney, was also aware of the difference in their new client.

Nikki was a whirlwind as she raced down the hall and around the corner to Alexis's office. She knocked softly and was told to enter. She did, her hands in the air, palms facing Alexis. "In a million years, no, a billion years, you are not going to believe what I am going to tell you."

Alexis sat up a little straighter, closed the book she had been studying, and stared at Nikki. "You have my undivided attention, boss."

Chapter 3

Maggie Spritzer looked up at the bank of clocks on the wall, which told her the time all over the world. Not that she cared what time it was in Australia or Japan, or anywhere else, for that matter. All she cared about was that it was only one o'clock in the afternoon, way too early to call it a day, in the Eastern time zone. And she was bored out of her mind.

It was a very slow news day. One of those rare days in the nation's capital when it seemed that absolutely nothing newsworthy was going on. And she was stuck here in the office as the once-again, temporary editor in chief of the *Washington Post*. She was sorry now that she'd let Annie de Silva talk her into taking over the post for a third time. But it was just so hard to say no to Annie. She hated sitting here and calling the shots for the reporters, since she was, plain and simple, a reporter at heart. She belonged *out there,* ferreting out the news stories that would make headlines, not sitting here in this plush chair, waiting for someone else to bring her a story that might or might not be newsworthy. Always and forever, she would be a newshound.

Maggie's gaze raked the room, coming to a full stop at the banker's box sitting by the door. Her *stuff*. Today was her last day sitting in this chair as the editor in chief. At least she hoped so. Annie had promised her that a new editor was taking over tomorrow morning. And the best part of it all was she didn't have to hang around to show him the ropes. As Annie had put it, he was a "seasoned pro who didn't need any help, thank you very much." But then, Annie had said that on three other occasions; yet here she was. This time, though, she'd been smarter. She hadn't lugged in a bunch of personal stuff to make her office her home away from home. Maybe secretly she knew this third time was really just temporary. Maybe. The banker's box held a few photographs, some notebooks, a plant that had more yellow leaves than green ones, some breath mints, a few batteries, and her slippers. She could carry it out of here with one hand, provided she taped it up to make a handle.

There was no sense in kidding herself; she was going to miss the perks that came with the job. Big-time perks: car service, driver at her beck and call, her outrageous salary, and the overly generous expense account. Yep, she would miss all that for a few days; then she'd be right back in the groove. Guaranteed.

Maggie looked around again. With nothing to do that her staff couldn't handle, and the hell with the time of day on the Eastern seaboard, she made the decision to call down for the car. Might as well head home and snuggle with Hero, her cat. She'd build a fire, pop something in the oven for dinner, then watch some silly shows on TV, hit the sack around nine, just so she could get a running start early in the morning as the investigative reporter she was. What she would investigate was still a mystery. Yep, that's what she should do, but before she did that, she decided to call the girls to ask them if they wanted to meet up for a drink to celebrate her being liberated from her desk-jockey job.

She'd start with Kathryn, because Ted had told her yesterday before he left with the guys for the Big Apple that Kathryn was back in town. That was another thing: all the guys had left for New York and hadn't invited her to go with them, and Ted was unusually tight-lipped about the reason for their trip. What was even more unusual was that Charles and Fergus had gone with them. Normally, Charles and Fergus stayed behind and left all the heavy lifting to the younger guys. Normally. It had been like pulling teeth to even get that much out of Ted, but she'd managed. Whatever they were up to, and she was absolutely positive they were up to something, she'd figure it out; she always did.

Kathryn picked up on the second ring. Maggie got right to the point. "Hey, you want to round up the others and meet up at the Squire's Pub for a drink to celebrate my last day on the job as editor in chief of this benighted publication? I know it's my third retirement, but this time it is going to stick. I've had it with sitting in an office. What do you say?"

The ten seconds of silence on the other end of the line did not go unnoticed by Maggie. "Gee, Maggie, I can't. I have to take Murphy to the vet. He's been sick the past few days. Not *sick* sick, if you know what I mean. His back legs are full of arthritis, and he is really having trouble moving around. I had to cancel my run. He's older now, and I don't want to leave him alone. You understand, right? Congratulations! Do you think it will work this time? I mean your going back in the field to work as a full-time reporter?"

Maggie blinked. She'd never heard Kathryn talk so fast or sound so jittery. She knew how much Kathryn loved Murphy, and it was true, the shepherd was getting up there in years. "Okay, no problem. I guess I'll just go home and hang with Hero. Let me know how Murphy does, and if you need me, call."

"Sure. Sure. You bet." Kathryn clicked OFF and shoved the phone into her hip pocket, unaware that the rough material of her jeans jostled the ON/OFF button to the OFF position.

Maggie blinked again as she stared at the phone in her hand. Talk about getting the bum's rush. Still, when it came to Kathryn, there was always some sort of drama going on. "Damn!" Well, she could always call the others and see if they'd be willing to help her celebrate her new freedom from the office. She called Yoko. Yoko was always up for a serendipity moment.

"I'm sorry, Maggie, I can't. I have to be here for my pumpkin delivery. And then I have to head over to the academy to do my volunteer duty at Lily's school. With Harry in New York, I'm stretched too thin timewise."

Maggie didn't know how she knew, but she knew Yoko was lying to her. But why? She bit down on her lower lip, and said, "Sure, I understand." *Like hell I understand.*

Yoko looked at the phone in her hand and shook her head. She tossed the phone on a pile of papers before she headed out to the greenhouse. Her work here in the office was done for the day. Yoko hated cell phones with a passion and was forever misplacing or losing hers. Harry was forever saying he was going to put a string on it so she'd have to wear it around her neck.

Maggie's next call was to Alexis, who cut her so short that Maggie was left speechless. When she finally found her tongue, all she could say was "I understand, business comes first, and, of course, you can't cancel two clients in a row for something as silly as going for a drink. Call me when you have time."

Alexis shoved the cell phone into her briefcase and headed for the conference room, where she was meeting up with a family to discuss a probate matter. The firm had a rule of no cell phones in meetings, and that included clients. There were signs to that effect plastered all over the firm.

Maggie was down to Myra, Annie, Nikki, and Isabelle. Was there any point to even calling any of them? Maggie chewed on the inside of her cheek, a nasty habit she'd picked up doing when she was frustrated. Before she could think about it, she called Nikki.

"Maggie, I'm out at the farm. I left work at noon. I have some things I have to take care of out here that Jack should have taken care of before he left for New York but didn't. I don't want to make the trip back to town. I hope you understand. I'm thinking I might even take a nap."

Maggie almost said out loud, *You're a terrible liar, Nikki,* but she didn't. Instead, she simply said, "Okay, another day then. See ya."

Nikki eyed the phone for a long minute. Now that she thought about it, a nap sounded good. Real good. She couldn't remember the last time she'd taken a nap in the middle of the day. More than likely, she'd never done it, and that's why she couldn't remember it ever happening. She literally galloped up the steps to shed her clothes and jump under the covers.

The word *conspiracy* jumped around inside Maggie's brain. Should she call Isabelle? Why the hell not? And Myra and Annie, too. Might as well go for a grand slam. If all three of them shut her down, then she'd know for sure she needed to look into a conspiracy. But to what end?

Maggie dialed Isabelle's cell. The only words she got out of her mouth were "Isabelle, it's me, Maggie," before Isabelle shut her down.

"I can't talk now, Maggie. I am up to my eyeballs and am in crisis mode. I'll call you back, probably sometime next year when I crawl out from under this mess I'm in." Aggravated with what was going on in the office and the prospect of going out to Nikki's at the end of the day was working on Isabelle's last nerve. She looked at the phone in her hand, debated all of three seconds before she turned it off. Ah, silence. Peaceful, wonderful silence. Until she turned it back on.

The only problem was, Isabelle forgot to turn it back on as she raced around to the offices, signing off on this and that and running interference with the two junior architects who had a big hate on for each other.

The connection went dead, leaving Maggie seething with anger. "Well, screw you, Isabelle. Just wait till the next time you need *my* help."

One down, two to go. Her call to Myra went straight to voice mail. She didn't bother to leave a message. The call to Annie's house was taken by her housekeeper, who said that Ms. de Silva had gone to see Mr. Easter and wouldn't be back till later in the evening.

"BullSHIT!"

Angry beyond words, Maggie pulled on her jacket and the backpack, which she was never without, then picked up the banker's box. Barely able to maintain a modicum of civility, she didn't say good-bye to anyone; she just raced to the elevator, which would take her down to the lobby and outside, where she would take her very last ride in her favorite perk. She crossed her fingers that her cat, Hero, would welcome her with his open arms so she could soak his fur with her tears.

She was right; it was a grand slam.

Maggie swept through the revolving door as fast as she could. She headed to the curb, but her car was nowhere to be seen. Traffic whizzed by at the speed of light. Where was her car? She craned her neck to look up and down for the shiny black vehicle and her driver, Eduardo. This wasn't like Eduardo. He was always early, and she'd never had to wait for him. Something must have happened to delay him. All of a sudden it dawned on Maggie that she had forgotten to call him. She told herself it wasn't the end of the world, that's why they had taxis, and she had yet to turn in her last expense report. She walked to the curb, with the banker's box still in hand. She'd have to jostle it somehow, prop it up on her hip someway so she could hail a cab.

The silver SUV came out of nowhere. Maggie heard high-pitched screams and saw people scattering as two small compact cars jumped the curb. She saw a young boy with a skateboard in the path of one of the cars. Her banker's box went flying through the air, the plant with the yellow leaves hitting the windshield of one of the cars, as she moved quickly to push the young boy out of the way. Just before her world went dark, she saw the frightened look on the face of the driver of the SUV. The time on the dashboard clock of the SUV said it was 2:10 when the crash happened.

The sound of police sirens and ambulances could be heard for miles. Cell phones were being held high in the air as pedestrians did their best to record what was going on. The driver of the silver SUV was slumped over the wheel, causing the horn to wail at a high-decibel level as blood poured from a head wound. Maggie Spritzer lay motionless, half on the curb, half off, her face as white as the blouse she was wearing. The young boy whose life she had probably saved was next to her. Both were unconscious.

Within minutes, a loud voice could be heard. "Stand back! Stand back!" a police officer roared as the emergency medical people rushed to do what they could before loading the victims onto gurneys to take them to the closest hospital.

They're too young, both of them, the veteran EMT thought. Mother and son? He didn't know. He told himself not to get personal, just the way he had told himself hundreds of times before in accidents just like this one. It looked to him like the boy was gone; the woman, touch and go; she was barely breathing. He hooked up the IV and said, the way he said each and every time, "Stay with me, lady, stay with me."

Then he prayed, because he always prayed in situations like this. He'd done what he was trained to do, and prayer was the only thing that was left. She looked familiar, he thought, and almost immediately realized who she was. He'd read countless articles written by her over the years. A reporter, and this accident happened right in front of the *Post* building.

The ambulance screamed its way through the streets as the EMT continued to pray over his patient. And then they were at the emergency entrance to Georgetown University Hospital. Nurses and doctors came running; the doors were held open. Seconds rushed by as Maggie was lifted down; then they ran at breakneck speed, pushing the gurney down the polished hallway to the operating room, where more doctors and nurses waited.

A second and third ambulance arrived, one carrying the driver of the SUV and the other the young boy. He heard one of the nurses say the boy was hanging on by a thread. *Thank God he wasn't dead. Thank God.* More doctors, more nurses, as they all rushed to do what they did best, try to save their patients.

The ambulance driver, whose name was Tony Spina, gathered up Maggie's backpack and walked into the hospital. He signed off on his paperwork and handed over the backpack. He knew better than to ask how the woman whom he'd transported here was. Now he had to put this behind him and head back to headquarters and wait for another call.

Later, how much later he didn't know, he'd call to see how the reporter was doing. Nine times out of ten, they'd tell him. Not that he'd be able to sleep any better—it was more to see if all the prayers he'd said had worked. He always wondered if God had time to get involved with the lives of the people for whom he prayed, and guessed that he would probably never know the answer.

On the ride back to headquarters, he allowed himself to think about the families of the victims and wondered if they even knew what was going on with their loved ones. Sometimes he wished he were the one who could go to them to soften the blow. Other times, he knew he couldn't handle the grief. That was the hard part, not knowing, and caring too much.

When his thoughts took him in this direction, Tony Spina always found himself wondering what his life would be like if he had decided to become a plumber. Of course, he knew without a doubt he'd have made a lousy plumber. On the other hand, plumbers did not find themselves praying for the lives of their customers.

Chapter 4

Ted Robinson was on his hands and knees looking for one of his contact lenses, which had just popped out of his eye. He didn't know why he was even bothering, since there was no way that he was about to put a dirty lens back in his eye. He always carried a spare, but still he looked for it. He could soak it and keep it as a backup. You always needed a spare if you were as blind as he was without his contacts.

The New York hotel room was chaotic as the boys railed, then complimented each other on how their interview had gone with the big industrialist who wanted to hire them. They were now packing up to head to Philadelphia on the late-afternoon train, and as usual they were running late.

"Your phone's ringing, Ted!" someone shouted.

"Well, answer it for me. Tell them to hold on." He needed that lens. You never knew when something like what just happened would happen again. If nothing else, Ted was thrifty.

"I got it!" Abner shouted. "C'mon, you guys, simmer down so I can hear."

The boys went instantly silent as they looked at Abner, as much as to say, *Make it quick then*. As one, they froze in place at the look on Abner's face as it went stark white. They couldn't help but notice that the hand holding the phone to his ear was shaking uncontrollably. "Ted, you need to take this call. Like *now*!"

"Tell whoever it is I'll call them back. I have to find my lens. I don't like not having a spare."

"*Now, Ted!*" Abner bellowed.

"All right, all right, I found it. Just let me drop it in some solution first. Just tell them to hang on. What's so frigging important, anyway?"

Abner didn't even bother to respond this time. Instead, he jammed the phone against Ted's ear and stepped back and whispered to the others, his voice as trembly as his hands. "It's Maggie. That was admitting at Georgetown University Hospital. Maggie was hit by an SUV when she was leaving the *Post* to go home. Ted and Annie are listed as her next of kin. The woman said they tried calling Ms. de Silva, but there was no answer. Maggie is being operated on as we speak."

No one said a word. No one moved. Not even Ted, whose face was as ashen as Abner's. Finally the silence was broken when they heard Ted say, "I'll be there as soon as I can." He shoved the phone in his pocket and looked around at his friends, who were staring at him. "I don't know what to do. Tell me what to do, someone. *Please.*"

"I know what to do, Ted," Dennis said as he busily tapped his cell phone.

"Georgetown University Hospital has a heliport. Go downstairs and hail a cab to take you to Kennedy. By the time you get there, I'll have your ride ready. You're in no shape to go alone, so take Espinosa with you."

Ted swiped at his cheeks as he gathered up his backpack and raced to the door, Espinosa on his heels.

"How did you do that, young man?" Fergus asked. "We need to get back, too. How soon can you get us there?"

Dennis, the multimillionaire major stockholder in Welmed and junior reporter for the *Washington Post,* continued to tap furiously. "There's an app for everything. Having money helps," he mumbled. "Okay, okay, I got us booked on a private jet, but we have to leave *now.* There's some Japanese businessman willing to take the flight if we're not on time. Move, guys!"

There was a mad scramble for the door as the boys barreled through.

Jack commandeered two cabs at the curb. Charles offered both drivers a hundred-dollar bonus to get them to Kennedy Airport in time to make their private flight.

Harry looked at Dennis, and whispered to him, "I like the way you stepped up to the plate, kid. Shows you have a kind heart. We'll pay you back out of the BOLO fund, so don't worry about that end of things."

"I'm not worried about it at all, Harry. I wanted to do it for Maggie. I owe her so much. I want to be there for her, just the way you all do. Do you think she'll be okay, Harry? Tell me the truth."

"The truth, Dennis, is I don't know. I wish I did. Maggie is special. She's one of us. By us, I mean the BOLO group. She's the only woman in our group. That should tell you how we feel about her."

"Ted's a basket case," Dennis said.

"Yes. I would certainly be, too, if it were Yoko in the operating room. Think positive, kid. We all need to think positive," Harry said loudly enough for the others to hear.

Jack swiped at his eyes. "Okay, then, time to roll. Move! That means you, too, Charles, and you as well, Fergus." The trite remark was in reference to both men's recent weight gain.

Charles and Fergus hustled and managed to keep up with the stampede.

* * *

Nikki Quinn woke at four o'clock, feeling groggy and out of sorts, a good reason why she didn't take naps during the day. Somehow she knew that she would wake up feeling just as she did now. The only remedy, she decided, was a hot-and-cold shower to wake her up. She thought about the simple dinner she was going to make for the girls when they arrived: soft-shell tacos and two pitchers of margaritas. All frozen. She was glad now that she'd taken the tacos and the drink mix out of the freezer before she'd headed upstairs.

Nikki danced under the hot spray, then cold, back to hot, then back to cold, followed by lukewarm water. When she stepped out of the shower, she was feeling more like her old self. While she towel-dried and dressed, she knew she should check her cell phone, but this precious time all alone was to be treasured because these moments were impossibly rare. Messages could wait.

Dressed now in warm, dove-gray sweats and sneakers, Nikki headed for the stairs to make some coffee, then a quick few minutes watching CNN to see if anything had happened in the world that she should know about before the girls came.

The moment she clicked on the TV, she was aware of how silent the house was, with Jack and Cyrus gone. Way too silent, she thought. She did like a quiet room, but one with just a smidgen of background noise. She worked quickly then, one eye on the TV and the other on the coffee she was measuring into the pot. Satisfied that things were all in place, Nikki reached for the phone. She came close to swooning when she saw that she had seventeen voice mails. She asked herself if she really wanted to listen to seventeen messages, most of them probably meaningless. She decided to stall a little longer, at least until she had her first cup of coffee. Then, and only then, would she feel fortified enough to deal with whatever lurked within the unheard messages. She supposed she should at least turn on the phone. Which she did. It rang almost instantly. "I knew I shouldn't have done that," she muttered over and over before she clicked it on to hear Jack's voice. She could barely hear, what with Cyrus barking and all the chatter going on in the background. What she could tell for sure was that Jack was very, very upset. Rarely, if ever, did he allow himself to lose control of his voice.

"Slow down. I can barely hear you. What's wrong? What do you mean, where have I been? I left the office early, came home, and took a nap. There's no law against it that I know of. The girls are coming over for dinner. What's wrong, Jack?" Nikki listened, her face going chalk white. "Oh, good Lord! I'll call the girls and tell them to meet me at the hospital. I'll leave now. Where are you? I hear Cyrus."

"At the airport. Reagan National. We just got back here. Ted should be at the hospital already. He left a good hour before we did. Dennis . . . the kid made it all happen."

"I'll probably get to the hospital just when you do. She's going to make it, isn't she, Jack?" Nikki blinked when she realized the call had ended.

What to do? Who should she call first? Myra and Annie, of course. Nikki moved by rote then; she put away the frozen food on the counter, searched for her keys and purse, and looked around for her jacket, all the while trying to reach the girls with no results. Even Myra and Annie weren't picking up.

Never one to wait around when she could be moving, through the tears that made it difficult to see what she was writing, Nikki penned off a note to stick on the door. It was a shame that everyone would make the trip all the way out here from town, only to turn around and head right back, which meant tonight's meeting to discuss Maggie wasn't going to happen. Maybe, all things considered, that was a good thing, she decided as she slipped into her jacket. She could already feel the guilt settling on her shoulders. Sobbing by now, she stuck the note on the kitchen door with a slice of electrical tape to ensure it didn't blow away, what with the way the October wind was gusting.

Nikki settled herself behind the wheel, wiped her eyes until it was safe to drive, and said a little prayer the way Myra had taught her and Barbara when they were younger, just a little prayer, asking God to watch over her and to let her reach her destination safe and sound.

Tears continued to roll down Nikki's cheeks as she drove against the traffic, glad she wasn't going in the opposite direction. She felt like she was flying blind. Jack hadn't told her anything other than Maggie was in surgery and had been hit by a car. How, what, when? It had to be serious if she was being operated on. Any accident was serious. Broken bones? What? She knew she would find out soon enough. The main question was whether she would be able to handle whatever she found out.

She thought about Maggie then, going back years and years to when she was an adversary, trying to expose the Vigilantes. And a worthy one, at that. She knew in her gut there wasn't a better investigative reporter walking the earth than Maggie Spritzer. But in the end, after weeks and months of trying to nail them, she'd given up and enlisted in the cause. It had been a red-letter day, to be sure. And along with Maggie came Abner Tookus, the friend, and now Isabelle's husband, who had helped them all out more times than she cared to remember.

Dear, sweet Maggie, with her crazy metabolism that allowed her to eat twenty-four/seven and never gain an ounce. Maggie was always the first one to get in line to help whoever needed help. And the boys had accepted her as the only female in their otherwise all-male boys' club. It was something that did not sit well with the girls, but they sucked it up. Maggie declared herself neutral, going so far as to call herself Miss Switzerland. The meeting tonight was to discuss forcing Maggie to make a choice, the boys or the girls. And now that wasn't going to happen. Maybe, after today, it would never happen.

Right now, however, none of that even seemed important. She hoped the others felt the same way. It was obvious the boys did, because they were all rushing to the hospital to be at Miss Switzerland's side.

Nikki forced her thoughts to go in another direction. Better to think about something more positive. Maybe not something, but someone. Someone like Selma Roland, aka Livinia Lambert. Now that she thought about it, she'd seen a message on her phone from Selma Roland. She hadn't bothered to listen to any of the other messages the moment she talked to Jack. Once she found a parking spot at the hospital, she would check her messages, because she did not believe in phone usage of any kind while driving. She wished more people felt like she did in that regard.

Ten minutes later, Nikki parked her red Jeep Cherokee next to a low-slung Porsche sports car. She whipped out her phone and listened to her messages. None from the girls, but there were nine from Jack, more from several colleagues checking in, and one from Selma Roland that simply said when she got home, she had gone straight to where she had hidden the tapes, and they were gone. She went on to say that the last time she'd checked them was about a month ago.

"What that means, Ms. Quinn, is this. You have to make all deliberate speed in filing my divorce papers—as quickly as humanly possible. I have to assume Wilson knows what I've been doing, and I do not think that will bode well for me. I think I might have to disappear for a little while. I will be in touch."

Nikki played the message twice more until she had it memorized, then she erased it, but she did store the number in her phone bank. She was out of the Cherokee a moment later, sprinting toward the main entrance of the hospital, where she saw Abner and Espinosa outside, puffing away on cigarettes.

She rushed up to them. They hugged and said they didn't know anything. Maggie was in surgery. Ted and the others were waiting to speak to the surgeon. And, no, none of the other girls had arrived as yet.

"Maggie had Ted and Annie listed as the people to be called in an emergency. That's why Ted was called. The hospital wasn't able to reach Annie."

"I didn't know you smoked," Nikki said, somewhat inanely under the circumstances.

"We don't. Some guy shoved the pack in my hand as he was leaving. He said he didn't smoke, either. Just something to . . . you know . . . to calm you down, I guess," Espinosa said.

Nikki shrugged. "I guess that makes some kind of sense. I wasn't able to reach anyone, either."

Abner's head bobbed up and down. "I know, we tried all afternoon. It's almost as if everyone took a day off from using their cell phones. Ted is a basket case," Abner said.

"Give us a little more time, and we'll all be basket cases, along with him, if we don't hear something soon. By the way, where is Cyrus?"

"Harry took him over to the BOLO Building. He should be back any minute. Harry, not Cyrus. Why?" Espinosa asked.

"Just wondered where he was. They don't allow dogs in hospitals. Sometimes, Jack gets just a little crazy where Cyrus is concerned. He thinks that Cyrus is almost human and wants everyone else to think so, too, and to bend the rules. I'm just not in the mood for another battle like that. Give me one of those cigarettes!"

Abner dutifully handed over the crumpled package of

cigarettes and held out a lighter to light her up. He laughed as Nikki coughed and sputtered, but she kept on puffing. "These darn things will kill you!" she gasped as she choked on the smoke.

"What you say is true, and that's why we don't smoke. This is a onetime event, just to get us over the hump. Here comes Harry!"

Nikki crushed out her cigarette and hugged Harry. "How is Cyrus?"

Harry laughed. "I think it's safe to say he was one ticked-off dog when I left him. I gave him a whole bunch of treats, and, believe it or not, he refused them. You know how he loves being where the action is, and he knows he's not being a part of it. He'll probably wreck the place, but Jack said to take him, so I did. He snarled at me when I was leaving. *Me!* That dog loves and adores me."

"*Did* love and adore you. That's one dog you do not want to get on the bad side of. I'm just saying," Espinosa said as he scampered away, far out of Harry's reach. "C'mon, let's go up to the waiting room. There might be some news by now. It's almost six o'clock."

Maggie Spritzer's friends stopped short at the doorway to the waiting room. They blinked and gasped at a wild-looking Ted Robinson, who looked like he'd just come through a hurricane. He was pacing up and down, muttering and mumbling under his breath. When he saw the group, he bellowed, "Nothing yet! It's been almost four hours! No one will tell me anything."

A nurse in a crackly, starched, white uniform appeared out of nowhere. She was an older woman with a disposition as crackly as the outdated uniform she was wearing. She homed in on Ted and went nose to nose with him. "Young man, we do not bellow, nor do we shout or cater-waul in this hospital. This is a place of sickness and healing. I want you to sit down now, and the doctor will be out shortly to give you a status report. Do not make me come out here again, young man."

The small crowd in the doorway moved quickly to get out of the way as the nurse snapped, crackled, and popped her way out to the nurses' station. From there on in, all conversation, what little there was of it, was made in whisper mode.

By seven o'clock, all of Maggie's friends, having gone out to the farm and seen the ominous note, were gathered in the small waiting room, having hushed conversations. It was Isabelle, sitting and holding hands with Abner, who spotted the weary-looking doctor, standing in the open doorway, dressed in green scrubs, face mask hanging askew around his neck, his stethoscope half in and half out of his pocket. She held up her hand and pointed to the doorway. All conversation ceased as the room became totally silent.

"I'm looking for Ms. de Silva and Mr. Robinson." Both Annie and Ted stepped forward, neither saying a word.

The doctor's brisk words belied the tired look in his eyes. "Ms. Spritzer is doing well. I had to remove her spleen. She had some internal bleeding, but we managed to stop it. Her pelvis is fractured. She has four fractured ribs. She also has a badly dislocated shoulder and two broken fingers on her right hand. She suffered a concussion, and we will be monitoring her minute by minute for the next twenty-four hours. She was awake and lucid in the recovery room. We have her on an IV morphine drip, and she is in a world of pain at the moment. That, of course, will subside as she moves forward with her recovery. She's sleeping right now, and I expect her to sleep through the night. What that means to all of you is that you are to go home and return tomorrow. There is nothing you can do for Ms. Spritzer at the moment. Nurse Handley informed the patient that all of you are out here, so she knows you're here. I feel safe in saying that right now she does not really care. She did, however, ask me to have someone look after her cat. I promised to pass on that particular request. She also . . . um . . . said she wants no visitors. She was as adamant as she could be, considering the condition she's in. She said absolutely no visitors until she says so. We always try to do what the patient wants. That's why I'm telling you to go home."

"I'll do that! I want to do that! Of course I will," Ted said in a voice that was somewhere between a sob and a curse, no one could tell which.

"Does that mean we can't go in to see her before we leave, Doctor?" Annie asked quietly.

"That's exactly what it means. You can, however, take a look at her through the glass. To a certain extent, I'm breaking a rule. Tomorrow, when you return, you will not be able to do even that. But, as I said, she's sleeping. Right now, that is the very best thing for her. There's nothing else I can tell you, so if you'll follow me, I'll take you to where you can see her."

Dr. Amos Latuda was like the Pied Piper of Hamelin as he led all of Maggie's friends down the hall to where a half-glass wall allowed visitors to see into a patient's room. "You have five minutes, folks, no more. The blind will be closed the moment you leave. Just so you know."

The gang moved as they lined up to stop and take a quick look at their friend. The doctor, who had seen scenes like this play out too many times to remember, was still choked up at the tears, the tiny gasps of pain as the visitors touched the glass, blew kisses the patient couldn't see, then stumbled away, blinded by their tears.

Once all the visitors had headed out to the elevator, Dr. Latuda moved off. He checked Maggie's chart one last time before he closed the blind on the window, and only then did he make his way to the break room to strip down and head home. Hopefully to sleep, but he knew that was wishful thinking on his part. He was on call twenty-four/seven, and he wouldn't have it any other way.

In the lobby, Ted Robinson dug his heels in and said he was not leaving, that he would sit in the lobby all night. "Don't you all get it? That's Maggie up there. Someone needs to be here in case . . . Look, someone just needs to be here, and that someone is me. I'm not leaving."

"Yes, Ted, you are," Annie said quietly. "You promised to go to Maggie's and take care of her cat, and that is exactly what you are going to do. Maggie is in good hands. There is not one thing you can do for her that isn't being done by her doctors and nurses. This is not negotiable. In the morning, we will swing by and pick you up and bring you here? Are we clear on this, Ted?"

Ted knew when he was beaten. Out of the corner of his eye, he saw Harry approaching, which hastened his positive reply, since Harry never took prisoners. He was just being a horse's patoot, and he knew it. He had said he would take care of Hero, and that's what he would do. "Okay," he agreed.

Annie looked around. "What's the plan here?"

"We're all heading to Philadelphia. We have a seven o'clock breakfast meeting in the morning. We talked about this on the way here earlier. We're going to take the nine o'clock train, which means we have to leave *now*. Espinosa, if you are agreeable, stay with Ted and give me a call in the morning. When I explain about Maggie, I don't think there will be a problem. If . . . if you need us, call, and we'll head back," Jack said.

"I called a taxi for Ted and a taxi-van to take us to the station," Dennis said. "They should be arriving any minute now." He moved to the entrance door to underline his point.

Kathryn, always the most verbal of the group, took that

moment to articulate her own point. "Sounds pretty cold and callous to me, if you want my opinion."

Jack clenched his teeth so hard he was sure he cracked one of his back molars. "I didn't ask for your opinion, Kathryn. I listened to what the surgeon said. He told us to leave. Maggie is in the best hands possible. In addition to that, he said Maggie did not want visitors. I repeat, *she does not want visitors.* What part of that aren't you getting, Kathryn? It's two hours from D.C. to Philly by Amtrak. It takes almost that long to get into D.C. from the farm during rush hour. If we have a charter plane on standby, we can be here in an hour. You do what you have to do, Kathryn, and we'll do what we have to do. Maggie wouldn't expect us to do anything different than what we're doing now. So stuff it, Kathryn." He then turned to his wife, and said, "Honey, walk outside with me, okay?"

Nikki sighed. She hated drama, and she hated guilt, two emotions that were consuming her at that very moment.

Outside, a large white van pulled up to the entrance, followed by a white cab. "Looks like our ride is here. Listen, Nik, the meeting in the morning is crucial. We came here prepared to let it fall by the wayside because Maggie is more important than any mission and dollar amount. Maggie is going to be okay. I know it in my gut. The doctor would have told us otherwise. He wouldn't have sent us out of there if he thought there was going to be a crisis of some sort. So we're leaving with a clear conscience. Ted, of course . . . is different. He's in love with Maggie. It would be wrong to make him leave with us. I don't like what I'm seeing on your face, Nik. All of you. We, the guys, talked about it earlier. Something is going on with you women where Maggie is concerned. I'm no seer, nor am I clairvoyant, but I have a feeling your little dinner party tonight had something to do with Maggie. Ted is the one who noticed how guilty you all looked, how stricken you were that Maggie was in the operating room.

"She wasn't invited to the dinner party, was she? A yes or no will be good, Nik. But before you answer me, I'm asking you to remember what happened with Abner a while back. Don't make the same mistake the guys and I made. Now you can answer me."

"Time to go, Jack, this guy has the meter running," Abner called out.

"Nik?"

"No, Jack, she wasn't invited. Go, they're waiting for you, and, no, I am not judging you or the others. Call me when you get to Philly."

Jack kissed his wife and sprinted for the van. The women stayed silent until the red dots of the van and the cab's taillights could no longer be seen.

Visitors walked around them, chatting as they rushed to get inside out of the blustery wind.

"I'd like to make a suggestion, girls. We all came in separate cars, so let's leave now and meet up at the Daisy Wheel and have some dinner. We can talk there. We do need to talk. I think we all agree on that, don't we?" Myra said quietly, but still loud enough to be heard over the gusting wind. There were nods, but no one said as much as *boo* as they separated to head for their cars.

Chapter 5

The Daisy Wheel was a hot spot in Georgetown, off a
side street with little to no parking. Guests were known
to park elsewhere and walk for blocks to be seen eating at
the famous Wheel, as customers called the eatery. It was a
favorite of Myra and Annie's. The menu was limited to
four specials: one meat, one fish, one poultry, and a veggie
dinner. The food was always perfectly seasoned, bountiful,
and doggie bags were under the dinner plates, colorful
bags with a large white daisy on both sides of the bag.

The owner, a flower child of the past who still looked
the part, greeted her guests, smiled, then went back to her
kitchen to cook each and every meal herself. She did, however, have four assistants. Starry Knight, as she called herself, and no one knew if that was her real name or not,
greeted Myra and Annie with a huge smile and a hug.
Myra and Annie were the only people Starry Knight ever
hugged. "How many tonight?" she asked.

"Seven, and can we have the table in the back?" Myra
asked.

"Of course, of course. Follow me, girls." Anyone under
the age of eighty was a girl to Starry Knight.

The sisters trickled in, one by one, and made their way
to the back of the eatery, where Myra and Annie were al-

ready sipping on Starry's famous homemade sangria, which had the kick of a mule, a very stubborn and strong mule.

"I ordered shrimp scampi and garden salads for all of us," Annie said in a no-nonsense voice, which meant, *Do not change the order.* No one disputed the order. They would either eat their meal or go hungry.

Annie took the lead. "Let's get to it, girls. This is not a good night. Nor was it a good day. One of our own is in the hospital. Having said that, I want all of us to think about why we're even here. Prior to . . . to what happened, we were all prepared, and I think I speak for all of us, to throw Maggie to the wolves because of her involvement with the boys and their . . . um . . . various . . . um . . . projects. There are some of us who have questioned Maggie's loyalty. I am not one of those persons. So let's get to it, air your grievances, whatever they may be, and we'll deal with it and move on." No one spoke for a moment as each of the sisters looked at the others, trying to decide who was to lead off. In the end, it was Nikki who spoke first.

"What happened to Maggie is a terrible thing. As you can see, we all rushed here to do whatever we could, even if it was just to be near her. Yes, we were having a meeting this evening to discuss Maggie's loyalty to the Vigilantes. I confess that a time or two of late, I myself wondered whose side Maggie is on. That's where I went wrong, because there are no sides. We're all one group, one family seeking justice. So the guys splintered off and are doing their thing, just the way we are. It keeps them busy. Let's face it, girls, we're all selfish. We want to do things our way, and we only called in the guys when we needed them for one thing or another. The show was ours to run, and we did. They sucked it up. None of them complained. But now they want more, so more power to them.

"Maggie somehow got downwind of all of that. She did what she does best, she investigated, and they included her.

From their standpoint, it was a wise choice, and there's absolutely nothing wrong with that. The guys did not swear her to secrecy as far as we were concerned. So why do *we* have to swear her to anything?

"The answer is, we don't. Maggie is a free agent. An *honorary* member of the Sisterhood. She adopted our cause after trying her damnedest to expose us to the world. That was her job. And that's the part we all forgot. We wanted *all* of her. We thought, wrongly so, that she belonged to us and should not be aligning herself with our counterparts."

"Nikki's right," Yoko said. "I love Maggie, and yet today, I lied to her. And you know what? She knew I was lying. I'm just sick over this. She called the rest of you, too, didn't she?" The others nodded, shamed looks on their faces. "I just know in my heart that's why she told the doctor she didn't want any visitors. It's just heartbreaking that we can't be there for her when she needs comfort the most." Yoko swiped at the corners of her eyes with her napkin.

"This hits me right between the eyes," Isabelle said. "It's just like when the boys turned on Abner. I saw firsthand what that did to him. I'm not ever going down that road. I will not do to Maggie what I saw done to Abner. Nor should any of you want to travel that road. There is nothing worse in this life than someone betraying your trust. Once trust is broken, it's broken. We have to fix this and make it right."

"I have an opinion, if anyone wants to hear it," Kathryn said quietly.

"By all means, share your opinion," Alexis snapped. "You never worried about voicing your opinions before, so why are you suddenly worried about whether we want to hear it or not?"

"Knock it off, Alexis. Meanness does not become you. That's my forte, and I'm working on that. I think we were all jealous of Maggie's being the only female in that newly formed boys' club. Being the superior force we think we are, not one of us asked or questioned her, now did we? We were waiting for her to volunteer information, which she did not do. I believe one hundred percent that had we asked her, she would have told us whatever we wanted to know.

"I know Maggie. She would never screw us over, and I feel like a pile of horse dung that I lied to her on the phone today. I agree with Yoko—she knew damn well that I was lying."

"I guess that leaves Myra and me to weigh in. Neither Myra nor I talked to Maggie, but had she gotten through to us, we would have lied also. I am ashamed of all of you, but I am more ashamed of myself, and I know Myra feels the same way. We are *NOT* divided. We are a whole. A whole family. Through a lot of hard work, we, all of us, girls and boys, made a family. There are always little skirmishes in families, little jealousies that have to be worked through, but in the end, the family pulls together and is stronger and healthier for the effort. That's all I have to say."

"That's good, dear, because our food is here. It does look delicious. I wish I were hungry, but I'm not," Myra said pitifully.

The others looked at their food, then at the daisy doggie bag under their plate. As one, they held out their glasses for Alexis to refill from the fresh pitcher of Starry Knight's homemade sangria.

"So what's our game plan here? Do we even have a game plan?" Kathryn asked as she poked at a pink shrimp on her plate. She looked at Alexis, when she said, "I, for one, vote to forget this whole Maggie-loyalty bit and move on."

"I agree," Yoko said, relief ringing in her voice.

"Me too," Nikki said. "I also think this is a good time to come to some kind of agreement where the boys are concerned. I would like us all to agree that we are not rivals. Let's also all agree that Maggie is indeed Miss Switzerland and is neutral. Before you agree or disagree, I want you all to ask yourself if you would trust Maggie to watch your back. If you answer yes, we're home free. Any dissenters? No! That's good."

"How are we going to get to Maggie to make this right?" Isabelle asked. All eyes turned to Annie.

Annie smiled. "I'll do my best. When an apology comes from the heart, it is usually accepted. Maggie Spritzer is no fool. Now, if we aren't going to eat, I suggest we pack up and go home. It's been a very trying day for all of us."

Because she was sitting next to Nikki, she was the only one to hear the low, guttural expletive that emerged from between her teeth. Annie looked to see what or whom Nikki was staring at. Nikki was glaring daggers at the Speaker of the House, who had entered with four other gentlemen, all of whom were being seated at a table at the front of the room. "What's wrong?" she whispered.

"That's Buzz Lambert, the Speaker of the House. Those four with him are the Chessmen. You've heard me talk about them. The Speaker doesn't know it yet, but he is about to be served divorce papers. As soon as I draw them up, that is. I imagine the Chessmen will be the ones to represent him in the divorce."

"Oh, dear Lord. Are you saying you are going up against those four?"

"Yep. I don't like that look I'm seeing on your face. Who are you putting your money on, Annie, me or them?"

Annie sucked in her breath. "Why, you, of course, my dear. Are you thinking what I'm thinking, Nikki?" Annie whispered gleefully.

"Oh, yeah," Nikki drawled.

Nikki led the parade out of the Daisy Wheel, with Annie and Myra the last in line. It was Annie who stopped at the table, and said, "Well, hello there, Wilson. Fancy seeing you here at this hour of the evening. How is Livinia these days? Give her my regards, and tell her I'll call." At the stupefied looks on the Chessmen's faces at the introduction, Annie wished she were wearing her tiara. "A pleasure to meet all of you. This lovely lady next to me is Myra Rutledge. Well, enjoy your dinner, gentlemen. Try the shrimp scampi. It's delicious."

Starry Knight appeared out of nowhere in her flowing robes and halo of fresh flowers wrapped around her hair, which hung down to her waist. She glanced with disdain at the men as she walked Myra and Annie to the door.

"It would not bother me or Myra one little bit, Starry, if all of those five gentlemen came down with a case of . . . something or other. Eating fish can be so unpredictable these days."

"You are shameful, Annie. I'll see what I can do. I so love your boots," Starry said, then cackled.

"Well, you aren't getting them, so there. Play your cards right, and I might, I say I *might,* loan them to you." Annie's rhinestone cowgirl boots were a standing joke between the two women.

Starry laughed. "One little question, Countess. How . . . um . . ."

"I think one bad week of sitting in the bathroom will do it." Annie laughed softly. "Pull it off, and I promise to at least let you try them on." Both women knew it would never happen; it was just a game they played.

"Promises, promises," Starry laughingly said.

"Get it in writing, Starry," Myra chirped.

Outside, huddled under the colorful awning, the girls were kissing each other and waving good-bye. Myra, Nikki, and Annie were the last to leave.

"I have an idea, girls. Let's stay in town tonight. The Georgetown Inn is just a block away. It's a long drive out to McLean, and it is getting late. I'll call my dog sitter, Steve, to run out to the farm to stay with the dogs. Neither Annie nor I have anything pressing for the morning. Nikki, you look whipped. You can go in late to the office."

Nikki pointed to her sweats and sneakers. "This is hardly office attire."

"Just announce that it's a casual day. I doubt if any of your clients will care what you are wearing. If we stay the night, we can check on Maggie first thing in the morning when the shift changes, then head out to the farm."

Nikki and Annie thought about it for all of two seconds, then quickly nodded in agreement.

Thirty minutes later, the threesome was ensconced in the last available suite in the small inn. Nikki took the couch, and Myra and Annie each got one of the two double beds.

"I can't remember the last time I slept in my clothes," Nikki said. "Good thing their treasure trove of amenities is plentiful. I can't go to sleep unless I brush my teeth. Who is going to call the hospital to see how Maggie is doing?"

"I'll do it while you two take turns in the bathroom. This really is a cozy little inn. I've never been here before, have you, Annie?" Myra asked.

"A time or two, back in the day," Annie drawled. "Don't look at me like that, Myra. I did have another life before I got married, then after I joined up with you girls. Well?"

"It was Nurse Handley, the head nurse. She said Maggie is sleeping and is being monitored constantly. She said she expects her to sleep through the night. At least she talked to me, so I guess Maggie's request for no visitors doesn't include phone updates, or maybe she didn't think about that. I just wish there was something we could do for that poor child. I feel terrible. She's there all alone. It's not right. It's just not right."

"Myra, there's nothing we can do right now. Tomorrow

is another day. Let's just try to get some sleep and, hopefully, the morning will be better, and Maggie will have a change of heart. If she doesn't, we can always write her a note. I'm sure the nurses or the doctor will give it to her. If she still doesn't want to see us, then we'll have to abide by her wishes. Good night, Myra. Oh, look, Nikki's already asleep."

"Poor thing, she's worn out, and she's taking full responsibility for this mess, and it is a mess. I am hopeful we can make it all right for Maggie. I don't want to dwell on Maggie right now, Annie, or I won't be able to sleep. What do you think about Livinia's finally getting a divorce from that bloviating hypocrite? That will set this town on its ear for sure. Wilson is so big on family values, and the two of them have been married about thirty years, I think. You don't suppose he's been fooling around on her, do you?" Myra asked.

"Good Lord, no. He's so much into money and power that he has no time for dalliances. What bothers me, Myra, is his relationship with the Chessmen. It stands to reason he'll use their firm for his divorce, and they will rip Livinia to shreds. We cannot have that, Myra. I'm thinking we are going to have to be preemptive here where Livinia is concerned."

"There's a little matter of Livinia's not having asked for our help, Annie."

"Oh, pooh, Myra. She doesn't know what we do, so how can she ask us? We're going to help her out of the goodness of our hearts."

"Just like that, eh?"

When there was no further comment, Myra craned her neck to see why Annie hadn't responded, but Annie had fallen asleep and was snoring lightly. Myra smiled to herself as she drifted into her own peaceful sleep.

* * *

It would be another hour before the sun crept to the horizon, when Maggie Spritzer woke to a world of pain coursing through her body. She knew she was whimpering and hated herself for doing it. Every bone, every ounce of flesh on her body, hurt. Her head was beating like a war drum. She then cried out and was immediately rewarded with a soft hand clutching hers. "Just press the button and you'll get some relief. Dr. Latuda has you on a morphine drip, honey."

Maggie did as instructed. She felt some immediate relief. "How bad off am I?"

"Bad enough, but you're here among the living. You're alive," the voice said softly. "The headache will ease soon. You have a concussion. Do you remember what happened?"

"Don't you know?" Maggie mumbled.

The soft voice held a hint of laughter. "Yes, I do know, but I want to know if you know. Like I said, you have a concussion. Try to remember."

"I got hit by a silver car that jumped the curb. There was a boy . . ."

"With a skateboard. Yes, he is here in the hospital, too. He has a broken clavicle, but he'll heal. He was very concerned that his skateboard got ruined."

"Tell him . . . tell him I will get him a new one. He tried to push me out of the way, I think."

"No, honey, that's totally wrong. *You* tried to push *him* out of the way. That's why your injuries are so much worse than his. You took the brunt of the collision. There were witnesses, I'm told, who backed up the boy's account."

"How often can I push this button?"

"As often as you want. It's time for some meds. I'm going to raise your bed a little."

"When can I go home?"

"You just got here, honey. Impatience does not work in

this hospital. You can ask the doctor when he makes rounds. He said if you were up to it, you could have some Jell-O and tea. Would you like some?"

The Maggie of old never ever turned down food because of her whacked-out metabolism. "No thank you." Just the thought of swallowing set her into a panic.

"That's fine, perhaps later. Now take these pills like a good girl, and before you know it, your headache will start to dissipate." Maggie dutifully swallowed the pills and knew immediately that she had made the right decision to pass on the Jell-O because even the pills hurt sliding down her throat. God, even her hair hurt. So did her eyebrows. And her toenails. How was that possible? When she was all better, she was going to research all of this, so it would make sense. She was so tired. But before she allowed herself to drift into sleep, there was something she needed to . . . do . . . say . . . ask. She struggled to remember. "My cat. Is . . ." She was asleep before the nurse could tell her the cat was being taken care of by someone named Ted Robinson.

Chapter 6

Nikki flexed her neck muscles, then rolled her shoulders to get relief from the sudden tightness she was feeling in her upper body. She'd been at the computer from the moment she entered the office, at a little after eight. She looked at the clock on her desk and saw that it read 2:10. She'd worked through lunch and had had no breakfast. The coffee in her cup, one of six cups she'd consumed so far, was cold, with the cream congealing on the top. Sighing, she gulped it down and winced at the bitter taste it left in her mouth. She had taken only one brief break, and that was to take a call from her husband, Jack, who had informed her he'd be home no later than nine, and to ask if there was any news on Maggie.

Nikki pressed a button on the phone console. "Carol, can you come in here for a minute?" Carol Peters, a motherly professional, had been with Nikki from the day she'd opened the Quinn Law Firm, working right alongside Nikki and never leaving the office before her boss. In the morning, she was usually the first one in, after Nikki and Alexis. Nikki considered her a true treasure.

Long years of familiarity allowed for first names and a loose conversational routine when they were alone. "What's up, boss? Just for the record, you look awful. You need to go home. I can handle things here."

"I am going home. I finished the complaint. Proof it and have it on my desk first thing tomorrow morning. I know I told you to hold all my calls, but did anything come in that was important? Is there anything that I need to deal with before I leave? Oh, and what's the latest on Maggie, anything?"

"The nurse I spoke to said Maggie had a good night. She said she was awake and had broth for a late breakfast. She reiterated that she was not accepting visitors. Someone named Starry Knight called, wanting to know if you could relay a message to Myra and Annie. The message is three words: 'Done and done.' " Carol rolled her eyes to show what she thought of messages like that. "Then there was one other call from a woman who said she was your new client. She wouldn't leave her name, but when I told her you couldn't be disturbed, she said to tell you she would call back at two-thirty. She refused to leave a phone number." Carol rolled her eyes again, then asked, "Is this something I'm not supposed to know about, or what?"

"Something like that," Nikki mumbled. "Call Myra and Annie and pass on the message from Ms. Knight. I have no clue what it means, but I am sure they will. When was the last time you called the hospital?"

"A half hour ago. Do you want me to continue calling this afternoon and report to you at home, or will you be taking over that responsibility?"

"I'll take over. I want to check with the others, anyway. Maybe some of the girls are at the hospital. No calls from Myra or Annie?"

"No, boss. It's almost two-thirty. Are you going to wait for your mystery client to call, or should I have her call you at home?" Carol sniffed, annoyed that she wasn't in on whatever was going on.

"I can wait five minutes. It will take me that long to pack up my spare briefcase and grab a sandwich. Please tell me there's something to eat in the kitchen. Please tell me that."

"I wish I could, but I can't, boss. I saw some bananas and cookies. I'll get them for you, if you want."

"No, it's okay. I'll grab a burger on my way home. Thanks, Carol. I don't know what I'd do without you. I mean that."

"Nikki, you're like a daughter to me. You hired me when I was in desperate need of a job, and you bent over backward to allow me the time I needed to be with my kids. Things like that mean the world to me, and the only way I can show my appreciation is through my loyalty to you and the firm. I'll get on this before we both get maudlin."

The phone rang. Nikki looked over at the clock. Right on the button. She picked up just as Carol closed the office door that separated her small space from Nikki's office.

"Nikki Quinn."

"You know who this is, right?"

Nikki felt her shoulders stiffen. Suddenly she wasn't in the mood for games. "Yes, Ms. Lambert, I know who it is. Now, before you can say anything, I want you to listen to me. No one in my firm cares what your name is. None of my people talk out of turn. There is no need for secrecy here in these offices. From now on, when you call here, tell them who you are. The fact that you refused to leave your name and phone number makes one curious. When people are curious, they whisper among themselves. Do you understand what I'm saying?"

"Yes, of course. I suppose I am just being foolish. I don't want anything to go wrong. It's just that Wilson is so powerful, and he knows everyone, and as you very well know, this town is full of 'secrets' that everyone knows about.

What this high muckety-muck is doing with that not-so-high muckety-muck and the like.

"Nothing is sacred or safe. It won't happen again. I called you for a reason. Wilson is sick. Because of who he is, a doctor from Walter Reed made a house call. As the dutiful wife, I was allowed to stand at the back of the room, so I heard everything. It seems he went to dinner, rather late for him, around eight, with the Chessmen last evening. They dined at a five-star restaurant, the Daisy Wheel. They are all sick. Two of the Chessmen went to the hospital to have their stomachs pumped. They are still in the hospital. The other two are as sick as Wilson. They're blaming the restaurant, but the owner provided the names of all the people who ordered the same dishes—shrimp scampi, lamb chops, and prime rib—and no one else got sick. Health officials showed up to investigate, and the report was glowing. They are, after all, a five-star establishment. Everything was in order, and they tested all the shrimp, as well as the meat, and everything that went into it. They couldn't cite the owner for a single infraction, not a single thing was amiss. From what I heard Wilson tell the doctor, the Chessmen want to sue the Daisy Wheel. They are lawyers, as you well know. Wilson agrees with them. Deep pockets and all of that. Are you going to say anything, Ms. Quinn?"

"I ate there last night, along with friends. We had the shrimp scampi, and none of us got sick."

"That's good to know, Ms. Quinn. I thought I should mention it, since according to the doctor who was here, Wilson will be housebound for about a week, and that will prevent you from serving him. And I won't be able to leave. I'm starting to get very nervous. And then there is that little matter of the tapes I had that disappeared all of a sudden."

Nikki struggled to digest all that Livinia Lambert was telling her. "We can always serve him at home, Livinia. Surely, you can think of something that will allow you to leave the house for the day without arousing suspicion— meetings, shopping, lunch with friends. We can wait to serve him once you're airborne. I don't want you to worry about that end of things. I do need a way to get in touch with you, and it will not work with your calling me on a burner phone. So give me a phone number where you can be reached twenty-four/seven."

Despite her client appearing amenable to her instructions, Nikki thought her new client would balk at this one, but she came through with the number, saying that the only other person who had the number was her son, Jeffrey. Nikki entered the number into her cell phone, then scribbled it on a piece of paper she pinned to her small bulletin board.

"There's one other matter we need to discuss. I need you to give me permission to talk about your case with my colleagues. I should have gone over all of this with you yesterday, but you were in such a nervous state, I didn't want to upset you even more. It has to be this way, or I cannot represent you. Do I have your permission?"

"Yes, yes, of course. Do you need something in writing?"

Nikki sighed. "That would be nice, Livinia. An e-mail will do it. Is there anything else?"

"When do you think . . ."

"This is Tuesday. By Friday, I think we'll be good to go. For now, do whatever you need to do and make your arrangements for Friday. If things change, I'll be in touch. By the way, does the owner of the Daisy Wheel have legal representation, do you know?"

"I don't know the answer to that question. It wasn't brought up. I would think a restaurant of that caliber would have the best of the best. Thank you, Ms. Quinn. I'm sorry I've been such a . . . whatever it is I'm being. I've never done anything like this before, and I'm a little jittery."

"You're no different than any of my other first-time clients, Livinia. You took the first step, and I'll finish the walk for you. Your job now is to sit back and wait. That is the hardest part. Can you do it? Tell me now if you think you might run into problems."

"I'm good. I'm good. I'll just . . . I'll just wait to hear from you then."

Nikki rolled her neck and stretched her shoulders again. She wondered what the chances were of her getting a last-minute reservation for a body massage. In this town, those odds were zip. Why was she even thinking about it? She rang for Carol to come into the office again. In five minutes, she had laid out Livinia Lambert's problem. "Watch for that e-mail and file it accordingly. I'm leaving now. Oh, if anyone from the health department calls or comes visiting, asking if I ate the shrimp scampi at the Daisy Wheel last evening, say yes, and I did not get sick. Share all of that with Alexis ASAP, please, because she was with us."

"Will do, boss. Now go home and take a nice bubble bath and have an equally nice glass of wine. Or two or three. *GO!*"

Nikki was halfway home to the farm when she realized that the stiffness and tension in her neck weren't due to sitting at the computer earlier. It was something else entirely, something she was missing. She thought back to when she first noticed the uneasiness, and all of a sudden, she knew the cause. It started when Livinia Lambert appeared in her office yesterday. She'd ignored her own internal antenna because of whom Livinia wanted to divorce. One of the most powerful men in Washington, D.C. It wasn't that she was afraid of Wilson Lambert. If anything, she was looking forward to the challenge he represented. So if it wasn't

Wilson Lambert, that left Livinia herself and, of course, Wilson Lambert's attorneys, the Chessmen. Was she a match for the Chessmen? Only if she played dirty the way they did.

Nikki had been named one of the top female lawyers in D.C. five years in a row. It had rankled that the people doing the survey felt compelled to put the word *female* in front of her name. Her twelve-member, all-female law firm had been in the top three firms seven years in a row. What that meant was she had more business than she could handle. Queen, King, Bishop & Rook held the top spot, followed by her firm. The third firm was one of the whitest of white-shoe firms: Rosen & Rosen, a husband-and-wife firm with nary a word of criticism thrown their way. That was a lot to say about a firm whose past and present clients were among the most elite personages in Washington society. She herself and the firm had their share of disgruntled clients, it went with the territory, but QKB&R, as she thought of the Chessmen, somehow managed to hang on to the top spot even though they had hundreds of complaints filed against them. The fix was in, and everyone in the know was fully aware of that, but no one cared enough to rock the boat.

Nikki felt a chill rush down her spine. Maybe she was the one who was finally going to rock Queen, King, Bishop & Rook's boat. And right now, right this minute, she had a fairly good idea of how she was going to do it.

The thought made Nikki's heart feel ten times lighter as she slowed to turn right onto the gravel road that would take her to Nellie Easter's old farm, which now belonged to her and Jack. She loved this place, the openness, the pasture, all the green grass, her flower beds, and the big old verandah, where she and Jack sat on summer evenings. This truly was the only place that felt like home to her. Jack agreed.

She realized her feelings meant she, more or less, sort of,

had a plan. And right now, that was good enough for her. A plan was a plan was a plan.

Nikki catapulted into the house, tossing her briefcase on the kitchen table, her keys on the counter, her sneakers flying in two different directions as she rummaged for her cell phone, only to give up and reach for the wall phone that was a landline. She called the hospital, voiced her query, and was told that Ms. Spritzer was resting comfortably. Her second call was to Carol, back in the office, where she let loose with a list of last-minute instructions on Livinia Lambert's divorce complaint.

"Nice going, boss," Carol chortled into the phone. "I see you're clicking on all cylinders again. I'll take care of it. Are you going to make the call, or do you want me to do it?"

"It's taken care of. Have a nice evening, Carol. I'll see you in the morning."

Nikki galloped up the steps, stripped down, and hit the shower, where she washed her hair, then lathered up. Twenty minutes later, she was back in the kitchen, contemplating a late-evening dinner with her husband, whom she'd missed terribly. She did love that man. Totally, deeply, and forever, and she knew Jack felt the same way about her. What to have for dinner? Jack's favorite, of course, stuffed pork chops, which had already been cooked, along with an extra portion for nights such as this, and frozen from the last time. They just had to go in the oven at the appointed time, along with a blueberry cobbler, also frozen, and one of Jack's all-time favorites. She was a whirling dervish as she set the dining-room table with her favorite dishes and the scented blueberry candles. Cloth napkins? Oh, yeah, since cloth napkins said this dinner was special. At least that's how Jack looked at it.

Done.

Now to work. She finally located her cell phone and

called Myra. She smiled. For some reason, she always found herself smiling when she heard her adoptive mother's voice, just the way she always laughed when she heard Annie's voice. The three givens, or the three constants, in her life, along with Jack. Who could possibly want more?

"Hi. I just got home. I called the hospital, and they said Maggie was resting comfortably. What's up with the Daisy Wheel, Myra?"

"Whatever do you mean, dear?"

"You know darn well what I mean, Myra. What did you and Annie do? Starry called the office and left a message for me to give you. The message was 'Done and done.' I assume that makes sense to you."

"I have no idea what that means, dear. I will call Starry and ask her what she meant. *We,* as in Annie and I, did not do anything, dear. Some pesky man from some health department questioned us both about our dinners last evening. He wanted to know if we got sick. I told him no. Did they call you? They called the others, who confirmed what I had told them earlier. Why do you ask?"

"Because I spoke to Livinia Lambert before I left for the day, and she said her husband and the Chessmen all had food poisoning and were blaming the food at the Daisy Wheel."

"That's ridiculous. We didn't get sick, and we had the same food."

"That none of us actually ate, Myra," Nikki snapped.

"Now you see, dear, that's where you're wrong. Annie and I brought our food home with us because you know neither one of us likes to cook. Those little mini fridges at the Inn are so handy. Anyway, we ate it for lunch, and it was delicious. I even called Starry to tell her, and she told me that there was an army of inspectors and health professionals going over the place with a fine-tooth comb. They could not find even one infraction, so she still has her five-star rating. She also told me that at the last minute, Mr. Bishop changed his dinner order from shrimp scampi to lamb chops. Mr. Lambert said he was allergic to shellfish and settled for prime rib. So you see, the Daisy Wheel is not responsible for whatever it was that made them sick. Annie and I think this is some kind of conspiracy."

"And the reason for their blaming the Daisy Wheel?" Nikki pressed. "And what about that cryptic message? What was it? Oh, yes, 'Done and done'? Sounds like some kind of code to me. Do you care to explain that to me, Myra?"

"I do not have a clue about that message, nor why those men would blame the Daisy Wheel. Nor does Annie, dear. Something devious, I'm sure. Since they are lawyers, and, I understand, not among the most ethical of the breed, I would assume a lawsuit is in the offing. Don't you agree?

"As for the message, who knows? Starry can be strange at times. If I had to guess, I'd say it probably has some-thing to do with a catering job for Annie. I'll check on it and get back to you. If there's nothing else, dear, then I'm going to cut this short and take Lady and the pups for a run. They just love romping in all those leaves. Then Annie is coming over, and we're going to play cards. At least that's the plan for the moment. Charles sent a text saying they're on the way home and should be here by nine. Is there anything wrong, Nikki?"

"Not yet," Nikki snapped again as she ended the conver-sation. "Not yet," she repeated under her breath, though she was tempted to shout it to the heavens.

Chapter 7

Jack Emery pushed his chair back from the table and looked down at his belt. He'd eaten too much, but Nikki's dinner, one of his favorites, was hard to resist when it came to second helpings. Cyrus had already accepted the fact that he'd also eaten too much of the chicken and veggies Nikki had cooked for him. He snoozed in contentment.

The pretty dishes Nikki only used for special occasions, along with her favorite blueberry candles, told him tonight's dinner was special and just for him; but for the life of him, he couldn't come up with a thing to account for whatever it was. "Good dinner, Nik," he said, stalling for time while he tried to come up with what special occasion it was.

"Give it up already, Jack. I can see your mind racing. There is no special occasion. I just felt in my blueberry mood. I've had a crummy couple of days, and I did miss you. How was the trip? This dinner was just my welcome-home present."

"We didn't commit, so that should tell you something. Industrial espionage. More like a personal vendetta, if you want my opinion, and we don't operate like that. Plus the supposed bad guy was, in my opinion, pretty much the good guy. The money was awesome, but I think we're going to walk away. Charles told our client, who really isn't our client yet, that we needed a week to do some due diligence. That's it pretty much in a nutshell. Then, if you factor in Maggie, it's a no-brainer. What about you? What has you in your blueberry mood?"

Nikki told him. When she was finished, she was out of breath. "More coffee?" she gasped.

"Sure, why not? I'm not going to sleep, anyway, so pour away, my dear."

Nikki poured coffee for Jack and more for herself. "Aren't you going to say something, Jack?"

"I'm thinking, I'm thinking. I think what you're asking me is what am I seeing that you *think* you missed. Two heads are better than one, that kind of thing. Something you can't quite put your finger on. Am I right?"

"Yes, and it's making me crazy. What do you think, Jack? I told you everything, so you have as clear a picture as I have. What did I miss?"

"I hate the word *coincidence* as much as you do, but don't you think the past two days do not pass the sniff test? Let's take it in order. Your new associate arrives bright and early yesterday morning. Not only is she your new associate, but you are handling what is probably one of the nicest, friendliest divorces of the century. The soon-to-be ex-husband arrives. They hold hands, everyone is misty eyed, soon-to-be ex is setting up a trust for her, which she doesn't want, but if she wants the divorce, which she does, she has to agree, and in the end, she agrees. Soon-to-be ex is rich, made *kazillions* in a start-up company, and has a trust of his own set up by his parents. Mom is rich, that's where the family money comes from. Dad is good old Buzz Lambert, the Speaker of the House of Representatives and second in the line of succession to the presidency. A man of distinction, in his own right, and one who might want to move into 1600 Pennsylvania Avenue down the road. No love lost between father and son, but we do not know why. Yet.

"Moving right along here. New associate leaves to go wherever she's going. Soon-to-be ex hightails it down to Margie Baylor to sign off on the trust, and who shows up, but good old Buzz? That's all we know about *that*.

"Moving further along, your second new client shows up, using an alias, no less. All hush-hush and secretive. And, lo and behold, it turns out that your second new client is the mother-in-law of your new associate, and mother to the Lamberts' only offspring, Jeffrey Lambert. Wife of good old Buzz Lambert. She wants a divorce, too. Lots of hoops to jump through here, but she lays down a hefty retainer. Lots of stories. True or false, who knows? What we do know at this point is that it is definitely weird.

"Oops, I forgot to mention the mystery tapes that involve Buzz and the Chessmen, Washington's hatchet lawyers. Said mystery tapes that suddenly disappear. Tapes, if they actually exist, that could put your client in jeopardy and damage the Speaker's reputation. How am I doing so far, Nik?"

"If nothing else, you're making me look like the idiot I feel like. Continue, Jack, since you are on a roll now."

"Okay, last night you and the sisters hit the Daisy Wheel for dinner to figure out what to do about Maggie. You all ordered a dinner of shrimp scampi, which none of you ate, but took home with you. When you were leaving, you noticed Buzz and the Chessmen at the front of the restaurant. Myra, Annie, and you were the last to leave. Annie, for whatever reason, stopped at their table and recommended the shrimp scampi. She knows Buzz, but not the Chessmen. Introductions were made. Then you leave, and Myra decides it's late and you three should stay at the Georgetown Inn, instead of driving out to the farm.

"Today, when you're finishing up to get ready to go out

to the farm, your new client calls to tell you her husband and the four Chessmen have a bad case of food poisoning. Two are in the hospital. A doctor from Walter Reed made a house call for Buzz. Unheard of in this town, but obviously it did happen because of his position. She's worried that you won't be able to serve divorce papers on him, plus she's jittery and scared now. I would assume because of the missing tapes.

"Half of Washington's health officials—hell, maybe all of them—descend on the Daisy Wheel to check it out for infractions. Because, after all, it is a five-star restaurant and is run by that aging hippie, Starry Knight. Who just happens to be best buds with Myra and Annie. That's where we are right now. Did I miss anything?"

"Only the part about Starry's leaving a message for Myra and Annie at the office. Myra blew that off and said 'Done and done' probably referred to a catering job Annie hired her for. Do I believe that? Look at me, Jack, do I look like I believe it?"

Jack laughed. "I have to say no, you do not. What's your next move, honey?"

"That's just it, Jack. I don't know. I know what I want to do, but don't know if I should or not. I'm thinking ahead here. It's going to be little ole me against those big bad Chessmen. No, they don't scare me. But they fight dirty. I go by the letter of the law. Yes, I have my whole firm behind me. I'm a damn good lawyer, Jack, you know that. Mrs. Lambert has the money. Buzz just has his salary. She's kept it that way all these years, so she obviously has some very astute financial advisors. The minute Buzz is served, first crack out of the gate, she'll get a notice that she is being audited by the IRS. That's years and years and boo-koo bucks defending. Next comes the muck. They'll have scores of people who will swear she has a penchant for little boys or something equally disgusting. I know this because they've done it countless times to other women. Some of the stories I've heard are really scary. Every lawyer in town knows this, and no one will go up against the Chessmen. They cave the moment their clients get served."

"Okay, coffee's done, now how about some wine? You have a plan of some kind, don't you?" Jack said, reaching for a bottle of wine from the wine rack.

Nikki leaned back on her chair to eyeball her husband. "It came to me right after you came home and went upstairs to shower. Cyrus and I were having a long talk. He agreed with me. When I had Carol prepare the complaint, I had her leave the last page blank. Sometimes, Jack, you just have to stack the deck. Let's see who buckles and runs for cover once that complaint is served to Mr. Wilson 'Call me "Buzz"' Lambert, also known as Mister Speaker of the House."

Jack grinned from ear to ear; then he let out a loud whoop of pure pleasure. "And the lawyer's name on the complaint."

"Elizabeth Fox. My secret weapon!"

"Did you call her? She's okay with it? I'm excited now."

"More than okay. She said she's been itching for years to take on those guys. She'll be here tomorrow."

"Way to go, Mrs. Emery," Jack said, high-fiving his wife.

"Those guys really have not been on my radar screen. I know what I know, but I also know I don't have the full skinny on them. Let's pool our knowledge and see exactly what we're going to be dealing with. We have all night, and this is a big bottle of wine. You go first," Nikki said as she poured wine into exquisite wine flutes, which she kept for special occasions. "Wait, wait. Before we get to all that, backtrack a bit. Do you think I'm being set up? Why? To what end? I'm not seeing it, even though I know something isn't right. Two divorces in the same family. Right now, that's pretty much all I see. Where are you seeing the problem, the young soon-to-be–ex Mrs. Lambert, or the older soon-to-be–ex Mrs. Lambert senior?"

"I don't have the answer right now. You know me, Nik, I need to think and stew and beat it to death before I come up with something. That's for later, anyway. Let's see what we know about the Chessmen. Maybe we'll find the answer there."

Nikki wrinkled her nose, an indication the subject was smelly.

Jack laughed. "Back when I worked as a prosecutor in the DA's office, that's all the young guys talked about. The way I recall it, most of them were just putting in their time till they got some experience under their belts; then they all, and I do mean all, were going into the private sector and make their fortune by billing six hundred bucks an hour, like the Chessmen. I was the lone exception, if you can believe that. I liked working in the DA's office, even though it was shitty pay. I just never had those kinds of aspirations.

"I read all the articles written about them because the young guys brought them in for everyone else to read. I skimmed through them, picked up a few things I still remember. I've seen them interviewed on TV.

"I think the four of them graduated from Harvard, then Harvard Law. They admitted they were nerds and had no friends other than themselves. What drew them together was they all belonged to the same chess club. They're all obsessed with the game. None of them are tournament players, but they do okay. Then they made a joke out of their names, saying they knew if they started up their own law firm, it would be a success. Think about it, Nik. King, Queen, Bishop, and Rook. One of the guys in the DA's office brought in a snippet he said his girlfriend gave him from some tabloid that said the four of them were better chess players than lawyers. Then I heard later on they sued the tabloid, forced a retraction, and the reporter was fired. I remember the reporter's name, too. For some reason, I never forgot it. I suppose because she was so young, and they ruined her life. She tried to defend herself, but those guys, even back then, had too much clout. We're going back a lot of years, Nik. After it happened, every time I heard a story about them, I would think of Lee Anders. She disappeared. The tabloid eventually folded, too. Rumor had it that the Chessmen saw to that."

"That's terrible. How did they get so powerful? And so quickly?"

"Good PR. And their own success. It was like overnight they became the go-to guys if you wanted to win a court case. Fear and intimidation. They actually worked at it back then. Now, today, they are the biggest firm in the District. They, as far as I know, do not try cases themselves anymore. They just sign off on them. Rumor is they always settle because no one wants to go to court. They have almost sixty associates, over a hundred drones, and I forget how many paralegals. They have forty thousand square feet of office space on K Street. Lots and lots of cubicles for the drones. They have the best benefits package going, and they pay top dollar to their people. The perks are unbelievable, or so I'm told. They have scouts they send out to recruit the cream of the crop from every graduating law class around the country."

"I heard they have a day-care center in the building, a real fish pond, a state-of-the-art gym, and a gourmet kitchen, with two five-star chefs, which caters to the entire staff and the four partners. I can see why they don't have any trouble with recruitment. I heard another rumor a while back about how they give all their new associates a pep talk and tell them when they bring in fifty—yep, *fifty*—million dollars, they will be considered for partnership. The monkey in that woodpile is that there were a few of the associates, real go-getters, who *almost* got to the fifty million. They were let go for whatever reason the Chessmen could come up with. No one fought back. *No one.* Did you hear that, Jack?" Nikki asked.

"No. But knowing what little I do know, I believe it. They rule by fear and intimidation, like I said. I'm also sure their severance packages were generous enough that none of those who were let go would fight it, knowing what they would be up against."

Jack looked across the table at his wife. He hated the worried look he was seeing on her face. "I know exactly what you're thinking. Do not go there, Nik. You're as fearless as Lizzie is. You can take these guys on and win, so wipe that look off your face. Once Lambert is served, and the Chessmen know who it is they're going to go up against, the tide will turn. In your favor. I know you're concerned about how they play dirty. Are you forgetting about your sisters? You girls have tricks in your bag that they can't even imagine. You win that one, and you can take down that firm. Do you have any idea how much Mrs. Lambert is worth?"

"She's up there with the endless zeros. Her family made their fortune in cotton and tobacco, just like all those other Virginia farmers. She has top-notch financial people handling her affairs. Buzz has never been able to get his hands on it. Everything grinds to a halt the moment he's served. Shut down. Shut off. He won't know what hit him, but the Chessmen will. I have Mrs. Lambert's power of attorney."

"You're kidding! She signed that over to you?"

"Yes, and it was her idea in the first place. I'm tired of talking about this, and we have finished the wine. We need to clean all this up and go to bed. Tomorrow is going to be a busy day. And didn't I hear you say something about being excited. What *exactly* does that mean?"

Cyrus reared up. He knew what that meant. It meant he was going to have one of those *I-am-not-going-up-the-stairs* moments. It meant he was sleeping right where he was. He thumped his tail on the tile floor, rolled over, and went back to sleep. At least he wouldn't have to make his bed in the morning.

"I say we just leave everything, and clean it up in the morning," Jack said, pulling his wife to her feet.

Cyrus cracked one eye open. He knew exactly how this was going to end.

Chapter 8

It was still dark out when Nikki made her way down the stairs, careful not to make a sound. She wasn't the least bit surprised when she saw Cyrus waiting for her at the bottom of the steps, his tail moving in a frenzy. She bent low, hugged the huge animal, and whispered in his ear before he trotted alongside her out to the kitchen. She turned on the outside light and opened the door. She shivered as the cold October air rushed through the doorway. "Don't take all day, Cyrus."

After she turned the heat up, Nikki eyed the mess she and Jack had left the night before. Gritting her teeth, she went at it, and, within minutes, the dishwasher was humming along, the coffee was dripping, and Cyrus's breakfast was under way: four scrambled eggs, four strips of bacon, and a hefty scoop of dry dog food. She eyed the perfectly scrambled eggs, knowing that she couldn't eat any. Breakfast had never been one of her favorite meals, and it still wasn't, unless she ate it at dinnertime. The best she could do in the morning was a slice of toast, a glass of juice, and two cups of coffee.

This morning, though, she was going to forgo the toast and stick with just coffee. No juice because she had forgotten to buy any.

While she waited at the door for Cyrus to return from his morning ablutions, her thoughts took her everywhere. What was she doing up so early? She'd tossed and turned all night, something that usually happened when she started a new case, so it really wasn't anything particularly out of the ordinary. What was out of the ordinary was that things were not lining up the way she wanted, which meant that she had to be missing something. Her gaze went to the clock on the Wolf range. Lizzie Fox's flight would be landing soon. Lizzie had the uncanny knack of looking at something and knowing instinctively what to do and how to go about it. Lizzie, she was sure, would make sense of all of this and tell her what she was missing.

Nikki opened the door for the shepherd, who waited patiently for her to test his breakfast to make sure it wasn't too hot, then went at it with gusto.

Nikki crouched with her back to the stove and waited until Cyrus was finished before she started to talk. Cyrus was always a good listener.

"Somewhere in this mess is an agenda, Cyrus. I know it. You know how you just know something. That's what this is. My gut is talking to me, but I'm not hearing the message it's sending. Is it my new associate? Is it Mrs. Lambert? To what end? Divorces are pretty cut and dried. There's always the nitpicking, the squabbles, the compromises. I just cannot, for the life of me, figure out the endgame here. I know in my gut that these two divorces are not your everyday kind of divorce. The only thing I can think of that is different is the law firm for the Speaker. That is my fly in the ointment right now. But . . . the Chessmen have nothing to do with Jeffrey and Amy, at least to my knowledge. I'm starting to think that Livinia might, I say *might*, have an agenda where they are concerned. She said she had tapes, which have now, presumably, gone missing, if they ever really existed in the first place.

"The Speaker's reputation is going to be severely damaged when the news gets out that his wife of all these years, his very rich wife of all these years, is divorcing him. Of course, the Chessmen will try to put a lid on it. What do you think, Cyrus? Am I even on the right track here, or am I just beating a dead horse?"

Cyrus reared up and licked at her cheek. He whined low in his throat, a sign that he couldn't help, even though he wanted to. Nikki stroked his massive head and hugged him. "I'm going to figure it out. I always do. I just wish it were going to be sooner rather than later.

"Oh, wow! Listen to this, Cyrus! I just had a thought. *Starry Knight!* Knight is the name of one of the chess pieces. Could that be my smoking gun? There are six pieces, pawn, bishop, knight, queen, rook, and king. Now if the last piece somehow comes to light and is named *pawn,* I am seriously going to be upset. All four of the Chessmen, plus Mr. Speaker of the House, got sick the other night after they ate dinner at Starry Knight's restaurant! Too much of a coincidence? I think I need to pay attention to this and see if I can hook it all together.

"Cyrus, go upstairs and wake up Jack. Don't let him roll over and go back to sleep. Bite his toes, if you have to. Go!"

The shepherd bounded out of the room the moment the words rolled off Nikki's tongue. *Permission to nip at Jack?* Doggie heaven after Jack made Harry take him to the BOLO Building and leave him there. Revenge is definitely a dish best served cold, preferably when its recipient is snugly nestled in a nice, warm bed.

Nikki was sliding a tray of sticky buns into the oven just as Jack stumbled into the kitchen. Nikki quickly poured him a cup of coffee and set it in front of him. "Good job, Cyrus!"

The shepherd barked to show he could follow orders. "I've seen you look better in the morning, honey." Nikki giggled. She continued to giggle at her husband's wild hair, which was standing on end, as well as the one arm in his robe, the other dragging on the floor. He wore one slipper and looked meaner than a cat caught outside in a rainstorm.

"I was having the best dream. I was at a pure white-sand beach swimming in crystal-blue waters. You and Cyrus were with me, and you were wearing a bikini that could fit in my ear. It was red-and-white polka dots. Cyrus was wearing a jeweled collar. A big wave was bearing down, then, *bam!* All I could see was your bikini washing away in the wave. Cyrus tried to get it, then he woke me up. That dog is relentless. What are you doing up so early? Oh, you cleaned the kitchen! Sticky buns. Is that a peace offering for waking me so early? Say something!" Jack demanded.

Nikki sniffed. "Well, for starters, I do not own a red-and-white polka-dotted bikini. Cyrus never fails. He would have retrieved my bikini if it really were mine, which it could not have been. How do I even know that *I* was the one wearing it in your dream? I just have your word for it, and right now, you look pretty shifty-eyed to me. So . . . who was it?"

"It was you, I swear. Now tell me why you had Cyrus drag me down here at this ungodly hour."

"Starry Knight. That's why. Think Chessmen. Think about their names. Starry's last name is *Knight.* Knight is one of the chess pieces. Six pieces to a chess game. Only pawn is missing. Think about how they all got sick suddenly at Starry Knight's restaurant. *Knight* as in *knight.* Think, Jack!"

"You're thinking what, exactly? That somehow that aging hippie is somehow involved with the Chessmen," Jack said as he tried to smooth down his bed hair.

"Don't you? It's the only thing that makes sense."

"That would have to mean that Starry is friends with their wives. We already know she is friends with Myra and Annie. And the agenda is . . . ?"

"I don't know, Jack. I'm just throwing that out there to see if we should run with it or not." The oven timer went off. Nikki slid the tray of sticky buns out of the oven and set it on the counter to cool.

Jack refilled his coffee cup. "This is getting weirder by the minute. I don't know why I'm saying this, but I think you might need to keep a sharp eye on your new associate when she starts work next month. Something is not right about all that."

"Yeah, I know. You think about that, and I'm going to hit the shower. Lizzie's plane should be landing any minute now. She sent me a text saying she was going to stop at the hospital to see Maggie, then head to my office. If you're bored while I'm showering, call Avery Snowden and ask him to run a full background check on the Chessmen, back to the days they were born. Then if you're still bored, call Charles and have him call a meeting tonight at Myra's. We need to get cracking on this and have all our ducks in a row before that divorce complaint is served on good old Buzz Lambert."

"Yeah, sure." Jack reached for his third sticky bun, then a fourth, which he slipped to Cyrus. He was about to pour more coffee in his cup when he heard the *ping* of an incoming text on Nikki's phone, which was on the counter. From Lizzie. The message was short and sweet: **I'm on the ground. See ya.**

"You know what that means, Cyrus, right? Lizzie's here!" Cyrus let loose with a sharp bark to show he understood that the cavalry had arrived.

Lizzie Fox had indeed arrived at Reagan National Airport. Incognito. Lizzie was a head turner, with her mane of silver hair, incredible long legs, and the longest eyelashes in the world. She always turned heads; men's glances, as well as women's, always followed her until she was out of sight.

During her years practicing law in Washington, D.C., she'd become a legend in her own time. There wasn't a lawyer who didn't groan in misery when they found out she was their adversary. She had the ears and eyes of every judge on the bench, and it was rumored when the court docket was worked on, the judges fought among themselves to hear her cases. Lizzie Fox never lost a case.

The nation's capital went all out to throw a going-away party, which was the envy of the White House, when Lizzie announced that she was relocating to Las Vegas, Nevada. It was rumored for months after Lizzie's departure that every judge in town went into a funk and took out their frustration on every lawyer to hit their courtrooms. It was further rumored that more than one judge had hanging on their walls a picture of the silver-haired goddess, who battled for the underdog, right alongside photos of dignitaries no one knew or remembered. *Everyone* remembered Lizzie Fox. Every politician on Capitol Hill knew of her personal friendship with President Martine Connor and the time she had spent working for her in the White House.

Today, though, at this hour of the morning, no one in the busy airport recognized Lizzie Fox. Today, she was dressed in faded jeans, sneakers, a dark blue hoodie, and a baseball cap. A plain black Lands' End backpack rode her shoulders. She carried no purse and wore no makeup. She was just another traveler getting off the red-eye.

With no luggage to declare because her husband, Cosmo Cricket, had sent it on an earlier flight with instructions to deliver it on to Pinewood upon arrival, Lizzie strode through the airport and out to the taxi line. She hopped into the third taxi in line and instructed the driver to take her to Georgetown University Hospital.

Lizzie arrived just as the shift changed. She walked down the hall as if she knew where she was going, which she did, and entered Maggie's room quietly. "Hey there, Miss Reporter, how's it going?"

Stunned that she had a visitor, Maggie gasped. "Lizzie! What are you doing here? Oh, my God, am I dying? Is that why you're here? Lizzie!" she squealed. "How did you get in here, anyway?"

"Shift change. No, you are not dying. You look better than I expected. Talk to me, Maggie," Lizzie said in a voice that she only used for her husband and son.

Maggie started to cry. Lizzie didn't move or say a word or try to comfort her until she felt that Maggie was done sniffling and sobbing.

"A family is a wonderful thing, Maggie. I, for one, know this. Even when that family isn't from the same bloodline. Family is family. Your family was here for you until they were forced to leave. I understand the boys had to use a crowbar to get Ted to leave. That isn't quite true, but close. I'm sorry I wasn't here. The reason our little family is so successful is because we're all sisters under the skin. Not one of us would knowingly hurt or harm any of the others. I'm hoping, Maggie, you see that now and regret preventing the most important people in your life from seeing you.

"Nikki told me about the meeting they had planned to discuss what they thought might be a problem where you were concerned. A *possible* problem, Maggie. The reason you were not included in that meeting was they pretty much knew you weren't a problem, but they needed to be sure. You can't fault them for that. Nikki said they would have gone to you immediately to bring you up to date. She also said, if anyone would understand, it would be you. I guess she was wrong. Is she wrong, Maggie?"

"I've had nothing to do other than lie here and think

and think. No, she isn't wrong. Yes, I did overreact because all I could think about was that goof-up with Abner and the boys. I didn't want that to happen to me. I really didn't, Lizzie. I'd give up my right arm for any of them, that's how much I love all of them. It just hurt so bad that they would think I couldn't be trusted. Me, of all people." Tears trickled down Maggie's cheeks, but Lizzie still made no move to comfort her.

"Forgiveness is a wonderful thing. I had to learn that the hard way many moons ago. To forgive is to be free. Coming from the gambling mecca of this country, I am willing to bet you five dollars that once you let it go, you'll feel on top of the world. And you need to be there, because the reason I'm here is to help the girls. They're going to need your expertise, so when are you blasting out of this place?"

"Are you kidding me? I've been begging them to keep me as long as possible, just so I wouldn't have to face . . . you know . . . everyone. This is just a guess, but I think I can leave tomorrow if I agree to stay housebound for a week or so. I've been ditching the pain meds. I hate not being in control. So, if I can handle what I've handled, then I can handle it at home. Besides, Hero misses me, I'm sure. Let's shoot for tomorrow, okay?"

"And the family?"

"I'll make it right. They might have to wait until I'm all healed, so I can grovel, but I will grovel. I promise. Now, tell me what the mission is, and don't you dare leave anything out."

Lizzie told her everything she knew. When she was finished, Maggie let out a loud whoop, which brought the nurse in the crackly uniform running. Seeing that her patient was okay, she homed in on Lizzie, who squelched her with one ferocious look. Miss Snap, Crackle, and Pop turned and went back to the nurses' station.

"Oooh, I wish I had that power. She makes me crazy."

Lizzie smiled. "And yet you wanted to stay."

Maggie rolled her eyes. "I have been wanting to go after those Chessmen for years. For whatever her reasons, Annie always killed my requests. Are you saying she's okay now with going after them? I have tons of research, and so does Ted. Lordy, Lordy, for sure I have to get out of here. You sure do look different, Lizzie."

"I'm going to take that as a compliment, Maggie. Look, I have to go. They're expecting me out at the farm, and I'm getting hungry. First, though, I did make a promise to drop in at Nikki's office. I must admit that I'm looking forward to one of Charles's gourmet breakfasts. Is there anything I can do for you before I leave? Do you need anything?"

"A cell phone would be nice. I don't know what happened to mine or to my backpack, and the doctor said I didn't need a phone. What does he know?"

"I have a burner I can leave with you, but I need it back when you get home."

Maggie's eyes popped wide. "The great Lizzie Fox has a burner phone! Wow! Why?"

"Cosmo got it for me. He has one, too. They're untraceable. You never know when one comes in handy. Like now. Here," Lizzie said, handing over a cell phone that looked just like every other cell phone in the world. "I taped the number on the back because I keep forgetting it. Remember, you have to give it back."

"Okay. Oh, man, this is going to be such a good day. I can feel it already. Thanks, Lizzie. I'll call to let you know if they'll be discharging me tomorrow. Uh-oh, here comes Miss Snap, Crackle, and Pop again. You'd better get out of here, since it isn't visiting hours."

Lizzie leaned over and kissed Maggie lightly on the cheek. Maggie almost swooned at the scent of gardenias and hibiscus that emanated from her friend. Lizzie always smelled like gardenias and hibiscus. "See ya tomorrow. Thanks, Lizzie."

"That's what friends are for, Maggie."

Maggie let out another loud whoop of happiness as she waved the burner phone in the air. A moment later, Lizzie Fox was gone, replaced by Miss Snap, Crackle, and Pop.

"Doctor said no phones, Ms. Spritzer. Hand it over."

"That's not going to happen, and I think we both know it. And don't think you're giving me a sponge bath, either. I'd like a really good breakfast this morning, if you don't mind. None of that mushy oatmeal that tastes like cardboard, either. Real eggs and real bacon and warm toast. Lots of coffee, and not decaffeinated, either. Please," Maggie added as an afterthought.

"I'll see what I can rustle up for you. A word of advice, Ms. Spritzer. I wouldn't let Dr. Latuda see that cell phone. You might want to stash it somewhere until the doctor finishes his rounds. He's on the floor, so he'll be in momentarily."

"Why are you being so nice to me all of a sudden?" Maggie asked, suspicion ringing in her voice.

"Maybe because you're a woman, and I'm a woman, and that lady that just left here has been my idol for a very long time. She might look like a hippie today, but I darn well know Lizzie Fox when I see her. She successfully defended the nurses' union some years ago. Like I said, she's my idol. Now, how do you want those eggs?"

"Sunny-side up," Maggie said smartly.

Nurse Handley gave her a thumbs-up as she waltzed through the door, crackling with every step.

Maggie threw her good arm up in the air. "Thank you, God, the Universe, Lizzie, and everyone else in the whole world!"

Chapter 9

Mitzi Doyle, Nikki's office manager extraordinaire, poked her head in the door, and said, "Got a visitor for you, boss."

Nikki created a draft when she bolted out of her chair to run across the room and wrap her arms around Lizzie. "Oh, it's so good to see you, Lizzie." She turned to Mitzi, and said, "Coffee, please, and send Alexis in." Then back to Lizzie, "Thanks for coming on such short notice. How'd it go with Maggie? Is she okay? Talk to me, Lizzie."

Nikki herded Lizzie over to the plush seating area and motioned for her to sit down. "Coffee and sticky buns will be here shortly. Tell me everything, and don't leave a single thing out."

Whatever she was about to say went unsaid when Alexis buzzed into the room to hug Lizzie. Squeals of pleasure and laughter took over as the three dear friends reunited after a long absence.

"Lookin' good, Lizzie!" said Alexis.

"Gotta say the same about you, Alexis. How's tricks?"

"Same old, same old. Sorry I can't stay—I have a client in the office who is acting like she stepped into an anthill. See you out at the farm tonight." A moment later, she was gone.

"You look tired, Lizzie, so I won't keep you. We can talk tonight." Nikki poured coffee and handed the cup to Lizzie. "Just tell me about Maggie, sign the divorce complaint, and you're good to go. You're okay with this, right?"

"Absolutely. Maggie is back in the fold. Her feelings were hurt, really hurt. Nikki, she would never betray you and the girls. Never. She'd walk away first."

"I know, but when there is even a shadow of doubt, we have to deal with it. Otherwise, it doesn't work. You know that."

"I do know that, and so does Maggie. It was a knee-jerk reaction. Then there was that episode with Abner, which was still so fresh in her memory. It's over and done with, and we're all moving on. There's a good chance Maggie will be discharged tomorrow. A week or so, with a home health aide, and she'll be almost as good as new." Lizzie popped a piece of sticky bun in her mouth and rolled her eyes in pure pleasure. "I haven't had one of these in ages. Okay, where's the complaint?"

"Right here," Mitzi said, handing it over along with a pen. Lizzie scrawled her signature and grinned at Nikki. "Done!"

"Mitzi, take this down to Billy in the mail room and have him take it to the courthouse. Put it in an envelope first. Peggy knows it's coming. Tell Billy to wait until she stamps it and bring it straight back here. Do we have our process server ready to go?"

"The minute you give the word, boss."

Nikki looked over at Lizzie. "I was going to wait till Friday until Alexis reminded me about courthouse leaks. We have to serve the Speaker right away, and at the same time give Mrs. Lambert time to get airborne. She said she would be good to go at a moment's notice, but I don't think she meant four days ahead of schedule. Mitzi, call her and tell her what's going on and see if she can leave now."

Lizzie was on her feet and gathering up her things. "I need to get some sleep, Nikki, or I won't be good for anything."

"One more minute, Lizzie. Um . . . I need to ask you something. In your opinion, am I a good lawyer? I mean *good* good."

Lizzie took a step back, far enough back that she could look Nikki in the eye. Her own eyes narrowed at the question. "What did I tell you years ago?" she asked quietly.

Nikki cleared her throat. "To never doubt myself and always go with my gut."

"And?"

"Take no prisoners."

"So what's our problem here?" Lizzie asked, puzzled at the question.

"I don't know what it is, that's my problem. My gut is telling me I'm missing something. That I'm not seeing something. I know it's there. *I know it.* If I was as good a lawyer as I think I am, then I would know. I can't nail it down, Lizzie."

"If it's there, you'll find it. Shift into neutral. I really don't want to ask this, but I am going to ask it, anyway. Are you perhaps a bit intimidated knowing you will be going head-to-head with the Chessmen? Trust me when I tell you that you are a better lawyer than the four of them put together."

"*NO!* I don't practice law the way the Chessmen do, Lizzie. They fight dirty."

"Did you forget who you are, Nikki? Did you forget who you have watching your back? Think about *that*! Enough said. Okay, I'm off to the farm. I'll see you tonight. One last thing, do not ever let me hear you doubt yourself again."

Nikki felt like she was being chastised by her favorite teacher, back in grade school. "Yes, ma'am. I hear you. I'll walk you out."

"You know, Nikki, even in Las Vegas we get District news. I subscribe to everything that will allow me to know what's going on here from minute to minute. I have so many apps, I can't keep track of them all. What I'm trying to say is your firm is triple-A rated. That puts you on the map. You know some very influential people here in town. And I know a few as well. Those boys don't have a lock on people in high places. Don't fall for their PR is what I'm trying to say here, because they're the ones who originated the PR in the first place."

"Gotcha." Nikki gave her friend a hard hug. "You're the best, Lizzie. Thanks again."

"What are friends for? See ya."

"Yeah, see ya tonight."

Nikki stood at the plate-glass door watching until Lizzie was out of sight. She felt sad and yet elated at the same time. How weird was that?

Nikki sprinted back to her office and whizzed by her secretary, who called out to her, "I have your client on the phone. Line two."

Breathless, Nikki identified herself and said as coolly as she could, "It's nine-thirty. How soon can you be airborne?"

"I can leave now and take the first flight I can get a seat on. I wasn't expecting to hear so soon."

"I know, I know. Things changed rather quickly. Call me when you're ready to board. It's crucial that I know as soon as possible. Has anything changed?"

"No, not really. Wilson spends all his time on the phone. I don't know who he's talking to, because he stops talking when I enter the room. His cronies would be my guess."

"Who is going to answer the door when the process server rings the bell?"

"The housekeeper."

"Before you leave the house, tell her someone called

who will be delivering something to your husband that he has to personally sign for. Just say you forgot to tell your husband. Will she tell him or just accept what you are telling her?"

"I don't know, Ms. Quinn. Wilson hired her. She's a terrible housekeeper, but he likes her. He probably hired her as a favor to someone. I can't believe this is happening so fast."

Nikki wanted to say she couldn't believe it either, but she kept that thought to herself. "Remember now, walk out of the house as though you were going shopping or to lunch. Don't take anything with you. You have your—"

"I have it all. I know what to do. I'll be out of this house in the next fifteen minutes. Thank you, Ms. Quinn."

Livinia Lambert was almost as good as her word. It took her eighteen minutes to gather up her envelope of false identities, cash, and traveler's checks. She was already dressed, because she was old-school, meaning that she dressed for the day regardless of whether she was going out or staying at home. Nothing she was doing now, or would do in the next eighteen minutes, should raise any eyebrows.

It was hard not to shout at the top of her lungs, to shoot her closed fists in the air, but knowing what was at stake was all the impetus she needed to do things the right way and leave her triumphant feelings unexpressed.

Livinia poked her head into her husband's study and asked if she could get him anything before she left.

Wilson Lambert clicked off the call on his cell phone and looked up at his wife. He didn't really care where she was going, but he asked, anyway. It seemed like the thing to do, and he'd been doing it for years. "A day out with the ladies, Livinia?"

"Not really." She sounded too cheerful, she thought. Toning things down a bit, she said, "Library luncheon, a little shopping. Dinner with our son's old professor, which I have been putting off. Ella will prepare something light for you. Are you feeling better, Wilson?"

"Actually, I am feeling better. Run along. I have a hundred calls to make here."

Livinia stood in the open doorway and stared at and through the man she fervently hoped never to see again. He was a handsome man, tall, well over six feet, and he carried his height and weight well. That was mainly because he loved being on camera and needed to present a robust image. He wore shell-rimmed glasses he didn't need because he thought they made him look scholarly. But it was his crop of premature snow-white hair, with a hint of a wave, that set him apart from his peers. And his year-round tan from the tanning bed he'd installed in the basement. Not to mention the pricey veneers she'd paid for so he could look ten years younger when he smiled into the camera. Wilson Lambert worked hard at looking distinguished, and, given his wife's money and his own vanity, he managed to succeed.

Speaker Lambert was dressed in a suit and tie, even though he was sick and at home. He said he owed it to himself and the world to dress like he was going to make the world better, each and every day, and therefore he had to dress to look the part. Livinia wanted to tell him that was all a crock of something or other, but she knew it would go in one ear and out the other. The only person Wilson "Buzz" Lambert listened to was himself.

"Is something wrong, Livinia? Why are you looking at me like that?"

"No, Wilson, nothing is wrong. I was just thinking that you do look much better today. Your color is coming back. I was also thinking about how you look sitting here in my daddy's study with all his books, his desk, the chair you're sitting in. Sometimes I think I can smell my daddy's presence. I guess it's because you smoke the same pipe to-bacco. Some days, I don't like it when I see you sitting in my daddy's chair. Some days, I remember and don't like that you would never let Jeffrey come into this room when he was a little boy."

"Well, you need to get over that right now, Livinia. Your daddy's long gone, and Jeffrey is a grown, married man. What's gotten into you today?"

What indeed? Uh-oh, I just stepped out of the box. Livinia forced a laugh she didn't feel. "For heaven's sake, a person can't control her memories. Memories are part of our lives, and I wouldn't have it any other way. Besides, I was just woolgathering. I'll be off now. Enjoy your day. Good-bye, Wilson." *You low-life, bottom-feeding son of a bitch. I am never ever going to set eyes on you again. Enjoy my daddy's room for now because you are going to be out in the cold on your bony ass within days. How's that for a memory, Mr. Speaker of the House?*

Nikki's phone rang at precisely 11:11 that same morn-ing. "I'm about to board a flight to Jacksonville, Florida, under the name Frieda Opala. I'll call again before I board my next flight. Everything went well."

Nikki ended the call and walked out to her secretary's office. "Call Billy and tell him it's time to head over to the courthouse. Remind him he's to wait for the signed stamp and bring it straight to me. Which process server are we using? I want him or her up here and waiting to go the minute Billy gets back. Get Ted Robinson on the phone for me, will you?"

"I'll get right on it. Take a break, boss. You're looking a tad frazzled right now. We'll get this done just the way you want it done. You want some coffee?"

"Guess what, I feel as frazzled as I look, and, yes, I want

coffee, but I'll get it myself. Take care of business. Buzz me when you have Ted on the line."

A minute later, Nikki was breathing evenly, her mind as sharp as a steel blade, as she spoke into the phone. "Ted, it's Nikki. Listen, Lizzie Fox is in town. She just left my office and is headed for the farm. We all plan to meet tonight at Myra's. Around seven, I think. No one mentioned dinner, so you might want to nail that down. But the reason I'm calling is to tell you that Maggie is probably going to be discharged tomorrow and will have home rest with a home health aide to help her out. A home health aide, Ted, not you. I think it might be a good idea to plan a little welcome-home party for her, say around three or four. That means you need to get in touch with everyone and put them on alert. Order in some food, whatever Maggie likes. Get some balloons, some streamers, you know, party stuff. I think that if you go to the hospital right now, you'll be allowed to see Maggie. Lizzie made everything right, thank God."

"Oh, man, I am so on this, you have no idea. I'm going to take a selfie of me and Hero to pave the way. Thanks, Nikki. I guess I'll see you out at the farm tonight."

Nikki stared at the phone in her hand. Dead air. Ted could move fast when he wanted to. When it came to anything to do with Maggie, he literally galloped. In spite of herself, Nikki laughed out loud. If ever two people were meant for one another, it was Ted Robinson and Maggie Spritzer. They both knew it, but still they fought it. Why? She had no clue.

"Ms. Quinn?"

Nikki swiveled her chair around. "Oh, Billy, I didn't hear you come in. You ready to go? You know what to do?"

"Yes, ma'am."

Nikki made shooing motions with her hand until the

young man figured out she meant for him to leave ASAP. Which he did, wondering what all the fuss was this time.

Nikki sighed. She was going to do something. What was it? Ah, yes, she was going to get some coffee. Which she really didn't need, but would drink, anyway. To her surprise, she found Alexis seated at the table, nibbling on a dry bagel.

"Everything okay, Nikki?"

Nikki quickly brought Alexis up to date. "I don't think I ever moved this fast on a divorce complaint in my entire career. It's just that the minute it's recorded, the leaks and gossip will start. I want the Speaker served before it gets out. Otherwise, he'll go to ground to avoid it. At least I think that's what he'll do. As we speak, our client is on the way to the airport and out of harm's way. I hate to admit this, Alexis, but this really kicked my fanny. I am going to figure this out one way or another."

"Spoken like a true lawyer. I'm excited for Maggie, that she's going home tomorrow. Are we going to video her for the meeting tonight? Abner knows how to set that up so she can talk and be part of it all. Of course, the hospital has to approve, but my money is on Maggie. I think she can get them to cooperate. And then a surprise party for her homecoming. Just perfect. I cannot tell you how much better I feel now that all of that is in the past. I hope we never have to go through anything like that again."

"Me too. It's like Lizzie always says. When all is said and done, things will end just the way they are supposed to end. I've never known her to be wrong, have you, Alexis?"

"Nope. If Lizzie says it, then it's gospel. Gotta run. I have that guy who makes me see red coming in about his eminent-domain case on a piece of property. The man refuses to take my advice or to listen to anyone else who tries to help him. He's not even complaining about the whopping bills he's getting from the firm. Some days like today, I cannot help but wonder if I really am supposed to be a lawyer."

Nikki laughed. "Trust me, you are meant to be a lawyer. This is just one of those days we all have four days a week. Wanna go to lunch, say around one?"

"Sure. You buying?"

"Nope, but the firm is."

"Well, then, okayyyyyyy," Alexis drawled.

Chapter 10

Boarding pass in hand, Livinia Lambert was on the third leg of her journey with her third phony ID. She'd traveled as Frieda Opala from Washington, D.C., to Jacksonville, Florida, where she boarded a flight to Houston, Texas, as Teresa Lyons. She was now about to board her third flight, out of Houston, as Mavis Journeyman. Her final destination, Honolulu, Hawaii.

As Livinia shifted her weight from one foot to the other, her gaze kept going to the huge airport clock hanging on the wall almost in front of her. Her flight from Houston had been late, so she'd had to scurry, which didn't leave much time for phone calls to the Quinn Law Firm. There were too many people around now to make the call. Perhaps once she was seated in economy class, she'd have a minute before the pilot ordered all cell phones to be turned off. Had Wilson been served? Was he pulling that lush white hair on his head out by the roots? She also needed to call her son at some point, but not right away. Maybe she'd have Nikki Quinn make the call to Jeffrey. She wouldn't put it past Wilson to pull out all the stops and find a way to check Jeffrey's phone records.

The time was four o'clock, central time, when Livinia,

aka Mavis Journeyman, settled back in her seat in economy class as the huge Boeing aircraft rose to a cruising alti-
tude of thirty thousand feet. It was an hour later, six o'clock
back in Washington, D.C., when Hunter Wayne, the process
server for the Quinn Law Firm, rang the doorbell at 2301
Clements Ferry Road, the home of Livinia and Wilson
Lambert. In his hand, he held a brown manila envelope,
complete with a red wax seal. The red wax seal meant
nothing and was for effect only. The red wax was from a
birthday candle he'd melted, then jammed his thumb in
the soft wax to make it look official. Hunter Wayne knew
every trick in the book when it came to serving papers on
people who did not want to accept service, because to do
so invariably meant a lawsuit of some kind was in their future.

Hunter was dressed in what he called his "server suit."
It was an off-the-rack suit, but he'd paid top dollar for it.
He was spit and polish from the top of his groomed head
to the shine on his black shoes. He could have easily
passed for a Wall Street broker, a banker, or even, God for-
bid, a lawyer. Or even one of the civilian workers from the
Pentagon or a denizen of the halls of the House or the Sen-
ate. He drove a Mercedes C-Class car—not too high end,
but not low end, either.

Hunter stepped back when the door opened just as the
porch light sprang to life. "Yes, can I help you?" the staff
member wearing a gray uniform with a white apron asked
in a reedy-sounding voice.

"I certainly hope so, ma'am. I have a delivery for a Mr.
Wilson Lambert."

The lady reached out to take the envelope. Hunter took
another step backward. "I'm sorry, ma'am. My instructions are to personally hand this envelope over to Mr.
Lambert and take a picture showing me doing so."

"Mr. Lambert has been ill. I can sign whatever it is that needs to be signed. I really don't want to disturb Mr. Lambert."

"Nothing needs to be signed, ma'am. I told you, I need to take a picture of Mr. Lambert accepting this delivery. I can leave and come back another time, but I have the feeling, and I do not know this for sure, that this is a very important delivery. Why don't you check with Mr. Lambert, just to be sure, before I leave?"

"Who is it from?"

"I'm not at liberty to say, ma'am. See this seal? Something pretty official, I'd say."

The housekeeper looked at the red wax seal under the porch light, then said, "Wait here. I need to speak with Mr. Lambert."

Hunter mentally patted himself on the back. He quickly slid his nail under the red wax seal, and the envelope opened in a second. His cell was in his other hand, all set to snap the obligatory picture. *Ho hum,* he thought, *just another day in my life as a process server.*

The door swung open, just as he knew it would. The Speaker of the House literally filled the open doorway with his presence. "What do you have for me, young man? Isn't it kind of late to be making deliveries?" Wilson Lambert eyed the envelope and the red seal and stretched out his hand.

"Are you Wilson Lambert?"

"I am. I am the Speaker of the House."

"I need to take your picture accepting this delivery, sir." Phone in place with one hand, as the other hand withdrew the contents of the envelope, Hunter Wayne had the situation under control.

Click.

"You have been served, Wilson Lambert!"

Done!

"Have a nice evening, Mr. Lambert."

"What the . . . Come back here! What is this?" Lambert barked. Hunter Wayne walked as fast as his legs would carry him. He did not look back.

Hunter continued to ignore the Speaker and climbed into his C-Class Mercedes and barreled down the long, winding driveway. At the end of the driveway, as he waited for a break in traffic to make a left turn onto the highway, Hunter sent a two-word text that said, **Lambert served.** The picture he'd taken accompanied the text. Ninety-five dollars for serving the papers and a fifty-dollar bonus for serving the papers so expeditiously. One hundred and forty-five bucks for one hour's work. Minus fifty-nine cents for the birthday candle. All in all, he was more than pleased with himself.

Back at the Quinn Law Firm, Nikki was waiting by the door for Alexis when the text, along with the picture of Wilson Lambert, came through cyberspace. Nikki's fist shot in the air. She quickly sent off a text to Livinia Lambert that Livinia wouldn't see until she landed in Hawaii. Far enough away so that Wilson Lambert couldn't get to her.

Nikki and Alexis high-fived each other when Nikki showed Alexis the text and picture.

"What do you think the illustrious Speaker of the House is doing right now, Nikki?" Alexis giggled.

Nikki laughed. "This is just a guess on my part, but I kind of think right now he's snuggled up with Jim Beam as he's dialing the Chessmen for a conference call."

If truth be known, Nikki was only half right in her assessment of what Wilson Lambert was doing.

Fifteen miles away as the crow flies, Wilson Lambert tilted the bottle of Jim Beam and guzzled till his eyes burned and he thought he would black out. He had read the complaint three times until he had it committed to memory.

When he felt like he had himself under control, he swore like he'd never sworn before.

"Son of a goddamn bitch!" he bellowed. He wanted to rip the papers on the desk, Livinia's daddy's desk, but he knew he couldn't. Then he was tempted to throw the same papers into the blazing fireplace, but he knew he couldn't do that, either. He started to pace then, the bottle of Jim Beam still in his hand. His eyes were wild and crazy as he stared at the room that he considered his own. Thirty days to vacate the premises. *Thirty days!* Thirty days to respond to this . . . this piece of crap. He'd be the laughingstock of the town. The White House was *not* going to like this. His face would be plastered all over the world. He had to do something. What? He tilted Jim Beam again and took a mighty swallow.

Wilson stopped his frantic pacing. He was dreaming. That's what this was all about, or else he was delirious from all the medication he'd been taking. He pinched himself. It hurt. His eyes narrowed as he recalled Livinia's standing in the doorway earlier in the morning. She'd talked more to him in that little window of time than she'd talked to him in years. And she'd actually said *good-bye.* Why hadn't he picked up on that? And all that talk about her daddy, and this being *his* room. That should have been a clue right there. He'd flubbed that, too. He bellowed for Ella, the housekeeper, who came on the run. "Has my wife gotten back yet?"

"No, sir, she's not home. Do you need something? Dinner is almost ready, chicken and rice, so it will be easy on your stomach. Some nice mint tea. Tell me when you want me to bring it in. I know how you like to eat by the fire."

"I'm not hungry. Don't look at me like that. Take the rest of the evening off, Ella."

The minute the housekeeper was out of sight, Wilson bolted from the study and ran as fast as he could to the second floor. He literally flew down the hall to his wife's bedroom. It smelled like her, all powdery and dry. He felt like a wild man as he tore through the room, looking for any sign that she was gone for good. Since he hadn't stepped foot in this room in years, he had no idea what he was looking for. Everything was neat and tidy, just like Livinia herself. The bed was perfectly made. The desktop was neat, with nothing out of place. All the clothes were neatly arranged in the huge walk-in closet. Luggage was on the top shelf. It didn't look like any of the matched set was missing.

The suite of rooms was so empty, *felt* so empty, that Wilson was positive that his wife was not coming back. Not while he was still in the house. She'd simply walked out of the house this morning, never to return. She was genteel enough, however, to say a final good-bye. And he'd been too stupid to pick up on it, and this was the result. He tipped the bottle of Jim Beam once again.

Livinia couldn't have done this, planned it all on her own. She had to have had help. *Jeffrey!* Of course. Jeffrey was in town to file for his own divorce. The two of them must have planned this together. He needed to call his son and straighten this out right now. Right this very minute. The only problem was he didn't know his son's phone number. Now, that was a sorry state of affairs.

Wilson stumbled his way over to his wife's tidy desk to look for her address book. He finally found it in the bottom drawer. But he couldn't read it without his readers. He spied his wife's reading glasses on a little tray on the corner of her desk. They would do. He quickly punched in the numbers and waited for the call to go through. Even before he could identify himself, he heard his son say, "Hi, Mom, what's up!"

"This is your father, Jeffrey, not your mother. I want you to put her on the phone so we can discuss what she's done before this gets out of hand. Now put her on the phone. I know she's with you. I also know you probably put her up to this."

"Put her up to what? I don't have a clue as to what you are talking about. Is Mom okay? Have you been drinking? You sound drunk, Mr. Speaker, sir."

" 'Put her up to what'? Is that what you said?" Wilson snarled. "Like you don't know. I just got served with divorce papers. I'm to vacate this house in thirty goddamn days. And your mother is gone. She walked out of the house this morning and never came home. Now I'm not going to tell you again, young man, put your mother on the phone. I know she went running to you. I know it. Where else would she go?"

"I'm not going to tell you again that Mom is not here, and I do not know what the hell you're talking about other than that you sound drunk. My advice is sleep it off, take two aspirin, and call me in the morning. Of course, when you do, my response will be the same. But perhaps once you are sober, you will be able to understand what I am saying. Good-bye, Mr. Speaker of the House. I'm hanging up now."

"Don't you dare hang up on me, Jeffrey Lambert! I know a lie when I hear one, and you're lying right now."

"I am not surprised at all that you know all about lying. That's all you've done your whole life, and, yes, Mr. Speaker, I am hanging up on you. Don't call me back because I won't answer the phone. On second thought, do not call me in the morning because I won't want to talk to you then any more than I want to talk to you now.

"And, incidentally, if what I think you're calling about is true, that Mom has decided to divorce you and throw you out of her house, then all I can say is good for her."

Since he'd made the call on the house's landline, Wilson could hear the phone's dial tone. His son was true to his word and had hung up. He cursed then, using words that surprised him as he wondered where they had come from. In frustration, Wilson finished off the Jim Beam and tossed the empty bottle across the room. "Take that, Livinia," he muttered as he stomped his way out of the room.

Back in *his* study, Wilson looked around, trying to decide what he should do next. A wise man would opt for the leather sofa by the fire to sleep off the Jim Beam. Right now, though, he didn't feel particularly wise, so he snatched the papers that the process server had handed him. He settled himself in *his* chair, reached for his reading glasses, and started to read. On his fourth read-through, he'd really committed every single word to memory, having realized he'd somehow missed paragraph seven on his third read-through. That was when he knew he'd crashed and burned. He heaved himself upright and staggered over to *his* leather sofa, fell into it, and was instantly asleep.

It was four-thirty in the morning when the Speaker of the House slid off the leather sofa onto the floor with a re-sounding thump. Stunned, Wilson struggled to his knees and was back on the sofa in seconds. He felt like he was in a sauna, even though the fire was nothing more than smoldering embers. He was soaking wet with his own sweat, and he was still dressed in his suit and tie. Somewhere along the way during the evening, he'd lost his shoes. He took a moment to wonder if that was important. He decided it wasn't as he contemplated his black socks, held up by garters.

Wilson Lambert knew he was now stone-cold sober. He had a moment of instant recall as to why he was where he was, in the condition he was in. He cursed again simply because it seemed like the thing to do at the moment. He leaned back against the buttery-soft leather and closed his eyes. He knew at that precise moment in time that his life, as he knew it, would never be the same. He looked down at the pricey, fancy watch on his wrist to see the time. He needed to know so he would remember later on when he finally realized he'd crashed and burned. The time was 4:59 A.M. The date was October 9.

At 11:59 P.M. Hawaiian time, the huge Boeing plane carrying Livinia set its wheels down on Hawaiian soil. Passengers moved then, some waking up, others reaching for their carry-on bags in the overhead compartments. Livinia remained seated until the line formed for the passengers to head toward the front of the cabin. It took her fourteen minutes to make her way into the terminal, and another fifteen minutes to find her way to the nearest exit, where she could get a cab.

When she'd left Washington earlier in the morning, the temperature was a brisk fifty-five degrees. Here, she thought, the temperature was probably in the low eighties. The air felt warm and sultry against her skin. She looked around, then just fell in line with the others who were looking for a taxi, the same way she was.

She had made it. Almost halfway around the world from where she had begun her journey. Free of her husband. She looked around again. Everyone had a cell phone in hand. She reached for her own, turned it on, and checked her messages. She sighed so loud when she read Nikki's message, she thought people would stare at her, but no one was paying the slightest attention.

She really was free. For the first time in almost thirty years, Livinia Lambert felt like if she waved her arms, she would fly off into the warm, sultry night, reaching so high she could touch the stars.

Free at last.

Chapter 11

Wilson Lambert made four phone calls, one after the other. He made them so fast that he felt a blister start to form on his fingers. His message was the same to all four partners at Queen, King, Bishop & Rook, short and succinct. *This is an emergency. I will be at your office in thirty minutes. Be there.*

"This had better be good, Buzz, or I will personally strangle you," Maxwell Queen said thirty-nine minutes later.

"What the hell has gotten into you, Buzz?" Eli Rook growled. "Now I have to shave in the men's room. I hate shaving in the men's room," he continued to growl.

"Do you have any idea how sick I've been, Buzz? Unless you're dying, you are going to wish you were dead," Leo Bishop snarled as he struggled with a sloppy-looking knot in his tie.

Josh King shot Buzz a look that was mean enough to raise the hair on the back of Wilson's neck.

"You all just need to shut up and stop with the threats. Do you think I'd be here if it weren't important? Let's head to that soundproof conference room you're always bragging about. Order some tea. Make it mint—it's good for the stomach."

It took some doing, what with the Chessmen getting in each other's way as they snapped and snarled at one another; then they all focused on Wilson Lambert and let loose with another volley of angry denunciations.

"All right, here's your damn tea, Buzz. Start talking," Bishop said through clenched teeth a few minutes later.

Wilson Lambert looked around the polished conference table at the four men he considered his closest friends. In truth, they were his only friends. They all looked terrible, just the way he looked and felt. He should cut them some slack. Should, but wouldn't.

He tossed the complaint down on the table. "I was served these divorce papers last night at six o'clock. I was going to call all of you then, but instead I ended up drinking a whole bottle of Jim Beam and passing out. That's so you know where I'm coming from and why I called for this meeting."

The Chessmen's jaws dropped as though they'd been choreographed, but no one spoke because Buzz wasn't finished. "Livinia is divorcing me. I was in shock last night when I was served these papers. For the record, I am still in shock. I have thirty days to vacate the premises and thirty days to respond to this complaint. A female lawyer, someone from Nikki Quinn's firm, I assume, is representing Livinia. Quinn herself also has Livinia's power of attorney."

"Good firm. All female," Eli Rook said grudgingly. "Not as good as us, though."

"Yeah, well, take a look at the signature on the last page, gentlemen!" Wilson shouted. "Just take a look!"

"Stop with the theatrics, Buzz. So some skirt with a law degree is handling your wife's filing. So what? Why did you wait till now to tell us you were getting divorced? Do you expect us to believe this came out of the blue? I thought we all agreed that you needed to be squeaky-clean if you're going to make a run for 1600 Pennsylvania Avenue. *Squeaky-clean* means no goddamn divorce. Are we clear on that?" Josh King thundered.

"What? How dare you blame me! A divorce is the last thing I want or need. I didn't have a clue. I was blindsided. I didn't see this coming. I had nothing to do with this, and, no, before you ask, I did not cheat on my wife. There is no one who will come forward and say I did, either. Who the hell has time for flings? Certainly not I."

"Well, what are you going to do about it, Buzz? If you're here to ask our opinion, that's one thing. If you're here to have us represent you, that's another can of worms. Which is it, Buzz?" Queen asked.

"This is going to screw everything up. We had a plan. What made her do this?" Bishop asked. "I think you need to give some thought to trying to patch things up. If even a hint of this gets out, it won't be good. We need to be preemptive here."

"I don't know. It came out of the blue, just like Josh said. I don't even know where Livinia is right now. Not the slightest idea. She walked out of the house yesterday and never came back. I thought she went to California, so I called my son, who said she wasn't there. I think he's lying, but I can't be sure. If I knew where she was, I'd be on a plane right now, but I can't do that, since I don't know where she is. That alone should tell you no amount of sweet-talking is going to make her change her mind. What do you want from me?"

"What you promised if we backed you for your run. Now it appears we can kiss that promise good-bye because you didn't see this coming," King said in a voice so cold it could have set Jell-O.

Wilson Lambert cringed at the words and the tone. "I thought you four were the best of the best. If you can't represent me, make me the injured party, what the hell good would you be to me if I was president? First of all, Livinia is no fighter. She's a lady. She would never get down and dirty. That's your specialty, isn't it, down and dirty? You need to pull out all the stops on this. I know you have a top-notch investigative firm at your disposal. Call them to find her. Start with my son. Hack into his phone, his e-mails, whatever you need to do. Just get on it *now*."

Eli Rook had his cell in hand and was busily punching in numbers. "We need to have a prepared statement ready to go when this hits, which will be like midmorning. The courthouse leaks like a sieve. I'm surprised it didn't make the early-morning news!"

"What exactly is your relationship with your son these days, Buzz? I know at dinner the other night you said that he was in town to sign off on his own divorce. I don't want you gilding the lily, either. Just tell us straight out so we are not blindsided. He's got a voice now, what with that company he founded and now that he is a billionaire. People are going to listen to him. We are going to have to tread very carefully here," Queen said.

"Jeffrey is a mama's boy. We were never close. Like I said, he was joined at the hip to his mother."

"So what you're saying is Livinia was both mother and father to your son all his life because you were too busy with your political career. Is that about right? I also recall reading somewhere, and not all that long ago, that your son called you Mr. Congressman, then Mr. Minority Leader, and, finally, Mr. Speaker. Not Dad or Pop or Father, but Mr. whatever. At your instruction, so he would show respect. That was a quote in some Silicon Valley interview. Is that true? And, Buzz, it is going to come out that your wife is the one who has the money. You have been riding her financial coattails ever since you married her right out of college," Leo Bishop said.

Buzz frowned. "It's true. Jeffrey and I had words concerning his divorce. I think his soon-to-be ex is a gold digger. I said it from the day he married her. Livinia was smitten with her. I wasn't. She had that look all gold diggers have. I have a question. What is our response to irreconcilable differences? That phrase could cover a multitude of things."

"We'll get into that a bit later. We can make that statement work for us. Right now, we have to call a press conference and be preemptive," Maxwell Queen said.

"You realize that the *Post* is going to come down heavy on Livinia's side. That reporter, Maggie Spritzer, and her colleague, whose name I can't remember right now, will have a ton of material in their archives to use as fodder for their stories. On us. The Chessmen. That in itself is not good, Buzz. They will portray Livinia as the second coming of Mother Teresa, and you will be the Devil Incarnate," Queen said, his voice sour and angry. "God alone knows how the two of them will blister this firm."

The Speaker threw his hands in the air in frustration. "Sounds to me like you're saying you aren't up to the job of making this come out right for me. Is that what you're saying?" Buzz barked.

"That's not what Maxwell is saying at all, Buzz. We can handle whatever comes our way, just the way we always do. We know people who know other people, as you know damn well. You have to know whose ass to kiss in this town. You, Buzz, should know that better than anyone in this room because you've done your share of ass kissing all these years," Josh King said, icicles dripping from his words.

"All of that, and a bag of chips," Buzz sniped. "So far, none of you have looked at the last page of that complaint. I suggest you do that right now, then tell me if what you just said will hold up."

The only sound to be heard in the conference room was the rustle of paper and chairs moving so that the four

Chessmen could view the signature on the last page of the document on the table.

"Son of a bitch!" the four lawyers said in unison.

" 'Son of a bitch' is right," Buzz agreed.

"You said Nikki Quinn was your wife's attorney!" Bishop spat.

"No, Leo, I did not say that. I said the Quinn Law Firm was representing Livinia. The first thing I said when we got in this room was for the four of you to look at the last page. You didn't do that until just now," Buzz said. For some reason, he felt pleased at the panicked look on his friends' faces. It was something he'd never seen before. The Chessmen always projected an appearance of victory and jubilation to those present. But the momentary pleasure he'd just felt turned to outright fear at what he was seeing.

Buzz cleared his throat when the others suddenly found themselves speechless. "I guess what your expressions mean is this particular lady lawyer is going to outlawyer you, and that I will be going down the tubes. Is that what I'm seeing, *boys*?" He sat back and waited for the air to clear.

And then the Chessmen were all talking at once in voices that were jittery and shaky and nothing like the sonorous and sometimes bombastic tone they used to use in the courtroom, back in the day. Buzz went back to feeling pleased again, but only until he realized that it was his reputation that was being put in the Chessmen's hands.

"You're afraid of her! Admit it! Well, I never thought I'd see this day, boys. Suddenly I am not feeling very confident about your representing me. Actually, you're scaring me. And don't even think about calling this particular lady lawyer a *skirt*. I know who she is. I know her reputation. I know she lives in Las Vegas and is married to that guy Cosmo Cricket, who just happens to be the lead counsel for the Nevada Gaming Commission. That's a lot of clout right there, boys! That means Cricket knows people, too. And his wife has had a direct pipeline straight into the White House for a long time, not to mention just about every damn courthouse in the country. For God's sake, will one of you say something already before I explode?"

The instant metamorphosis Buzz was seeing rocked him back on his heels.

"Don't ever compare us to that gambling attorney in Las Vegas!" Maxwell Queen barked. "As for Elizabeth Fox, we can take her with our hands tied behind our backs if she doesn't play dirty."

"Well, you should know all about playing dirty, but I think you're confused here, boys. Elizabeth Fox does *not* play dirty. She doesn't have to. She has every judge in this town, civil as well as criminal, totally wrapped up in her court. She has more legal knowledge in that beautiful head of hers than the four of you put together, and do you know how I know that? I know it because my old golfing buddy, federal judge Ambrose Feldman, told me that on the ninth hole back in May of this year. Cosgrove, Spinelli, and Jepson all agreed. We were a foursome that day. They love and adore her, fought among themselves to get to hear her cases. Their wives all want to be like Elizabeth Fox.

"Just for the record, all four of those judges hate your guts. Spinelli referred to you as clowns. You know I'm right. So, having said all that, let's all own up to our failings and get down to business. There has to be some way to outsmart that bitch."

"Maggie is going to be so surprised by this little welcome-home party," Myra whispered to Annie, who was busily tying the last cluster of colorful balloons to the dining-room chandelier.

"Why are you whispering, Myra?"

Myra laughed. "I was, wasn't I? The element of surprise, I suppose. Ted outdid himself with the decorations. He even got a hospital bed and set it up in the family room, so Maggie won't have to climb the stairs. As far as I can see, he didn't miss a single thing. He said the nurse would be here at two, when the party breaks up, and will take over immediately. The food looks delicious, doesn't it?"

"Yes, it does, and I plan to try a little of everything. Maggie doesn't know about the nurse yet. I expect she'll kick up a fuss at first. I hope she doesn't, because I hate wielding my authority."

Myra hooted. "Since when? You love issuing orders! You were probably a Prussian general in one of your previous lives, admit it!"

"They're one mile out!" Jack shouted to be heard over the TV that someone had turned on in the kitchen. "Dennis just sent me a text. Everyone, in the family room! The minute Maggie comes through the door, we whoop it up."

"I hope she isn't upset with this little welcoming party," Isabelle fretted.

Annie shot Isabelle a look that clearly said, *She'd damn well better not be upset.* Isabelle blinked and followed Yoko into the family room.

"Reminds me of a sweet-sixteen surprise party." Lizzie giggled.

"They're about to turn the corner," Jack said, looking down at the incoming text from Dennis. "For some reason, I don't think this confetti is a good idea, but Ted insisted. Okay, I heard a door slam. Get ready!"

"Then Ted can clean it up, since it was his idea," Espinosa said.

"Doorknob is turning," Jack hissed.

"*SURPRISE!*" the gang shouted as confetti flew in all directions. "*WELCOME HOME, MAGGIE!*"

"Oh! Oh! Oh, you guys are too much!" Maggie cried out. Tears rolled down her cheeks, and she clung tighter to

Ted. They all watched as he settled her carefully on the sofa with a mound of pillows.

"He's handling her like she's a national treasure, and in some ways, I guess she is," Abner whispered to Isabelle. "At least where he's concerned."

"There's only one Maggie, just like there's only one Abner," Isabelle said, hugging her husband.

"Party time!" Nikki said as she headed toward the magnificent buffet, which had been set up by the caterer.

"I am so hungry," Maggie said.

Ted almost killed himself rushing to the dining-room table to fill a plate for his beloved.

They ate, drank, talked, and laughed. All was right with their immediate world as Myra said, tipping her glass of apple cider upward.

"For now!" Annie said.

The camaraderie and laughter continued until it was time to start the cleanup process. Dennis West was the one who whistled sharply to get everyone's attention. "Ted, quick, turn on the big TV. The Speaker of the House is due to have a press conference with the Chessmen! Hurry up!"

Nikki looked over at Lizzie, who met her steady gaze. She shrugged.

"This can't be good," Nikki hissed as Ted turned up the volume on the TV.

"I think you're right," Lizzie whispered. "I didn't expect a reaction this soon."

"Those guys are not dummies. This is a preemptive strike."

"I don't like this. Look how they're lined up. I bet we're looking at a hundred grand in apparel alone. Suits, shoes, Hermès ties, monogrammed shirts, Rolex watches! The big guns. They don't look like they've been sick," Annie said.

"That's because they're wearing makeup," Alexis observed.

"They wear makeup for a press conference!" Myra said in awe.

"Welcome to the world of the Chessmen, Myra. Those guys were probably up all night rehearsing this little ten-minute interview. They're experts at this. It's all about the show they're putting on," Lizzie said.

"Shhhh, here comes the Speaker. Looks rather dashing, if I do say so myself," Maggie commented. "I don't think I've ever seen him look this good, and I've interviewed him dozens of times. Ted has, too. He's really put together, like someone dressed him from some chic, high-dollar haberdashery."

"That's exactly what they did, Maggie. He's going to give a flawless performance," Lizzie said, and her eyes narrowed in speculation.

"They look like they're at a funeral," Dennis said.

"And that is to give you the impression that this is indeed the end of something that we are about to hear about. See how solemn they all look. It's a game. A chess game to these guys," Lizzie said.

"Where is this taking place?" Yoko asked.

"The Chessmen's offices. Outside the front door, actually," Nikki responded. "Shhh, he's talking, and we do not want to miss a word of this."

"Ladies and gentlemen, thank you for coming on such short notice. I have something I want to share with you all, and I did not want gossip and speculation out there when I can stand here and give you the straight story.

"As you all know, I am a public figure and have been in politics my whole adult life. Because of that, there are those of you who like to write about matters like what I am about to tell you and put your own spin on things.

"My wife and I have decided to go our separate ways.

Yes, that means we are divorcing after many, many years of married life. I'm standing here now feeling lower than I have ever felt in my whole life. Because this divorce is my fault. I let my job consume me because I was bent on doing what is right for my country and my fellow man. Along the way, I forgot about my wife, who was sitting at home raising our son. I regret that now, but I cannot un-ring the bell. My wife is an exceptional woman. She never complained, she kept our home fires going and saw that our son had a good life. I was, at best, an absentee hus-band and father. I take full responsibility for shirking my duty to my family.

"My wife wants a life outside of the political arena. She wants to live an artist's life, to paint, to read, to write in surroundings of her choice. She wants to be available to babysit grandchildren, if they come along. She's tired of luncheons, dinners, photo ops, and seeing me plastered all over the television and newspapers. I understand that. *Now*. At first, I didn't, because I'm a man, and sometimes can't see the forest for the trees, as my wife put it.

"There is nothing dark or shady in our decision to di-vorce. There were no extramarital affairs. There will be no ladies coming out of the darkness, no boy toys to titillate the media. Livinia and I are simply two people who de-cided that it was time to move on and enjoy what's left of the rest of our lives. I will be vacating the marital home and moving into a condo in Crystal City. I don't think I can handle staying in our home without my wife there. The memories would just consume me, and I wouldn't be any good to anyone. What I am trying to do here is tell you my situation, so you all don't go digging and dragging up anything you can think of just for the sake of gossip. I'm being as honest and forthright as I can be right now, even though it is beyond painful. Even more so for myself since I am the one at fault here.

"This is the only interview I will be giving on this matter. I imagine, but I do not know this for sure, my wife might decide to speak out. I seriously doubt it, since she is such a private person. I'm asking all of you to please let us get through this painful, emotional time the best way we can. Please give us some privacy to make our way to the next stage in whatever life holds in store for us both. Thank you for coming and, no, I will not be taking questions. Oh, one last thing, yes, it is my intention to run for the presidency. Thank you, again."

The last camera shot of the five men was of the Speaker swiping at his eyes as he followed his attorneys into the building outside of which the press conference was held.

"That was sickening," Nikki said.

"I did like the eye swiping," Lizzie said. "I told you they choreographed this whole thing, right down to the teary eyes. He's stepping up to the plate, admitting he did wrong and taking all the blame. People love hearing stuff like that. The Chessmen never miss a trick."

"What is this going to do to your client, dear?" Myra asked.

"Right now, Myra, I don't know. Lizzie, what do you think?"

"I'm going to reserve my opinion for the moment. I want to think about this. For now, though, I think you should call Livinia and tell her to turn on her television. Just in case she is tempted to blow her cover and do an interview, tell her not to. Before we make a move, we need to see what she has to say and what her reaction is to her husband's statement."

"I think we all need to leave now so Maggie can get some rest. Her nurse will be here shortly," Annie said, looking down at the oversized Mickey Mouse watch on her wrist. The doorbell took that moment to ring. Annie smiled from

ear to ear as Maggie sat up straighter in her nest of pillows.

"What *nurse*? No one said anything about a nurse. I
don't want a nurse. I can take care of myself. Ted said he
would help out. No, no, no!"

"Look at me, dear! That wasn't a question, nor was it a
request for permission. It was a statement of fact. I have a
busy schedule for Ted and Joseph, so they won't be any
help to you."

"But, Annie . . ."

"This is not up for discussion, Maggie. The nurse stays
until your doctor says she is no longer needed. Please tell
me you understand."

Maggie looked toward the door, where her nurse was
standing, suitcase in hand. If she was intimidated by the
large group of people and her patient, she gave no outward
sign. She smiled, and said, "Hello, everyone. My name is
Ming Su."

"Mercy, Annie, she looks like she's twelve years old,
and she can't weigh more than ninety pounds soaking wet.
Wherever did you find her?" Myra whispered.

Annie laughed gleefully. "From Harry. That little slip of
a girl has a black belt and could toss Charles and Fergus
across the room and never break a sweat. She won't take
any sass from Maggie, either. Trust me when I tell you we
are leaving our intrepid reporter in excellent hands."

"Well, then, in that case, I say we leave the two of them
to get acquainted. Time to go, people!"

There was a mad scramble as everyone searched for
their briefcases, purses, and backpacks before they stood
in line to hug and kiss the patient, who was fuming like a
dragon bent on breathing fire.

"We'll check in, from time to time, to see how you're
doing," Yoko said.

"Twice a day, no more," Ming Su said in a musical voice.

"Now, see here, that's not going to work for me," Maggie started to sputter.

"But it works for me, and I'm the one in charge," Ming Su said softly.

Nikki bent over to kiss Maggie's cheek as she was the last in line. "Give it up, Maggie, she's here to stay, and always remember, Harry trained her, and she has a black belt. And you are slightly incapacitated. Enjoy the attention and get on that computer and do what you do best. Find us something that will be beneficial. See ya. Call if you need anything."

"Yeah, see ya," Maggie said as she settled down to accept the inevitable.

Chapter 12

Annie de Silva blew into Myra's country kitchen like the hounds of hell were on her heels. Her hair was standing straight up in the air, thanks to the ferocious October wind, and her cheeks were cherry red, thanks to her wild dash across the courtyard to the kitchen door. Bright orange leaves were on the shoulders of her jacket. She shook them off and looked down at the floor, then at Myra. "Where's the broom?"

"Where it's always been for the past forty years, in the laundry room. How cold is it out there?"

"The thermometer in my car said it was fifty-two degrees. It's going to rain later. I feel it in my knees. Actually, it's rather misty out right now, and the leaves feel wet. Do you have any news, Myra? It's been three whole days since Maggie's welcome-home party. I thought we were going to have a meeting. What's going on?"

"You missed one," Myra said, pointing to a yellowish leaf lying next to the stove. Annie made a face as she bent down to pick up the offending leaf. "Nothing is going on, that's the problem. Charles and Fergus are down in the war room, where they've been for the past three days. I have no clue as to what they are doing. Didn't you miss Fergus? I think he's been sleeping here in your room."

"Of course I missed him. He's Scotch, you know, and tight-lipped. The reason I came over here was to see if he was still alive. Is he, Myra?" Annie asked with a tinge of anxiety in her voice.

Myra was in a devilish mood. "Do you think we should go down to the war room and check? Now that you mention it, I really haven't seen Charles, either. Nothing has been going on in the kitchen. No one has cooked anything. Sniff the air, Annie. Do you smell the remnants of anything?"

The sudden look of alarm on Annie's face made Myra laugh out loud. "Got you that time!"

"What *are* they doing down there?"

"We could go down and see for ourselves. That's if we really want to know. I've seen Avery's car coming and going, so whatever is going on must involve him and his operatives. At our last meeting, the reports were still coming in on those lawyers they call the Chessmen. Nikki hasn't called. Lizzie is still here. She's staying with Nikki and Jack. That, I am very much afraid, is the sum total of what I know."

"Maybe we should go out to lunch instead of going down to the war room. Charles hates it when we pop in uninvited. It's almost Halloween. We could stop at Yoko's nursery and pick up some pumpkins. Or we could just sit here, drinking coffee. Or you could continue to knit on that three-mile-long scarf you've been working on for God alone knows how long."

"You know what, Annie. That's a good idea. Let's go to the Daisy Wheel."

"They don't do lunch, just dinner."

"I know that. It's just two-thirty now. They open at four. By the time we get there, it will be after four. I'm game if you are."

"I don't think the Daisy Wheel is a good choice. Let's just order in and start our own investigation. I'm tired of waiting around for things to happen. We need to jump in with both feet and stir the waters."

"Ya think?" Myra drawled. "What exactly did you have in mind?"

"Good Lord! You forgot already. You said start at the beginning. Isn't that what you said? So we start at the beginning. That means Nikki's divorce client and her new associate, Amy Jones Lambert. I just had a better thought. Let's pack up and head for Georgetown. I think it's time to visit Maggie. She knows how to do all that social-media stuff. We can sit there and watch her do it. What do you say?"

"I say let's do it. We can stop for takeout and have an early dinner with her. She's probably going out of her mind, being stuck in the house with that nurse. Just give me ten minutes to change, take the dogs out, and put down some food for them."

"Make it snappy, Myra. I know how you dawdle. I don't want to get caught up in rush-hour traffic."

"Ten minutes, Annie. Not a minute longer."

Myra was as good as her word. She was downstairs, purse in hand in exactly ten minutes. "You driving, or am I?"

"Is that some kind of trick question, Myra? I said we want to get there before rush hour. If you drive, we'll be lucky to get there by eight tonight. I. Am. Driving!"

It was a little past four-thirty, with two stops for take-out, when Annie rang the doorbell at Maggie's Georgetown house. They were greeted by Ming Su and Maggie's cat, Hero, who brushed against Myra's leg so forcefully that her purring sounded like the opening bars of a Rossini overture.

"Company! Thank God!" Maggie squealed. "And I can smell the food. Oh, lead me to it, you dear ladies!" Then, sotto voce, she said, "Please, you need to get rid of her. I'm starving. She makes me eat like Harry eats, sprouts and weeds, and she's driving me crazy."

"Just a few more days, dear," Myra said as she headed to the kitchen to get the food ready.

Annie looked around the neat, tidy family room. She nodded to Ming Su, and said, "Myra and I will be here for a while. Go into town and do some shopping, have tea or dinner. I'll call you when we're ready to leave." It wasn't a request, it was an order, and Ming Su recognized it as such. She nodded, smiled, and bowed. Five minutes later, she was out the door.

"Quick, Myra, hit the dead bolt so she can't get back in. Please. Look at me, I'm half crazy. If it wasn't for my laptop, I would be all the way crazy. Oh, this food looks so good. I want some of everything. A lot of some of everything. Hide the leftovers."

Annie and Myra picked and stirred at their food as Maggie gobbled hers and went back for seconds. Everyone knew all there was to know about Maggie's whacked-out metabolism.

"We need your help, dear," Annie said.

"Sure, what do you want me to do?"

"We want to get the skinny on Amy Jones Lambert."

"Really!" Maggie said, fork poised in midair. "When you were here for my welcome-home party, I did hear you, Myra, when you told Nikki to start at the beginning. I already did that. It's what I've been working on these past three days. Ted and Espinosa, too. I had to do something, or I would have gone out of my mind. Do you know *that person* actually trimmed my toenails! She did."

Myra and Annie both leaned forward. "What have you found out?" they asked in unison.

Maggie's expression turned crafty. She laid her fork down, and asked, "What's it worth to you?"

"You are on my payroll, Maggie!" Annie sputtered.

"No, I am not. I am officially on disability. So, ladies, what's it worth to you?"

"Is what you have any good?" Myra asked. "Won't Charles and Avery be able to find out the same thing?"

"Yep. Nope." Maggie speared her sixth mini meatball and popped it into her mouth. She reached out for an egg roll and took a good look at it before she bit down. She smiled at Myra and Annie and was as certain as she could be that Ming Su was as good as gone.

"All right! All right! Ming Su was for your own good, Maggie," Annie said. She looked like she'd just bitten into a sour lemon.

"Say it! I want to hear the words," Maggie said as she crunched down on the shrimp egg roll.

"Ming Su goes."

Maggie clapped her hands in glee. "Call her to come back and pick up her gear. You might want to give her . . . you know, a bonus of some kind for putting up with me."

"You drive a hard bargain, dear," Myra said. "I do understand where you are coming from, however. I do not like people fussing and fretting over me, either."

"Well, I just happen to love it!" Annie said. "It makes me feel important." Annie then called Ming Su and told her that Maggie was feeling stronger and felt that she could take care of herself. Therefore, her services would no longer be needed. She thanked Ming Su for taking care of Maggie and said that even though she was being dismissed early, she would be paid for the complete length of time she had been hired for, plus a bonus. Ming Su said she would return shortly to pick up her belongings and Annie ended the call. "All right, she's on her way back. Now tell us what you found out. That's an order, Maggie."

Maggie giggled. "Annie, there are orders, and then there

are orders. I'll tell you the minute she walks out the door with all her . . . her . . . stuff. Let's have a drink, ladies!"

"You can't drink with all the medicine you're on," Myra said.

"What medicine? I spit it out as soon as she turned away. I'm doing just fine without it, can't you tell? I have a bottle of Advil under the cushions, and when she wasn't looking, I would take a few. I absolutely do not like taking prescription medicine. Now, about that drink?"

"Give it up, Annie, you know we can't win here. Besides, I think I'm also ready for a drink. And you look like you can use one, too," Myra said as she rummaged in the cabinets until she found a bottle of Kentucky's finest bourbon. "Maybe we should hold off drinking this until after Ming Su leaves."

"Maybe we shouldn't," Maggie snapped. "Pour, Myra!"

Myra poured.

The ladies were on their second round when Ming Su poked her head in the kitchen to announce that she was leaving. She smiled sweetly at all three women. And then she was gone.

"Talk!" Annie roared.

"Okay, okay! I've been digging and digging. So have Ted and Espinosa. They sent Dennis out on a mission. He isn't back yet, but he has checked in with what he found out. Me first. According to social media, Ms. Amy Jones Lambert's life began when she was eighteen years old. The hall of records and every other database in the country say Amy Jones Lambert did not exist before then. That's when she joined the world. Either she's in the Witness Protection Program, or she's adopted, or she was growing up under another name in foster care. Those are the only three reasons why nothing shows up before she turned eighteen. I'm going with adoption or foster care because it's the only thing that makes sense to me. When she came of age, she must have taken off on her own and changed her name, which leads me to believe she was in foster care and not legally adopted. If she had been legally adopted and had adoptive parents, there would be some sort of paper trail.

"She got a Social Security number when she turned eighteen. She had many jobs, most part-time, as she was working her way through college. I suspect she's smart. I couldn't get her high-school transcripts. Abner will have to hack into the college system to get those records for us. Whatever is there has probably been dummied up somehow. If she wanted to leave her old life behind her, for whatever reason, she wouldn't leave any footprints behind.

"I checked the college yearbooks, but didn't find much. From what I can tell, she had two friends. I use the term loosely. That's where Dennis is, trying to find out what, if anything, they can tell us that will help. In her junior year, the same year she met Jeffrey Lambert, she was voted the girl most likely to make her dreams come true. Her dream was to be a criminal-defense lawyer."

"That's very interesting," Annie said. "I wonder what kind of story she told Jeffrey Lambert about her past. I would think he'd want to know something about her background if he was going to marry her, especially with who his father is. We should definitely call Nikki and ask her to call Mrs. Lambert senior and ask some pointed questions. She might be able to shed some light on Amy's background."

"Maybe not. If she was ashamed of her background, she might have made up some story about her parents' deaths, she's on her own, blah blah blah. They make movies and television shows about things like that all the time. I'm thinking she'd be careful, knowing exactly who she was marrying and the family he came from," Myra said.

Maggie reached for the last egg roll on the plate. She sprinkled salt on it, then dipped it in some spicy red sauce before shoving it in her mouth. "Do you think Mrs. Speaker will give anything up?"

"Only if Nikki were to tell her that the Chessmen will go after her and savage her reputation. Then she might spill whatever she knows, if anything. But after that press conference, it seems highly unlikely that Nikki can tell her that. It seems pretty obvious that, for whatever reason, the Speaker is not about to fight the divorce.

"Anyway, her son might have kept her in the dark, for all we know. Young men are pretty protective of their mothers, especially when their fathers are like Buzz Lambert," Myra said.

Annie called Nikki at the office and explained the situation and their thinking. Nikki said she would get back to them after she thought about it for a while. "We'll be at Maggie's for a little while longer. Call us back here."

"What did Dennis find out, dear?"

"Nothing that is going to help us. At least I don't think so. He found one of Amy's friends and actually spoke to her in person. She works as an administrative assistant at Georgetown University Hospital. She said she was a study buddy of Amy's in college. Not best buds or anything like that. She also said they never got personal about their backgrounds, but she had the feeling that Amy didn't have any family. She said it was just a feeling and nothing she would want to swear to. Her name is Grace Zarata. She said Amy never attended any of the reunions after graduation. She knew she was going to go to law school. Said she was extremely smart and had a very high IQ. Mensa material. She hasn't seen her since graduation.

"Oh, she did say she was head over heels in love with some guy whose father was a big-time politician. Once he entered the picture, Amy was done with her. Heard she married the guy, but she wasn't invited to the wedding. That's it. Dennis will have it all typed up and hand it over to Charles."

"What about the other friend?" Annie asked.

"Dennis is with her now. She was Amy's roommate up until Amy got married. Her name is Elise Moore. Dennis called about a half hour before you got here. He's still with her because he took her to lunch. He's on his way back now. Elise is a vice principal at a middle school in Reston, Virginia. She said that while they were roommates, they almost never saw each other. Amy worked two jobs, and when she wasn't working, she was in class or the library. She had very few clothes. Never received mail, didn't even have a phone or car. She worked in the cafeteria, so she could get free food. They never confided in each other. They simply shared a room.

"Then, one day, she said, Amy told her she was getting married. She said that was the longest conversation she'd ever had with her. She did say she was incredibly smart. She aced all her subjects, and that's what allowed her to hold down two jobs.

"It's possible Dennis might come up with something else, but right now, that's all he had to report," Maggie said as she nibbled on her thumbnail.

"A loner. By choice," Myra said.

"Wait a minute. Didn't Nikki tell us that Amy and her husband were more like brother and sister, and it was an amiable divorce?" Annie said.

"Yes, she did say that. But Grace said she was head over heels in love with the guy she met and married. Maggie, call Dennis and ask him to ask Ms. Moore if she knows anything about the marriage or the courtship that led up to the marriage. While you do that, Myra and I will clean up the kitchen. It doesn't appear that there will be any leftovers, so you might want to have Ted bring something by on his way home," Myra said.

"You know what, Myra, all of a sudden I'm getting a really itchy feeling between my shoulder blades. There is something there, you know, like when something is on the tip of your tongue, and it just won't surface. That kind of feeling. Are you sensing it, too?"

Myra sat down on one of the kitchen chairs and started to knead her hands. "Yes. What's banging around in my head is what Nikki said when she was telling us about the civilized divorce of that young couple. She never alluded to the fact that they were head over heels in love. Granted, that was a few years ago. Young people are so different these days, but I had the impression from what Nikki said that they were just friends, from the very beginning. Friends who wanted to belong to someone. Not crazy in love.

"And Nikki said Amy cried and that the young man's eyes were moist. It's not computing, Annie. No one said anything about their having grown apart after being crazy in love with each other. Well, that's not quite true. Amy said she wanted to spread her wings or something like that. Oh, look, Maggie is off the phone. Let's see what young Dennis has to say."

"Well?" Annie barked.

Maggie threw her arms in the air, then winced. "Ms. Moore said she personally did not know anything, but she heard, and she said to Dennis that what she was going to say was rumor only, that Ms. Moore's boyfriend at the time, who is now her husband, belonged to the same fraternity as Jeffrey Lambert. The boyfriend/husband said Jeffrey was so in love, he couldn't see straight. He started staying away at night, missing classes, and his grades suffered. He didn't care. He said that the guy was the joke of the house. The guys got sick of hearing about Amy twenty-four/seven. He said he brought her by the house a few times and couldn't keep his hands off her. She was the same way with him.

"Then his parents showed up and read him the riot act.

The whole house heard it. Jeffrey moved out that same day. She thinks he and Amy got an apartment and guesses that's when they got married. That's it," Maggie said. She almost started to wave her arms, but thought better of the idea. "So, are you thinking what I'm thinking, ladies?"

It was Annie's and Myra's turn to turn crafty. "What are you thinking, dear?" Myra asked.

"That it was all an act. A way for Amy Jones Lambert to weasel her way into Nikki's firm. And it worked. Remember that little scene Nikki told us that she and Alexis witnessed in the parking lot. Amy and Jeffrey holding hands and kissing. If you're going to divorce your husband, do you cry, hold hands, and plant a lip-lock on him the way Nikki described? I think the two of them played her. I don't know why, though."

"It must have something to do with Mr. and Mrs. Lambert senior and their divorce. What in the world could it be? I'm feeling incredibly stupid right now," Annie said irritably.

"I feel the same way, Annie, so don't feel bad," Myra assured her as she fingered the pearls around her neck, her lifeline to sanity, as Annie was prone to say at least once a day.

"Where does that leave us, ladies?" Maggie asked, just as Annie's phone rang.

"It's Nikki." Annie clicked on and listened, her face expressionless. When she ended the call, she had a strange expression on her face.

"What?" Myra and Maggie asked at the same moment.

"Nikki said Livinia seemed reluctant to say anything. And Nikki had no leverage to pry anything out of her. She admitted to not knowing anything about Amy's background. She said if Jeffrey knew anything, she is certain he would have told her. She did say Amy was a sweet girl, very smart and kind and generous. She liked her. Said her husband did not like her and called her a gold digger, which just widened the gap between him and Jeffrey. She also said her son was hopelessly, and she stressed the word *hopelessly,* in love with Amy, and Amy appeared to love him in the same way. She said she prayed that Amy wouldn't break his heart. She's just sick over their divorce."

"Did she say she saw her husband's press conference?" Maggie asked.

"Yes, she saw it and said it was what she expected. She also said good old Buzz does not have any tear ducts, so it was all an act. She agreed to lie low, according to the plan, and not to get in touch with anyone. She did ask when Amy was going to start working at the firm, which I find a little strange. She also wanted to know if Nikki had gotten in touch with Jeffrey. Which she had. Nikki said he just listened to her, but didn't offer up anything, which I think is a tad strange. For all intents and purposes, he appears to be okay with everything. This is giving me a headache," Annie said as she massaged her temples.

Myra fingered her pearls as Maggie stared off into space.

The three women turned when they heard the front door open. Hero jumped off Maggie's lap and ran to the foyer. "Hey, anyone home?" Ted Robinson called out as Hero leapt into his arms.

"In here, Ted," Maggie called out.

"I guess we can leave now," Myra said, relief ringing in her voice.

As Annie slipped into her jacket, she turned to Ted. "Do you know anything we don't know?"

"It's all a work in progress. I'll call you later. My pack is full of printouts. Oh, my God, where's the nurse?"

"Gone, never to return! You are now officially in charge of me, Ted Robinson."

"Oooh, I like the way that sounds. Nice seeing you

ladies. I'll take over now," Ted gurgled as he shooed Annie and Myra toward the front door. "I'll call you later."

"I have to say, that was the fastest shuffle I've ever seen. I feel so unwanted all of a sudden," Annie said.

"Get over it." Myra laughed.

Chapter 13

It took two more days of Myra's and Annie's acting like angry hornets before Charles finally called an emergency meeting, and that was only thanks to Fergus, who warned Charles that the two of them had exhausted the patience of their beloved partners.

The war room was full to capacity, with Avery Snowden in attendance, sitting in on the emergency meeting, something that had never happened before.

The electricity in the climate-controlled room was palpable. There was little to no conversation, just angry, surly looks. From time to time, feet shuffled, and the only sound to be heard was Espinosa cracking his knuckles, which to all of them was a clear indication that the next thing to get cracked would be Charles and Fergus if they didn't start the meeting.

Fergus stepped down from the dais to hand out colorful yellow folders. "Sunshine yellow. I don't see anything sunshiny about this meeting at all," Isabelle grumbled under her breath, but still loud enough to be heard by the others.

Lizzie Fox was the only one in the crowded room who appeared relaxed and comfortable with what was going on and what was to come. Jack eyed her with suspicion until she winked at him. He looked over at his wife, who simply glared at him. Then he got flustered. *Women!*

"I think we're ready now, ladies and gentlemen," Charles said as he took his place directly behind Myra's chair at the head of the table. "What you have in the yellow folders in front of you are the dossiers on the Chessmen, as well as the Speaker of the House. The contents of the folders are what took so long to get us to this place in time. A lot of what you will read, some of you will already know. There are quite a few things that no one is privy to, except the Chessmen themselves and Avery Snowden. As you read and absorb the contents, you will all come to appreciate the time and effort, as well as the expertise, Avery has employed to secure the information.

"I have here in my hands a set of red folders, which contain material on Livinia Lambert, her husband, the Speaker of the House, and Amy and Jeffrey Lambert, soon to be divorced, as are the senior Lamberts. There are two folders for the Speaker, just so we're clear on that. On my desk, there are three other folders, which at the moment do not need to be discussed. That's for later, but I will tell you the names on those folders—Jeffrey Lambert, son of Livinia and Wilson, and soon to be the ex-husband of Amy Jones Lambert. The second folder bears the name of Amy Jones Lambert. And the third folder carries the name of Starry Knight.

"Having said all that, do you want me to talk this through while you follow along with the reports, or do you just want to read in silence, after which we shall discuss the contents? Either way is all right with me."

"Talk us through it, dear," Myra said sweetly. "I left my readers upstairs, and I think Annie did, too."

Charles waited a few moments to see if anyone was going to object. When the room remained quiet, he cleared his throat and started to talk. "The first of the Chessmen is named Maxwell Queen. He's the leader of the pack. His name is first on all things Chessmen. He's forty-nine years old. He wears absurdly bright blue contact lenses, has had some minor facial surgery and a few Botox injections. He's incredibly vain. He wears a hairpiece. Of the four, he graduated with highest GPA, which, by the way, is not saying much, given the academic performance of the other three.

"According to this report, he has a bit of a Napoleon complex. Meaning he is a short man, only five feet two inches tall. He wears lifts in his shoes. He spends a fortune on custom, designer clothing. His passion in life is not the law but chess. He wants to believe he is championship material. He definitely is not. His idols are the grandmaster Magnus Carlsen, the reigning world chess champion in all three major categories; Bobby Fischer, who I am sure you have all heard of, and, of course, Judit Polgár, the female player generally acknowledged to be the best ever of her gender.

"Everything he does in life, in the courtroom, in private, in social settings, has to do with chess. Everything he does is likened to a chess move in one way or another. Mr. Queen is obsessed. He is very wealthy. A good portion of his wealth was inherited. He, of course, has revenue from the law firm over which he presides. And the man has a sideline, as all the Chessmen have. Mr. Queen has a chess club, which he started fifteen years ago. One four-day weekend a month, nine months a year, he runs a tournament. The entry fee is twenty-five thousand dollars. He keeps his entries to fifty players per weekend tournament. June, July, and August are blackout months. We do not know why that is, it just is. Personal reasons, I assume.

"The prize at the end of the four days is one hundred thousand dollars. According to these records, he has a

CRASH AND BURN   141

waiting list of people who want to enter one of his tournaments. He even publishes a magazine, of sorts, that is free to all contestants. He also publishes a quarterly newsletter for which he charges. A subscription is one hundred dollars. He did all this in the hopes that somehow, someway, he would become a household name in the world of chess. It has not happened, nor will it happen. At best, he is a mediocre player. Probably somewhere near my own ability with a chessboard. He makes well over a million dollars a year during his operational months with his little club. As I said, he's been doing this for fifteen years or so. Do the math. The first seven years were not as lucrative as the later years. At this point in time, he makes more money than he could ever possibly spend.

"Still, he is not a happy man. The other three partners look up to him, and, by the way, all three partners and he himself enter the tournaments he sponsors. None of the four have ever won or even come close to being in the top three.

"Mr. Queen is married, and to a very nice lady, according to this report. They have one child, a son who lives in Rhode Island. He is a principal at a high school there. He is married, but has no children, so there are no grandchildren. Yet.

"Mrs. Queen does what most rich wives do—she plays tennis and golf. She lunches, shops, and goes to spas. The report says there have been no dalliances by either one. Strangely, the wives of the Chessmen are not close friends. They do the obligatory dinners, the photo ops, but then go their separate ways.

"That's pretty much it on Maxwell Queen. Oh, and he does not like to be called Max by anyone, even his closest friends.

"As I said, that's pretty much it on Maxwell Queen unless any of you have questions."

Dennis raised his hand. "What kind of lawyer is he? Corporate, real estate, probate, what? Is he any good?"

"According to this report, he is mean and bombastic. He uses fear and intimidation to get what he wants. Is he a good lawyer? According to this report, the consensus is that he is about as good a lawyer as he is a chess player, which means that he is less than mediocre. That latter is just my personal opinion. Any other questions?" Seeing there were no more questions, Charles shuffled the papers in the folder he was holding.

"Though Eli Rook's name comes last in the name of the firm, the order of the names in the title of the firm was decided upon at Queen's insistence. I suppose it has something to do with the order of importance of the pieces in a chess game, but that is just a guess. Anyway, Eli Rook is actually the second partner in the pecking order at the firm. He's also forty-nine years of age. He's a tall man, with a deeply receding hairline. He wears shell-rimmed glasses. He is the only athletic one of the four. By that, I mean that he not only works out at his health club one day a week, but he runs every day before work. A five-mile run. He plays chess, but, like Queen, he is just a mediocre player.

"He also has a passion in life, which is racing cars. He bought up a racetrack that had gone bankrupt, around the same time Queen started his chess club. Like Queen, one weekend a month, he holds races. He invites big names like Kyle Busch, Danica Patrick, Jeff Gordon, Dale Earnhardt Junior, just to name a few to show up at the track. He pays them one hundred thousand dollars to appear, do a photo op, sign some autographs, and maybe take a spin around the track. The entry fee for competitors is the same as for Queen's chess club, twenty-five thousand dollars. He has a fleet of racing cars that entrants can use, or they can bring their own race car. Also, like Queen's, it's a four-day weekend, once a month. He, too, closes up shop during June, July, and August. He's pulling in as much money as Queen is. He's just as privileged as the other three. His parents are still alive, but in very frail health. He'll inherit a vast fortune, but he also has a robust trust fund. His lawyering skills leave a lot to be desired.

"Rook is married, no hint of scandal, pure as the driven snow. According to this report, his wife does a lot of volunteer work at different hospitals. They have twin girls, who live in California. Neither twin is married. One is an aspiring actress and the other one earns a living reading tarot cards for people on the beach. Both girls are what you would call free spirits. They never come back to Washington. The wife goes to California to see them once a year. They Skype.

"That pretty much sums up what we have on Eli Rook. Are there any questions?" When no one spoke, Charles again shuffled his papers.

"All right, then, let's move on to Leo Bishop, the third man in the pecking order. He is described here as looking like a cadaver on steroids. I can't quite visualize that, but if Avery says that's what he looks like, then that's what he looks like. I will leave it up to each of you to visualize someone meeting that description. He is the same age as the others, forty-nine. He's married to a sickly woman, who is pretty much housebound. She has a nurse or aide who sees to her needs on a daily basis and lives in the house with the family. The report says that Mrs. Bishop is actually a hypochondriac.

"She became this way when their only daughter died in a car accident at age sixteen. There are no other children. There are no indications that either she or her husband strayed off the reservation. Leo Bishop's passion in life is a survival camp he runs in the Adirondacks. He has the same deal as the other two. He runs a four-day package for those who like survival training. He and the others participate on his chosen weekend. He also closes the camp during June, July, and August. None of the other three are what you would call fit and robust, with the exception of Rook.

"He, like his two partners, patterns everything after chess moves. He's not a good player, either, but he does like to play. He, too, has a waiting list of people who want to spend four days proving they're the fittest of the fit. Like his partners, he offers a prize to the competitor who aces the course. Some weekends, there are no winners. In that case, the prize that month carries over to the next month. The prize is one hundred thousand dollars.

"As you can tell, the Chessmen do everything the same way. The cost for the four-day weekend is, you guessed it, twenty-five thousand dollars, which he happily carts to the bank on his chosen Monday morning. According to this report, the course is so hard, so rugged, it's almost a guarantee that no one will complete it, yet some do. He also publishes a magazine, of sorts, along with a newsletter. One needs to subscribe to the newsletter for a fee, but the magazine itself is free and issued quarterly, along with the newsletter. Not even Bishop himself has successfully mastered the course, which is a goal of his, according to what I am reading here.

"Again, the course is designed after chess moves. Of the four, he is the best lawyer, but he is no F. Lee Bailey or Clarence Darrow. There is a note here that says that other than the four-day weekends, the partners do not socialize. By that, I mean they do not visit each other at home for dinners or parties, that kind of thing. Bishop inherited a string of high-end hotels, along the line of the Hilton chain. That's it on Leo Bishop. Any questions?"

Dennis again raised his hand. "Are all four of these guys Harvard grads? If their lawyering isn't all that great, how did they get admitted to Harvard?"

"Their parents endowed the school, how else?" Jack snapped. "Am I right, Charles?"

"Yes, Jack, you are absolutely right. Not one of the four was in any way extraordinary when he finished college. Their GPAs were less than stellar. Any other questions?" Charles shrugged, moved, and sorted his papers.

"I guess we're ready to move on to the fourth and final partner, Josh King. This report refers to him as the weak link of the four. He's a pleasant-looking man, has a ready smile, and is quick to shake hands with anyone he meets. In other words, he's a likable chap, unlike the other three. He appears to be what I would call the normal one of the four. He has a nice family. Four children, all off on their own and earning a living. He has two young grandchildren, whom he would like to see more of, but with his schedule, he does not. His wife never worked at a job. She ran the household, took care of the kids, went to all the PTA meetings, alone. Attended all the dance recitals and ball games. She likes to garden and has won some awards for her roses. Josh, according to this report, is nerdy, geeky, terms used today for a bookish person. Josh hails from Alabama, a Southern boy. The other three are Yankees through and through.

"He inherited his money from his grandparents, who raised him. His parents died when he was seven years old in a train derailment. His wealth comes from cotton and several golf courses. He is a frugal man, and so is his wife. Neither one is into material possessions, unlike the other three. Their children were not raised with silver spoons in their mouths. They all held jobs after school to earn spending money. Josh owns a bookstore that specializes in out-ofprint books and rare editions. He's lucky to earn enough to pay the taxes on the building at the end of the year.

"His four-day weekend is for book discussions, poetry readings, and the like. And it's all free. He even provides a continuous buffet for the four days. He does draw huge crowds. Sometimes he does readings himself. The other three partners suffer through that particular weekend. As to his lawyering skills . . . this report refers to him as a family lawyer. Neighbor problems, real-estate transactions, dog bites, car accidents. He buys his suits off the rack, drives a six-year-old Subaru. There is nothing to distinguish him from the millions of men walking around out there.

"He's fair-skinned, with light brown hair that is starting to recede. He wears wire-rimmed glasses, bifocals actually. He's six feet tall, not muscular but not fat, either. His profile doesn't fit the others', so it's anyone's guess as to what drew him to the other three back in the day. Like I said, his family is like the family next door. That's it on Mr. King. Any questions?"

No one had any questions.

"Then that brings me to Mr. Wilson 'Call me "Buzz"' Lambert, the Speaker of the House and would-be president of the United States. He is a year older than the others, fifty, to be exact. The report I have is unclear as to how Buzz got tangled up with the Chessmen. It does say that Buzz likes to play chess and entered one of Queen's tournaments. It is speculated here that that is how they came to know one another, but it has not been proven. There is a note in the margin that indicates he might have known the others early on in his career or possibly even during their college years, but that has not been nailed down, either, so we cannot take it as a given. They were not classmates. He has sent many politicians, friends of his, to the firm to have their divorces handled by the Chessmen.

According to this, they were successful each and every time and became the go-to lawyers if you wanted to win.

"Buzz married Livinia Roland fresh out of college. He worked his way through college and got several grants and scholarships. Summers were spent working two jobs. He did not come from money. In fact, his life was pretty hardscrabble until he went off to law school, paid for by Livinia's money.

"He adapted to Livinia's money very well. Not only did she put him through law school, but she bought him fancy cars, as well as taught him how to dress and how to speak. She was very much in love with him and could not do enough to help him get ahead. It's not clear how intense Buzz's feelings were, but it is noted here that he absolutely loved her money.

"Livinia's family was very politically active, and that helped him enter politics and succeed in every way possible. They had one son, Jeffrey, who a few years ago went public with a huge software company and is nipping at Mark Zuckerberg's heels.

"Father and son were never close. The son is a fine young man, thanks to his mother. Mother and son are extremely close. It's been rumored for some time that Buzz is going to make a run for 1600 Pennsylvania Avenue, which, of course, he confirmed at the sham press conference he held. A run for the presidency would come with the backing of the Chessmen and all the politicos they have in their pockets. Maxwell Queen was heard to say, possibly in jest, possibly not, that the White House would hold a chess tournament Buzz's first year in office. Leo Bishop was heard to say that the president, along with all his Secret Service detail, would be a regular fixture at his survival camp. Eli Rook promised to have a new race car painted and designated as 'Air Force One on the Ground' for the president to let off steam.

"Buzz earned his reputation as a man who can deliver. He's a true politician and loyal to his party. He's a lousy husband and father. He's never been involved in a scandal of any kind. He's known to go days without sleep if he's needed on the Hill. He gets on well with everyone who is at his level and in a position to help him, and is considered very likable by those he needs to impress. Despite his wife's assessment of his chances of becoming president of the United States, those in the know say he is very likely to take up residence at 1600 Pennsylvania Avenue.

"Which brings us to this point in time. His wife is suing for divorce. His son and daughter-in-law are also in the process of divorcing. Buzz has hired the Chessmen to handle his divorce. Nikki and Lizzie are handling both Livinia's and the daughter-in-law's divorces. Buzz had his attorneys call a press conference so he could state his case, which he did quite eloquently and preemptively before the media got hold of it and blew it out of proportion.

"That turned out to be a brilliant move on the part of the Chessmen and Buzz. So far, there has been very little coverage of the pending divorce, and I don't expect to see any from here on out. It's contained for now. The divorce will go off quietly, unless something unforeseen crops up."

"Well, if that's the way everything is going, why are we here? Two divorces with nothing out of the ordinary is not a reason for all of us to be here. People get divorced every day of the week, and we don't call special meetings. What is it we're trying to do?" Espinosa asked.

Nikki slapped her hands flat on the table, her eyes furious. "There is something wrong here! My firm has been played, for one thing. First by the young Mrs. Lambert, then by Mrs. Lambert senior. I take the blame for that. Whatever it is, I did not see it, missed it somehow. Something is wrong," she said fiercely. "That's why I called Lizzie. We're trying to figure out what it is and how the

Chessmen are involved. Maggie and Ted are digging into their backgrounds, especially Amy's, who seems to have no background prior to her eighteenth birthday. You did say that you have a folder for Amy Lambert, didn't you, Charles? Is there anything in it that we don't already know?"

Lizzie Fox spoke for the first time. "I might be going out on a limb here, but I don't think so. I think our answers lie with Amy Jones Lambert. That's the beginning, the middle, and the end of it."

Charles reached for the red folder that Fergus was holding out to him. "Let's hope you're right, Lizzie, because if you aren't, we're right back to square one."

Chapter 14

"I think we need to go upstairs and take a break, people," Myra said. "Coffee and apple pie sound good to me right now. We always seem to think better when we have coffee and something sweet. That means you, too, Charles, since you were baking those pies at five o'clock this morning. They're just waiting to be devoured."

"With ice cream?" Dennis asked, smacking his lips in anticipation.

"Of course, Dennis. You can't eat apple pie without ice cream, everyone knows that." Myra smiled at him. She really did love this rash yet shy young man, who was now one of their flock.

As they were all seated at Myra's oversized dining-room table, the conversation turned to the Speaker of the House and how the media were downplaying his announced divorce.

"The Chessmen have clout, that's for sure," Ted said. He fixed his gaze on Annie, and said, "So that has me wondering why you would never let me do an article on the firm. I really don't understand, Annie."

"I don't, either," Dennis chirped.

"That goes for me, too," Espinosa said through clenched teeth. "The *Post* is the best forum right now. Why are you holding back? Just for the record, Maggie is pulling her hair out in frustration."

"Because we don't want the Speaker to know I'm involved, and that's the first conclusion he and his attorneys will come to. We were all at the Daisy Wheel the night all of them were there. In fact, I stopped at their table to speak to them on our way out. Our day will come, and you'll get the exposé, I promise. I would also like to remind you that patience is a virtue."

Espinosa looked properly chastised as he dug into his apple pie.

"I'm leaving tomorrow," Lizzie said. "I can come back at any time. My plan is to stop at the Chessmen's office on the way to the airport tomorrow just to . . . make an appearance."

"What time is your flight, dear?" Myra asked.

Lizzie laughed, her special tinkling laugh that was so musical sounding that everyone smiled. "It's whatever time I want it to be. Cosmo chartered a plane for me, so I wouldn't have to rush. All I have to do is call the pilot to tell him I'm on the way. I'm thinking noonish.

"This is really good pie, Charles. I love the yellow raisins and the crushed walnuts. Cosmo likes to cook and bake in his spare time. He's actually teaching Little Jack, who is taking to it like a duck to water. He makes the best, and I mean the best, macadamia-banana pancakes, with banana syrup and melted butter. Neither one likes to do the cleanup. They leave that to me."

The others openly stared at Lizzie as they tried to picture the elegant attorney in an apron doing kitchen duty.

"And while they're doing that, what do you do?" Kathryn asked.

Lizzie giggled, something the others had never heard her do before because Lizzie Fox simply did not giggle. "What do you think? I watch, then I eat." She giggled again.

"All right then, ladies and gentlemen, our break is over. Time to finish up our meeting. Fergus and I need to get some sleep, since we've been at this for over three days now, not to mention we were baking these pies at five o'clock this morning. Let's just leave everything, and I'll clean it up when the meeting is over."

No one had a problem with that as they filed out of the dining room and headed to the secret staircase, which would take them all to the catacombs and the war room, which ran under the old farmhouse.

Back in place with the three red folders in hand, Charles took the floor. He opened the folder that had Amy Jones Lambert's name on the cover. "I don't see anything new in here that Nikki hasn't already told us about her client and newest associate. Maggie's input is pretty much the same. The young lady doesn't appear to have existed before she was eighteen years of age. All I see here is that she comes from New York, went to George Washington University, and worked her way through college with several small grants. She married Jeffrey Lambert and moved to California. She graduated, took two years off to work and save money so she could attend law school. During those years, her husband was struggling to start his company. Maggie's research tells us she was madly in love with her husband, and he with her, which is a direct contradiction to what she told Nikki. Ms. Lambert told Nikki it was two friends who got married, just to belong to someone. In other words, there was no passion involved. A platonic marriage, for want of a better term.

"No amount of digging or research has turned anything else up. So my suggestion, and the reason Avery is here, is this. Tomorrow morning, Nikki, I want you to show up on Ms. Lambert's doorstep at the safe house we have her staying in and take her out to breakfast. Make sure she brings nothing with her but her purse. Avery and his people will do a little breaking and entering to see what it is she's hiding. And she is hiding something, or her early years would be documented. I'm thinking she'd keep it on her person or perhaps in a lockbox of some kind. Possibly in a safe-deposit box or a storage rental company. Now comes the tricky part. Avery and I discussed this, and he feels his people can do it successfully. They will mug the two of you on your way out of the parking lot of wherever you go for breakfast. You'll have to be a part of it, Nikki, and do your part, which means a full police report. Ms. Lambert will have to file one, too. I think this will work. We need to vote on this."

"That's a great idea, Charles!" Dennis said enthusiastically. "You're thinking there might be keys on her key chain that we can duplicate, right? Like for a safe-deposit box or storage unit. Did anyone ever see a birth certificate?"

"Very astute, young man. That's exactly what I'm thinking." Charles smiled.

"To answer your question, Dennis, no, we did not ask to see her birth certificate. We don't ask for that when we interview. And, yes, Charles, I can be at the safe house bright and early. I assume this is a surprise visit and to not call ahead?" Nikki said.

Charles nodded. "Where do you think you'll take her to breakfast?"

"There's a pancake house not far from the safe house, right as you turn onto the boulevard."

Nikki directed her next question to Avery. "What time do you want to mug us?"

"I think eight o'clock sounds good. I can have my people in place, and I'll be close enough to the house that I can enter the moment you leave." Avery looked up at Charles, and said, "I don't need any instructions, Charles. The moment I'm finished, I'll head right back here. Nikki, make sure she has your business card on her so we can return her purse to the firm, since the police will not be in possession of your purses. I think it will pass the sniff test. As it is, if she is hiding something, she isn't going to want to have anything to do with the police. Pay attention to how she acts when she gives a statement to them."

"What if we're wrong?" Ted asked.

"Then no harm, no foul. Her handbag will be returned, and we move on to the other two names on the red folders. I'm going to leave now, since I have to call my people and get this all set up so it comes across as legitimate," Avery responded.

Charles looked around the room to see if anyone had any comments. Seeing no one who wanted to comment, he opened the folder that said Starry Knight on the cover. "The contents of this folder are thanks to Maggie. Avery did a quick background check, which pretty much duplicated Maggie's research. I'm not sure how Starry Knight and her restaurant, the Daisy Wheel, enter the picture other than that the Chessmen claim they got food poisoning from her food, which was proven not to be the case by three different health inspectors.

"Ms. Knight owns the Daisy Wheel. It's one of the hot spots to dine in, in the District. The Daisy Wheel is considered a five-star establishment. Ms. Knight does all the cooking herself. She's a bit of an outdated flower child and likes to dress accordingly. Neither Maggie nor Avery was able to pin down much on her background. There are no college records or even school records to be found. She never gives interviews to food magazines or to food critics. She also refuses to have her picture taken. It's rumored that she screens the people who call for reservations. The waiting list is forever long. The Daisy Wheel only serves dinner. She charges outrageous prices, but people are willing to pay what she charges. She owns the building outright. Nine years ago, she paid cash when she purchased the building. By cash, I mean green money. Not a check of any kind. Avery's people talked to the previous owner, who sold her the building. The owner's name is Nathaniel Wannamaker. He currently resides in an assisted-living facility in Arlington, Virginia. His wife passed away last year. Mr. Wannamaker has good days and bad days. Avery's investigator got him on one of his good days, and he remembered the woman who bought his building very well. Said she looked like a nymph, a spirit of some kind, and she had bundles of money in two shopping bags. He said he ate at the Daisy Wheel one time, and it was the best food he'd ever eaten in his whole life. And that's all we have on Ms. Starry Knight."

"Do we know if Starry Knight plays chess?" Dennis asked. "I'm thinking about this because her last name is Knight. And do we know if the Speaker plays chess?" Dennis asked. "The four lawyers have names of the chess pieces. If you play chess, you know there are six names: Knight, King, Queen, Rook, Bishop, and Pawn. The only name we don't have involved here is Pawn."

The others looked at Dennis like he'd suddenly sprouted a second head.

"That is so clever of you, Dennis, to come up with that. I never would have put the names together. Very good thinking," Alexis said approvingly.

"We know that's why the four attorneys are called the Chessmen. Because of their names. Starry Knight was never in the picture, and I think it's just a coincidence that her last name is Knight. The word *Pawn* as a name has never come up anywhere that I am aware of," Nikki said. "In fact, the morning after Jack got back from Philadelphia, Cyrus and I had a discussion about this very possibility, that all we were missing was someone named Pawn. But nothing I have seen since supports the idea." The others agreed.

"Just because the name never came up does not take it out of the realm of possibility," Myra said at Dennis's deflated expression. "Personally, I think Dennis is onto something here, whatever Cyrus thought about the idea, and we should not ignore it. And I do know something else. At least I think I do. Starry Knight does not play chess. Off the ladies' room, there is a little private alcove with a chessboard all set up. Starry told Annie and me that the chess set is for the staff and a few favorite customers. Starry said she never had any interest in learning the game."

"What kind of name is Starry Knight?" Kathryn asked. "It sounds like a hooker's name or, at the very least, the name of someone in the theater. Maybe she was a showgirl in her other life before she took up cooking. I don't think that's her real name. I just think she chose it to go with that getup she wears. A gimmick. And it worked for her. And why do we even care?"

"I don't know if we should care or not," Annie said. "Myra and I are friends with her. Not true friends, the way we all are. We used to dine there a lot. Starry always saved a table for us. Sometimes she would sit at the table with us over dessert, and we got to know each other. One time she was lamenting that she had a problem, something with the zoning board, and Myra talked to some people she knew, and the problem went away. After that, we more or less went on a first-name basis. She's a very pleasant lady, but if you look into her eyes, they are the saddest eyes I've ever seen. They remain sad even when she smiles."

"So what does all that mean?" Nikki asked.

"It means Starry Knight knows how to play chess and has sad eyes. It also means we leave no stone unturned, and we have Avery and Maggie dig up anything they can on Starry Knight, because I think young Dennis is onto something here. I just don't know what that something is," Annie said. "And I am not sure it has anything much to do with the game of chess. But I might be wrong about that, too. And if Mr. or Ms. Pawn shows up, then I will know that I am wrong."

Ted was already texting Maggie to get on it, and Fergus was texting Avery for the same reason, when Charles closed the red folder.

"Anyone want to hear about Jeffrey Lambert? Nothing here, really, other than he is a stand-up guy. Devoted to his mother. Crazy in love with his wife, according to his fraternity brothers. That's it in a nutshell. I say we adjourn for the evening and pick back up tomorrow after Nikki's mugging," Charles said as he stacked all the folders into a neat pile.

Chairs were pushed back as the group prepared to leave the war room. Talking was at a minimum, with Dennis asking who was going to do the cleanup in the dining room.

Harry turned, fixed his steely gaze on Dennis, and said, "Guess."

Dennis laughed. "I knew you were going to say that, Harry. Hey, I don't mind, really I don't. Because that means I get to take all the leftover pie home with me."

"Wiseass," Ted said as his mouth started to water just from thinking of the pie he'd consumed earlier. "Listen, kid, if you want some brownie points with Maggie, cut her a wedge and I'll take it to her."

"It doesn't work that way, Ted. I clean up, I get the pie."

"You know what, kid, you drive a hard bargain, but seeing a smile on Maggie's face is going to be worth stacking the dishwasher. Don't be chintzy when you cut that pie, either. Night, everyone," Ted called out to the others as they stampeded through the kitchen door.

Nikki looked at the kitchen clock, then at the watch on her wrist, after which her gaze swiveled to Lizzie and to her husband. "As much as I would like to stay here and talk, I have a mugging to get to and possibly a pancake breakfast. Lizzie, thanks for coming. Let me know how the meeting with the Chessmen goes. Fly safe, my friend. And, Jack, make something good for dinner tonight. Cyrus is getting tired of the same old, same old." She kissed and hugged both of them and was out the door within seconds.

"That girl can move!" Lizzie said in awe.

"Yes, she can. Listen, thanks for coming. You're lookin' good this morning, Lizzie. You are going to blow those guys' socks off when you show up at their offices. I gotta ask, though, what is that sparkly stuff in your hair and eyebrows?"

Lizzie laughed. "It's a girly thing. I left some for Nikki. A girl has to pull out all the stops when she goes on the hunt. You know that, Jack."

Jack took a step back to admire his friend and colleague. As always, he was dumbfounded at Lizzie's sheer beauty. If she was wearing makeup, it was hard to tell, not that he was a beauty expert, but he could recognize beauty. "You look like one of those models in the glossy magazines Nikki subscribes to."

Just for a moment, Jack let his mind travel back in time to a wet, snowy night when he found Lizzie at her fiancé's grave, with a bunch of frozen violets in her hand. At that moment in time, he knew that the friend he loved and adored had gone to that place to die. He didn't think twice; he scooped her up and took her home with him. And then he'd made her whole again. Secretly, he liked to think that he was responsible for all that she had become. Happily married, with a husband she idolized and a son she adored. He hoped she didn't look back to those dark days.

"I know what you're thinking, Jack. I can always tell.

Let's not go there—the past is the past. I owe you my life, it's that simple."

"Nah. I had nothing to do that night and was just wandering around."

"In a cemetery! In the snow, with almost freezing temperatures!" It was always the same comment and a way to get past the moment.

Jack took one last look at what he and Nikki both called perfection when it came to describing Lizzie Fox. She was tall, an even six feet, with a mane of pure silver hair, which now glistened like diamonds in the snow. It curled to her shoulder, causing men as well as women to turn around for a second look. She was long-legged and still wore spike-heeled shoes, which brought her to an imposing six feet three inches in height. She carried herself regally. Today she wore a winter white suit that made her seem all of a piece, from her glorious hair to the tip of her custom-crafted shoes and one-of-a-kind handbag, which shrieked dollar signs. And she smelled so damn good, like the summer sun, an ocean breeze, and all things Lizzie Fox. Jack grinned. "Knock 'em dead, Lizzie."

"I'll give it my best shot. Any advice, Jack?"

"That was a trick question, right?" Jack laughed.

"Actually, Jack, I'm serious. I've been in Vegas awhile now, so I am not up on the day-to-day legal goings-on here in town."

"Those guys never change, that's pretty much a given. I'm thinking all you will have to do is stand there and smile. I've found out the hard way that sometimes the less you say, the better off you are."

"Funny you should say that. Cosmo says it all the time. Guess it's gotta be true if my two favorite adult men in my life think the same way. Okay, I have to get moving. Thanks for your hospitality. See ya next time."

Cyrus, sensing this was Lizzie's exit line, stirred and walked up to her and held out his paw. This, after all, was the mother of the son who now owned his offspring. He let loose with a soft woof.

"I'll pass it on to Cyrus Junior, big guy. He's in good hands." Another soft woof.

And then she was gone.

Jack looked around the empty, silent kitchen. It seemed like all the air, all the energy, all the electricity, went out of the room, along with Lizzie. "It's okay, she's coming back, I just don't know when. Why don't you go look at that picture she brought you of Cyrus Junior, while I figure out what to make for dinner? Nikki said you are tired of the same old, same old, so this is what I think. We pick up a rotisserie chicken and some salads on our way home from the BOLO Building. And a cake of some kind. We'll put the chicken in the oven right before Nikki gets home, and she'll think I roasted it. Works for me. How about you, Cyrus?"

The huge shepherd turned and barked four times in rapid succession. Translation: *Puh-leez! Do you really think she's going to fall for that?*

"Yeah, guess you're right. We did that last week, and she got wise to it right away. Okay, then we are having lamb chops. You get the bones!"

Cyrus barked as he headed to his lair, where he kept all his treasures, especially the new one, his picture of his son, Cyrus Junior.

Jack moved then, doing everything he had to do so he could spend the better part of the day at the BOLO Building. As he worked, his thoughts traveled to Nikki and the mugging that was probably taking place at that precise moment.

Chapter 15

Nikki Quinn walked up the flagstone path leading to the front door of the safe house, where Amy Jones Lambert was temporarily living. She was walking against the blustery wind, trying to shake off the bright golden and orange leaves that were swirling about the property because of the many trees that, compliments of the autumn wind, were shedding their leaves. She wondered now if perhaps she should have called ahead, but Lizzie had said no, it was better to take Amy by surprise. And that's what Nikki was doing.

The question now was, would Amy open the door, since she wouldn't be expecting visitors? In the end, if she didn't open the door, then a phone call would be in order. The doorbell was loud, jarring, a tinny rendition of "When the Saints Come Marching In." A grin stretched itself across Nikki's face. She was marching in, but she was no saint. She waited. And waited. Then she jabbed at the bell twice more as she tapped out her new associate's cell number.

The door opened. Amy Jones Lambert stared at Nikki, a shocked expression on her face as she struggled for something to say. Nikki beat her to the punch, saying, "Get your jacket, I'm taking you to breakfast. I always take my new associates to breakfast before they start to work. This is your day. C'mon, snap to it, Amy. Time waits for no one, and I am starving. I'm taking you to the pancake house out on the boulevard."

"But . . . I just had . . . I'm not really . . . Coffee and juice, plus a vitamin, is . . ."

"Not today. Today we are dining on pancakes. Hurry, or it will get too crowded, and then we'll have to wait in line. I hate waiting in line for food." Nikki's eyes narrowed when she said, "Unless you are flat out refusing to have breakfast with me, which is not a good thing to do to your new boss. So, are you coming or not?"

"Yes, yes, of course. Just let me get my backpack and a jacket."

"No, no, no! No backpacks. Just your purse. This is a social event, not work related. I shouldn't even let you bring your cell phone. Absolutely no business of any kind is going to be transacted over breakfast." This last was said with an edge of steel to Nikki's tone.

"It's just that I never leave . . . I always carry . . . Okay, I get it. I'll just be a minute."

Nikki counted off the seconds as Amy disappeared down a short hallway that Nikki knew led to the master bedroom. *She's suspicious. And wary. Not good.* Nikki waited, her thoughts taking her to Lizzie and her soon-to-occur visit to the Chessmen, then back again to the mugging that would take place shortly.

"Well, you certainly look nice. Pretty jacket," Nikki said, eyeing the designer jacket and mentally calculating the cost, along with the Chanel RED handbag shaped like a pouch. It looked heavy to Nikki, like it was weighing down one shoulder. *She put her laptop in her purse. Why?*

"Jeff insisted on taking me shopping earlier this year on my birthday. He bought me the jacket and purse. He insisted. I'm not into designer this and that. I shop at J.Crew or Talbots."

This last was said so defensively, Nikki's eyes widened, but she didn't say anything other than "Let's go. Are all the doors locked?"

"Yes. I'm ready."

"Me too," Nikki said, heading toward her red Jeep. "I love pancakes. My mother used to make them in different shapes for me when I was little. I always looked forward to weekends because meals were special then. How about you?" Nikki asked, hoping to draw Amy out to admit something, anything. It wasn't working. Nikki prodded. "So what did your mother make you for breakfast?" There, it was point-blank; Amy had to respond one way or another.

"My mother wasn't much for cooking. She was . . . sick a lot. We had a cook. In the winter, it was oatmeal with raisins. In the summer, it was box cereal and milk."

"Guess that means you aren't a pancake aficionado like me then. I could eat pancakes every day. My husband loves them, too. These days we're both so busy, we just have special dinners and breakfasts on weekends. That's if we're not tied up on cases, then it's like the rest of the week, and we eat on the fly," Nikki said lightly. She knew she needed to tone down her rhetoric because she was starting to babble.

"Jeff likes pancakes. I can eat them, but I'm just not a breakfast person," Amy said flatly.

"You are raining on my parade here, Amy. Here I thought I was doing a nice thing, something I've done for all the new associates, a way to get to know one another at least a little outside the office. Perhaps I should just take you back to the house and apologize for bothering you. Yes, that's what I'm going to do. I'll just turn around in the parking lot, since we're almost there, and head on back." *Well, this certainly throws a monkey wrench into our mugging plan. Unless . . .*

Amy flushed a rosy pink. "I didn't mean to sound . . . No, it's all right. If I eat something now, I won't have to worry about lunch. The few errands I have to do can wait. Let's just have breakfast. I'm sorry for being such a putz. I have a nasty headache. Maybe I do need to eat something."

"That always works for me. Eating something, I mean." Nikki hoped the relief she was feeling didn't show in her expression or her tone.

"Well, I certainly didn't expect the parking lot to be so full, so early in the day. Then again, it is a strip mall, so other store customers park here, too. I'm going to have to park way in the back. You don't mind the hike, do you, Amy?"

"No, not at all. Exercise is exercise. Something I need to do more of."

Nikki's gaze was everywhere as she slid out of the car and waited till Amy closed the door before she pressed the digital key holder attached to her key ring. "I think it's even windier than it was at your house, and it feels like the temperature is dropping." Nikki gasped. She looked over her shoulder and immediately spotted her soon-to-be mugger.

"Ah . . . Amy, listen to me carefully. At your two o'clock, and don't look now, there's a strange-looking guy heading toward us. I could be wrong, but I think . . . Shoot, he's gaining on us. Hurry, dodge between that van and the pickup. I think we're going to get mugged."

"We'll just see about that. I have a gun in my purse, and I do know how to use it, too! Jeff insisted I get it and learn to shoot," Amy said fiercely.

"I have a gun, too, but I do not intend to use it, and neither should you. Law enforcement says to give them whatever they want so you can walk away. *Alive.* Are you listening to me, Amy? Crouch down, inch forward a step at a time. You go first. He's behind me. Make a mad dash for the entrance."

"Are you kidding me! That distance is half a football field. Look, I can't . . . I won't give up my purse."

He came out of nowhere, probably from the bed of the pickup truck, Nikki later told the police. The gun was black and ugly, just as ugly as the man himself, who wore a black ski mask. "Nice and easy now, ladies. Just toss me your bags and you walk away to enjoy the rest of the day. Don't make me say this twice."

Nikki worked to make her voice as jittery and frightened as she could. "Do what he says, Amy. Here, mister, take mine." There, that was a clue to the mugger that weapons could be put into play. She hoped the pretend mugger could tell how wired Amy was.

The mugger leaned out of the bed of the truck and had Amy's shoulder bag in his hand before Nikki could blink twice. Amy jackknifed to her feet and lashed out at him. The mugger gave a chop to her shoulder, and she was on the ground, moaning. Nikki screamed at the attacker, "Look what you did! Look what you did! You hurt her! You have our bags! Leave us alone!"

"Take it easy, lady. All I did was give her a good cuff. You look like smart women and should know better than to mess with me. She messed with me. She ain't going to die, so stop fretting. Look, see, she's coming around."

"Just take our money and leave our bags. There's nothing in either bag you can use."

"Oh, I can get some heavy-duty money for those two guns. I can sell your identities on the Internet and make a small bundle. Who knows? Some chick might be willing to pay top dollar for these here designer bags. Now turn around and stay down. You move, and it will be your last move of the day, maybe forever. You stay like that for a full ten minutes. Tell me you understand what I just said." With that, the mugger took off.

"We understand," Nikki said as she leaned over Amy,

protecting her with her arms. "Amy, don't even breathe. Let's just do as he says. Our lives are worth more than ten minutes. I can't believe this is happening." Nikki forced herself to cry, making sure some of her tears dripped on Amy's hand.

"I am so sorry, Amy. I thought I was doing a nice thing by taking you out to breakfast. How did doing something nice go so horribly wrong? The firm will, of course, reimburse you for the contents of your purse, the purse itself, and any cash you had in your wallet. We have to notify the credit-card companies and motor vehicles. Good Lord, you have no idea how much stuff I have jammed in my wallet," Nikki moaned. *She's too quiet.*

Amy shrugged Nikki off her back and rolled over. She looked around and thought it weird that there was not another human being in the parking lot. She said so.

"You know something, Amy, you're right. Are you . . . Are you thinking what I'm thinking?"

"What are you thinking, Ms. Quinn?" Amy asked coldly.

"That someone has been watching us. Probably you, since I'm just a lawyer. Think, why would someone want to watch or set you up? What the hell did you have in your handbag, anyway, that has you so jittery? I get the gun, sure. But you have a license to carry it and can always get another one. Your cell phone? You can get another one in an hour. I told you the firm will replace anything you lost. Is there something else I should know before we go inside to call the police?"

Amy got to her feet and dusted off the knees of her jeans. "My laptop was in the bag. Some personal papers. Things I will have trouble replacing." Amy's tone of voice was so flat and cold, Nikki winced.

Nikki pointed out toward the boulevard. "That explains why no one is in the parking lot. See the flashing police lights? There's been an accident."

"No one left the pancake place, either."

Nikki stared at her new associate. "What am I missing here, Amy? It's like suddenly you're someone I don't even know. Granted, we interviewed three times, but I didn't see this side of you. I guess you have two personalities."

"Doesn't everyone?" Amy shot back. "I've never been mugged before, and you certainly are taking this well."

"I'm alive. That's all that matters to me. That means I get to go home tonight to my husband and our dog. I get to eat the dinner he's cooking for me. I get to have him wrap his arms around me when we go to sleep. That's all I care about. What I don't get is why you don't feel the same way. Never mind, I don't want to know." Nikki held the door for Amy, then entered the restaurant. She asked the hostess for the manager and explained what had happened. After calling the police, Nikki called Alexis and asked her to bring her go bag, stored in the bottom of her desk drawer. She always kept a spare go bag, complete with cell phone, car keys, credit cards, duplicate driver's license, and cash. The only thing she didn't duplicate in the emergency go bag was her handgun.

Ten minutes later, both Nikki and Amy were back in the parking lot, giving their statements to the officer in charge.

Just as they were finishing up, Alexis pulled up to the front of the restaurant and got out of her car, a snappy silver BMW. She listened to Nikki's explanation, then handed over the go bag. She commented that no more than an hour had passed since Nikki walked out of the office to pick up Amy. It was a clue for Nikki that Avery and his people needed more time.

Nikki squared her shoulders. She thanked Alexis and turned to Amy. "I said I was taking you to breakfast, and I am going to do just that. Turn around and follow me. We are dining on pancakes, like it or not. Do not argue with me. That's an order, not a request!"

Resigned to the inevitable, a surly Amy trudged behind Nikki back into the restaurant. "Let's give our order, then head to the ladies' room to clean up a bit. Is that okay with you?"

"Would it make a difference if it wasn't?"

"Not one little bit. Not one little bit," Nikki repeated cheerfully. "Think about this. We are cut off from the cyberworld. I turned off my backup cell phone, so our phones aren't going to ring. No one can get in touch with us. It's just us and this place, and we're going to be dining on pancakes within minutes. How wonderful is that? Think about it, Amy. Peace and quiet. We can sit, eat, and talk and drink coffee and talk about our growing-up years. Or we can talk about our hopes and dreams. Whatever you want to talk about, with no interruptions. I think we should both treasure this little window of time because who knows when we'll get another chance." Nikki's voice dripped cheerfulness. She then noticed the waitress hovering and motioned to her they were ready to order. After placing their order, they headed to the ladies' room to freshen up.

Amy stared at herself in the mirror over the long block of sinks. She eyed Nikki, and said, "Are you for real? I've never met anyone like you." She splashed warm water on her face and wiped it with the rough brown paper towels. She did her best to finger comb her hair. Nikki was doing the same thing. Both women straightened their clothing, then looked at one another. Nikki smiled. Amy glared at her new boss.

"Of course I'm real. I refuse to let what happened get to me. And, of course, you never met anyone like me because there is only one *me*, and you're looking at her. We did what we had to do. There is nothing more we can do for now. We have to trust in the police that they will catch that guy. I know the chances of that are slim, but you never know, they might catch a break."

Back at their table, Nikki opened the go bag and withdrew one of the firm's credit cards. She checked the wad of currency and peeled off three hundred dollars. She handed them over. "When I drop you off back at the safe house, you can head out to get a new phone. Here is a spare key to the safe house that you need to return. Motor Vehicles is a mile down the road, on the right. You can get a new license within the hour. You do have a spare set of car keys, don't you?" Amy nodded. "Use the credit card to get a new laptop. Be sure to keep the receipts for anything you buy." Amy nodded again. "See, everything is working out. Think of it as hitting a speed bump. Oh, look, here come our pancakes."

Ten miles away as the crow flies, Avery Snowden was cursing under his breath as he waited for his operative to make an appearance. He'd been through the house with a fine-tooth comb and had come up with absolutely nothing. Bubkes. Ms. Amy Jones Lambert traveled light. Other than two suitcases full of clothing and two boxes of nothing, the safe house was just that, a temporary place to bed down until other accommodations became available.

Avery ran to the door and thrust it open the moment he heard the three *rat-a-tat* knocks. "There's nothing here. I hope what you have is what we're looking for."

The operative shrugged. "Lambert wanted to put up a fight, so my guess is that there's something in her purse she didn't want to give up, even to a mugger."

Avery was already dumping the contents out on the coffee table. "Why women carry so much junk is beyond me. I'll take the laptop. You check those two phones. Why does she need two phones? We'll save the packet of papers till last. How much time do we have, Adam?"

"At the most, an hour. If that. I guess it depends on how fast they eat. It's been my experience that women like to dawdle over meals. To answer your question, one of these phones is a burner." The operative's fingers swiped at the face of the phone. "She only uses this to call two numbers. She receives calls from the same two numbers she calls on the burner, too, so I'd say the burner is her phone of choice. The other phone has four bars and no calls to amount to anything. Spaced far apart. Days, actually. On some days, no calls come in or go out. There are several over the past ten days to the Quinn Law Firm. A few to take-out restaurants. What do you want me to do, Avery?"

"This computer is password protected. It's going to take me a bit of time to crack it. I have to first install Wizard so it can run a check. I can't download anything until I get in to see what she's got here. This is just run-of-the-mill protection. It's not like the CIA or what the FBI uses. Wizard can crack it in twenty minutes, but do I have twenty minutes? Then I have to upload it all and send it on to Nikki. So, to answer your question, common sense is telling me we need to split right after I check out the house for the last time. We can find a parking lot somewhere, and I can let Wizard do its thing while we head back to wherever the ladies want us to go. I'm thinking that young lady is going to gobble her food to get back here, so time is of the essence.

"I'm going to take a last look-through to make sure I didn't leave any telltale signs that someone has been here. I'm almost thinking that about now she might even be a little suspicious. Too many years in the field have my antenna flapping in the breeze."

"Works for me. There's a Shell station a mile or so down the road," Adam said as he gathered up the contents of Amy Lambert's purse, other than the laptop, and replaced them in the Chanel bag. "I'll park in the back."

Avery finished his check of the house. Satisfied that there wasn't so much as a thread lying about, he drove to the Shell station, where he installed the Wizard program on Amy Lambert's computer. Twenty minutes to go. He got out of the car and paced, his thoughts running in several directions. Before he made another move, he needed to check in with Nikki to see if she had changed her mind, yet again.

His first suggestion to her had been to drop off the handbags at her office. After careful thought, she switched up and said to drop them off at the police station, a Good Samaritan doing his or her duty. Her reasoning, and he was hard pressed to dispute it, was it might seem too pat for some nameless person to find and return the purses to her firm. This way the police would call her, and she would call Amy Lambert, and together they would go to pick up their respective handbags. She was right in that a police report had been filed, two purses were snatched, and then two purses would be turned in by a Good Samaritan. One plus one equals two. Amy Lambert couldn't dispute anything. The only thing Avery was uncertain about was whether he was supposed to leave Lambert's computer in her bag or take it with him. Once he uploaded everything on her computer, there was no reason to take it. But would a mugger leave a pricey laptop and just take phones, money, and credit cards? Not the kind of muggers he knew. They'd take everything. In the end, it would be Nikki's call.

Chapter 16

"Well, here we are, right where we started from. Got you home safe and sound, even though we were mugged. I wish it hadn't happened, Amy, but it did, and we have to move on," Nikki said as she tried to put as much cheerfulness as she could muster into her voice. "Do what you have to do. If I hear anything from the police, I'll call you when you get your new phone. Or you call me. Stay in touch."

"Sure thing," Amy said, getting out of the car. "Thanks for breakfast." Her tone of voice stopped just short of being snarly.

That you didn't eat. Nikki nodded and looked at her watch. Lizzie should be at the Chessmen's about now. She shifted into REVERSE, then DRIVE, and was out on the boulevard within minutes and on her way back to the office.

Nikki parked in her reserved parking space just as she heard a light tap of a horn to her right. In spite of her disheveled appearance and the current situation, with a thoroughly disgruntled Amy, whom Nikki now thought had not been fooled by the phony mugging, Nikki found herself laughing out loud as Avery Snowden emerged from a nondescript-looking van that had seen better days. She shivered as she waited for him to approach. In his hand, he had a small manila envelope. She felt a wave of elation as he handed it over.

"I didn't have time to read through anything. Call me when you're finished. You might give some thought to turning it over to Charles or Maggie, and have Charles call a meeting. My gut is telling me what you're looking for is in your hand."

"Will do. Thanks, Avery."

"It's what I do." Avery looked at his watch, and said, "Right this minute, my operative is probably turning those two handbags over to the police. When you didn't respond to my text, I decided to leave the laptop in Ms. Lambert's bag. You can tell her that the thief probably felt it too cumbersome to run around with, or something along those lines. Also, leaving it in the bag will give her a small measure of relief that her secrets are safe. At least for the moment. It was a judgment call, Nikki."

"No problem. I think you're right. I'll be in touch." Nikki stood in the howling wind and watched Avery's van until it was out of sight. She sighed, pulled the collar of her coat a little tighter around her neck, then headed for the rear door of her office building. "And this is just October," she mumbled under her breath.

The minute she had her coat off and a cup of coffee in hand, Nikki rang for her secretary, Carol. "I want you to take this over to Maggie Spritzer's house right now. Tell her to upload it and send it on to Charles. We're okay here, right?"

"Right as rain, boss. Everything is set up for your eleven-thirty depositions. I'll be back by the time you're ready to start. Anything else while I'm out?"

"No. I have it covered. It's really cold out there, so dress warmly."

"Okay, Mom." Carol giggled.

I just need five minutes. Five minutes to sit and stare at . . . nothing. Nikki felt pleased that her devoted secretary already had a fire going in the private seating area of her office. Five minutes to stare at the dancing flames. She sat down, propped her feet on the coffee table, and closed her eyes just as her cell from the go bag, which she had turned on after leaving Amy's temporary home, rang. *Lizzie.* Her feet hit the floor as she bolted upright, almost spilling the coffee in her cup.

"Just listen, Nikki. I'm here. Leave the line open, and you'll be able to hear everything. Everything go okay?"

"Couldn't have been more perfect if we had rehearsed for days. Avery left the laptop in her bag and one of his operatives is turning it over to the police as we speak. But I think Amy suspects a put-up job."

"All right, I'm in the lobby now. Don't say another word."

Lizzie Fox swooped into the luxurious lobby, propelled by the ferocious wind, which caused the silvery hair to move a little and put a natural glow to her cheeks. The overall effect was breathtaking, so much so that the young receptionist was instantly tongue-tied when Lizzie approached the desk.

"Good morning, young lady. My name is Elizabeth Fox, and I do not—I repeat, *I do not*—have an appointment with the partners of the firm. Having said that, I need to speak immediately with either Mr. Queen, Mr. King, Mr. Bishop, or Mr. Rook. I'm afraid I cannot take no for an answer, so if you would be so kind as to notify them I'm here, I would appreciate it. I can only wait seven minutes, so please advise them of that fact."

The young receptionist tried to unglue her tongue from the roof of her mouth as she stared in awe at the woman standing in front of her issuing orders. If she did what she was being asked, she was going to be fired on the spot.

"Um . . . I . . ."

"Oh, dear, we are eating into those seven minutes. I'll do it for you," Lizzie said, walking around to the back of the desk. She eyed the elaborate console; then one rosy-tipped nail hit the button that would broadcast her message throughout the building. "Hello, everyone! This is Elizabeth Fox. I represent Livinia Lambert and I am standing in your exquisite lobby waiting to meet the men known as the Chessmen, who are representing the Speaker of the House in the matter of his divorce from said Livinia Lambert.

"The reason you're hearing me over your sound system is that I think your receptionist just left the building or she quit. When I came in here, I said I would wait for seven minutes. Two of those minutes have expired. I'm waiting, gentlemen."

Lizzie looked around and saw the young receptionist grab her purse from under the desk and then walk away from the area at a very fast pace. She wasn't sure, but she thought she heard feet stampeding in some faraway hallway. She decided to amuse herself by tapping all the buttons of the console, then hitting the loudspeaker, where all manner of curses and expletives could be heard ricocheting throughout the building.

Lizzie stared down at her treasured Mickey Mouse watch on her slender wrist, a gift from Annie de Silva. She turned just in time to see the door to her right burst open with such force that it banged against the faux-marble wall. A chunk of marble-streaked Sheetrock fell to the floor as four breathless men barreled into the lobby. "Right on time, gentlemen. I like that. Punctuality is an art, did you know that? First things first, let me lock the door so we aren't interrupted." Once again, the rosy-tipped finger pressed a button. The sound of the locking mechanism was so loud, it sounded like thunder in the silent room. Then, just to be ornery, she let the same rosy-tipped finger run over all the keys on the console again. She smiled.

"We have an office, Ms. Fox. We do not conduct business in the lobby," Maxwell Queen blustered.

"You do now, *Max*." Lizzie walked over to the squat little man, reached down, and straightened his hairpiece. "Ah, that's so much better. You were looking a little lopsided there for a minute, Counselor. Yes, yes, I know you have offices. I have one myself, but if your offices are in any way indicative of this ostentatious lobby, I have no desire to see them. Ostentatiousness offends me to no end. Especially when it is done so poorly. You could take some lessons from Las Vegas.

"So, gentlemen, I just wanted to drop by to introduce myself, since we've never met in person. I am Elizabeth Fox. I know who you all are, so there's no need for you to introduce yourselves. I also wanted to advise you that I will not tolerate any dirty tricks where my client is concerned, and also to tell you in advance that I am delving into your backgrounds. *All* of your backgrounds, including the Speaker's, from the moment that you all dropped out of your mothers' wombs. I can do this, as you well know."

Lizzie moved a step closer and lowered her tone so the Chessmen had to strain to hear her soft, melodious voice. "I *know* that you all have a secret. And I'm going to find out exactly what that secret is. The wheels are in motion as we speak." The appearance of four deer caught in the headlights was Lizzie's reward for announcing her intentions.

"Are you threatening us? Because that certainly sounded like a threat to me," Eli Rook barked.

"Good grief, no, Mr. Rook. Why would I threaten you? That was simply a promise. A statement of fact. That statement, that fact, that promise extends to your client, Wilson 'Buzz' Lambert, the Speaker of the House, too. You are, of course, perfectly free to delve into my past to your heart's content. I'm an open book.

"Now here's our deal, gentlemen. Mrs. Lambert and her son, Jeffrey, are off-limits. This is a straightforward divorce case. I will not tolerate any 'he said/she said' comments. Play your cards right and you still might make it to the White House on the Speaker's coattails. Resort to your dirty-tricks MO, and we'll have a serious problem. Oh, dear, my time is up. I really have to go now. It was such a pleasure meeting you all in person."

"Blackmail is against the law," Leo Bishop snarled.

"I know! Did you just figure that out, Mr. Bishop? So, do we shake hands, hug, or spit and snarl at one another? Which is it to be?" Lizzie's eyes were twinkling.

Josh King, the handshaker of the group, as well as the weak link of the partnership, stepped forward and held out his hand. The other three Chessmen backed up a step just as Lizzie's index finger hit the door-lock button. Then, just for fun, she let her fingers run across all the other buttons on the console again. Lizzie laughed all the way to the door, the sound tinkling off the marble walls.

"What in the goddamn hell just happened here?" Maxwell Queen thundered.

"What happened was that Ms. Fox straightened out your hairpiece. You did look quite silly, Maxwell." Josh King grinned. "That lady is everything everyone says she is. I can still smell her perfume. A hint of hibiscus and a smidgen of gardenia. Very pleasant."

"She wears a goddamn Mickey Mouse watch," Eli Rook all but screamed.

"She's delving into our past! You did hear that, didn't you? We need to put a stop to that right now!" Leo Bishop hissed, spittle flying in all directions.

"I do believe we are being broadcast throughout the building, Leo. You need to forget it. If Ms. Fox said it, that means she's already on it," Josh King said. "You all said it would never see the light of day. Guess you were wrong, gentlemen. Looks to me like it's time to pay the piper." With that said, King turned on his heel and walked toward the front door. He turned, and called out, "I do not know yet if I'm coming back. I seriously doubt it, so just consider this my notice. I would be terribly remiss if I didn't say I warned you this day would come. I also told you I would walk if that happened. Well, that day is here, boys!"

"Son of a bitch!" the three Chessmen cursed in unison.

"Shut that goddamn thing off!" Maxwell cursed.

Eli Rook looked down at the elaborate console and had no clue how to turn it off. Leo Bishop reached down and yanked the wires loose from the outlet. Blissful silence filled the lobby.

"One of you call Buzz and tell him to get his ass over here right now," Queen said through clenched teeth. Eli Rook looked pointedly at the dismantled phone system. Queen slapped at the desktop, and said, "That's why we have frigging cell phones." Leo Bishop was already punching in numbers on his cell phone.

The two partners watched as Bishop's face went from red to white and back to red. "Listen, Buzz, I don't give a good rat's ass if you're sitting on the president's lap and licking his ear. Get your ass here right now or get yourself new lawyers. Your wife's attorney just left the building. How's that for a reason?"

"Now what?" Eli Rook asked, his hands flapping in the air.

"My office. *NOW!*" Queen bellowed so loud that his hairpiece shifted on his head.

* * *

Four blocks away, in her office, Nikki's closed fist shot in the air. "Way to go, Lizzie!"

"They *do* have a secret. I just threw that out there to get a rise out of them, and I got it in spades. It must be a pretty awesome secret by the looks on their faces. Now, all we have to do is find out what that secret is. I had some fun in there, Nikki." Lizzie chuckled. "Sometimes you just have to do something wicked, stir the pot a little, you know. When you hang up, call Charles and have him put everyone and their brothers on ferreting out the Chessmen's secret."

Nikki burst out laughing. "Will do. I heard it all, and may I say you were quite masterful."

"I'm signing off now. I have a plane to catch and a husband and son who are waiting for me, and whom I can't wait to see. You need me, call."

"Will do. Thanks, Lizzie."

"My pleasure, Counselor."

Ted Robinson opened the door to see Nikki's secretary shivering in the cold October air. He invited her in, but she declined, saying she had to get back to the office. "Nikki said the material from Amy Lambert's laptop is on this USB drive, and she wants Maggie to go through it and to call her the minute she knows anything. She also said to tell Maggie to upload it all to Charles."

"Okay, thanks."

Ted raced back to Maggie's family room, where she was cuddling with her cat, Hero. "I have here something you can really sink your teeth into, Maggie. Straight off Amy Lambert's laptop, courtesy of Avery Snowden. First, though, you have to upload it to Charles, then do the same to me. We can work side by side, and this way I won't be interrupting you to tell me what it is you're seeing. Okay?"

Maggie nodded.

"On the count of three, flex those fingers and dive in," Ted chortled. "This is just like old times, eh, Maggie?"

Maggie's eyes turned dreamy. "Yes, just like old times," she said softly. "Let's do it, lover!"

Ted almost fell off the sofa. *Lover.* That's what Maggie always called him back in the day when they went from being an item to engaged, then unengaged, then to rivals, and now back to friends. Friends with benefits. *Lover. Yippee!* Maybe there was hope, after all.

Two sets of fingers tapped out a symphony of sound so quick and fast, Hero leapt from Maggie's lap and ran to quieter quarters.

Twenty minutes later, the symphony stopped as both Maggie and Ted threw their hands high in the air. "Well, hello, Emily Holiday!" Maggie squealed, her closed fists shooting in the air. She winced at the pain in her shoulder, but she ignored it.

"Nikki and Lizzie were right when they said start at the beginning, and the beginning is Amy Jones Lambert, aka Emily Holiday. The name change appears to have taken place when she turned eighteen. Just as she entered college. I'll check the records to see if the name change was done legally. Keep working on what you have there and talk to me as soon as you see something we need to know," Ted said happily. Right now he was in what he called *Maggie heaven.*

The symphony of sound started up again. "Oooh, listen to this. Emily/Amy was adopted when she was five days old. Nothing on who the birth parents were. Her adoptive parents are Bradford and Pamela Holiday. Bradford Holiday manages a hedge fund in the billions. Pamela was a stay-at-home wife and mother. She passed away when Emily was approaching her eighteenth birthday. The Holidays had divorced when Emily was fourteen. A bitter divorce, and Pamela got skinned, thanks to . . . drumroll, please!!!!"

"The Chessmen! I knew it! I knew it! She changed her name legally. It's all right here. I'm sending all this on to Nikki," Ted said jubilantly.

"This is sad, Ted. I feel terrible reading it. It's Emily/Amy's diary. Why she would put it on a computer, though, is beyond me."

"Maybe she was worried about someone's finding an actual diary. It's pretty hard to lose a computer, and yet that's what happened this morning with the pretend mugging. What else is there?"

"Mother and daughter moved into a two-bedroom apartment. The husband paid his ex a pittance every month to live on. He did pay for the daughter until she reached the age of eighteen. Again, a pittance. His defense was she wasn't his blood, she was adopted, and, therefore, he owed her nothing. A court of law would say differently, but the wife didn't have the resources to fight it. Once he filed for divorce, father and daughter never saw each other again. He remarried shortly after the divorce to, I would say, a trophy wife. Eye candy. According to what is written here, Emily/Amy hates her adoptive father's guts for what he did to her mother. Because . . . the mother couldn't accept going from living in a mansion with servants to a two-bedroom apartment, where she had to do everything herself. She started to drink. Heavily. She also took pills to go to sleep, pills to wake up, pills to fight her depression. In the end, she died of a combination of alcohol and drugs. She left a paid-up insurance policy of ten thousand dollars to Emily/Amy. The girl had to use part of that to have her mother cremated.

"Emily/Amy, with the aid of one of the counselors at her high school, found a rooming house where she stayed until

it was time to go off to college. She worked two and sometimes three jobs to save up money. She got several grants
and scholarships to ease her way. Very smart, with a high
IQ and a 4.0 GPA. She's a very frugal person.

"She grew up in the Tupper Lake area in the Adirondacks. At first, her father commuted to work in Manhattan. He'd make the four-hour drive and stay in the city for
a few days, then go back home for a day or so, then do it
all over again. Says it was the perfect place to grow up.
They moved to Manhattan when she was eleven years old.
Mother hated it. Parents started fighting a lot, and the father didn't come home every night. Mother became convinced he was having an affair. At least now we know
where she came from.

"In this narrative, she says she cries herself to sleep every
night. By that, I mean at that time in her life. What kept her
going was the thought that somehow, someway, she could
find a way to get back at her adoptive father. That's when
she knew she would have to go to law school to make that
happen.

"In her spare time, and there was not much of that with
her work hours and studying, she spent hours and hours
researching the Chessmen. Her original plan was to see if
she could get a job with them. Later entries, in current
time, said that did not happen, although she did interview.
Under her new name, of course. Her next bet was to go
with the Quinn Law Firm and try her luck from there.
Which she has succeeded in doing."

"Anything on the marriage?"

"Yes, right down to the wedding night. We aren't going
there, Ted. It's bad enough that I'm reading this; I am not
repeating it. Suffice it to say, she met her soul mate, the
man she wants to spend the rest of her life with, to grow
old with. And she writes here that Jeffrey feels the same
way. She says she doesn't feel whole unless he's next to her.

He echoes the feeling. He writes her beautiful poetry professing his love into all eternity. They are compatible in every way.

"She adores Jeffrey's mother, Livinia, but she detests his father.

"There are no entries after she interviewed with the Quinn Law Firm."

"That's odd. What do you think that means, Maggie?" Ted asked.

"She wasn't taking any chances of whatever she was up to coming to light. We can now rightfully assume hiring on with Nikki was a means to an end. The divorce was all a setup. I'm sure if she has to, she'll go through with it, and when the dust settles, the two of them will remarry. Tall tales to tell their grandchildren someday. I'm guessing here, Ted."

"Right now, a guess is as good as a given. That's just my opinion. Look, you call Nikki, fill her in, and I'm going to text Dennis to come over here. I think he's the one who should perhaps have a talk with Mr. Bradford Holiday. Then let's see what you and I can uncover about whatever it is that the Chessmen are hiding. If Lizzie says they are hiding something, you can take it to the bank. With all of us working on it, we're bound to come up with the goods. At least I hope so."

Maggie flexed her fingers. "Let's do it!"

Chapter 17

The three Chessmen stomped their way down one hallway after another until they came to the partner wing and Maxwell Queen's elaborate suite of offices. Leo Bishop was the last man to walk through the door. He slammed it so hard, the other two Chessmen turned around to see if the door had come off the hinges. All three men were breathing fire as they verbally attacked one another, shouting obscenities to the four walls.

"Maxwell, you need to head to the lavatory and glue that damn rug back in place on your head. You look like some freaky cartoon character," Eli Rook bellowed.

"Don't you dare speak to me in that tone, Eli. You should talk. You look like you've been embalmed, but don't have the good sense to admit you're dead."

"Just chill out and calm down, everybody. This snapping and snarling is not going to get any of us anywhere. That witch wins if she drives a wedge through us. Use your damn heads, and, Maxwell, this is not one of your damn chess games. You need to deal with the here and now. We're in trouble. I'm contacting our investigators and calling them off. That Fox woman meant exactly what she said about Buzz and the divorce. And let me be the first to say I'm all for cutting Buzz loose this very minute. He's the reason we moved from safe territory to dangerous territory," Leo Bishop said, his tone of voice a tad lower than a full bellow.

"Now, who is the stupid one, Leo?"

"I need a drink. Fix me one, will you, Eli? Buzz isn't who you should be worrying about. You need to get Josh back here ASAP."

"What? You think I'm your slave? Fix it yourself. This is your office. For years, you've been holding it over our heads that you're the man in charge, the managing partner, even though all four of us are full partners. Partners in everything. Since you're the managing partner, then you damn well need to take charge and manage the situation. Don't you think it's a little early to start drinking?"

Maxwell Queen waved his arms about. "See all this! Your offices are just the same as this one. Look at me! We are a hair away from losing it all. Buzz will fall into line. Josh will not. Do I need to remind you that Josh did not participate in that event twenty-seven years ago? He split, wanted no part of it. That doesn't mean he isn't culpable, because he kept quiet. Now someone call him and get him back here. Do whatever you have to do."

Eli and Leo stared at their partner as he poured himself a half tumbler of scotch, but neither one made a move to do anything. The moment they saw him swallow the scotch in two gulps, both partners knew for certain that it was time to get upset.

Just to have something to do, Leo called Josh King, while Eli paced across the spacious office and back. Maxwell Queen poured himself another drink and took it neat. Then he marched over to his antique desk and sat down, his eyes watering. He reached up to see if his hairpiece was in place. Satisfied that it was, he leaned back and closed his eyes.

"The call went straight to voice mail. You heard the

message I left. Knowing Josh as well as I do, I think it's safe to say he removed the batteries and tossed the phone."

"You said that when we bought that property, we were safe," Eli said, slapping his hands down on Maxwell's polished desk. The sound was so loud, Maxwell Queen's eyes snapped open. "That's what you said, Maxwell. You convinced us to dismantle all five campgrounds and that hippie community. You said let nature take over."

"And that's exactly what happened. Everything is gone. Nature took over. All five educational campsites are gone. The hippie community is gone, and the people have moved on. It's been almost twenty-three years. Close your eyes and imagine what twenty-three years of forest growth would look like today. It looks like a damn jungle is what it looks like," Maxwell said, his words slurred. No one bothered to comment.

Eli started to pace again as Leo tried calling Josh at his home. No one picked up. He scowled at his two partners just as Buzz Lambert burst into the office, his face a mask of hate and frustration. He hated the degree of control that these men had over his life.

"Now what? I knew I should have gotten a different law firm to handle this divorce. You screwed it up, didn't you? Admit it!"

"Sit down, Buzz. *We* didn't screw up anything," Leo said wearily. "Look, you need to calm down and listen to what we're going to tell you. Lizzie Fox was here, all charm and smiles. She made no bones about your divorce going through with no hitches. We called off the investigators because . . . because she informed us she knew we had a secret and was going to expose us. Now, was that a scare tactic? I don't think so. She meant every word she said. That means that somehow, someway, she is going to find out what happened twenty-seven years ago. You were a party to that, Buzz, just the way we were.

"You might as well know right now—Josh bailed on us. He said he wasn't coming back. He can run, but he can't hide. He is as culpable as the rest of us. I've been trying to call him, but there is no response. As you can see, our self-appointed leader and managing partner is three sheets to the wind, which should tell us all something. We're in trouble. If you want to say something, now would be a good time, Mr. Speaker."

Buzz's arms flapped in the air as though he were about to take flight. "I must be stupid, because I'm not getting any of this. Okay, okay, I get the part about the divorce going through with no hitches. Livinia gets what she wants, and I walk off into the sunset. I can live with that, since I have no other choice, and the way I see it, I still have a chance to succeed in a bid for 1600 Pennsylvania Avenue, as long as I don't make waves. Explain the rest of this crap to me. Would you, please?"

"That question alone makes you too stupid to take up residence in the White House," Maxwell Queen said in a singsong voice from his position behind his antique desk.

Eli and Leo rolled their eyes for Buzz's benefit. "Your wife's attorney of record, Elizabeth Fox, as well as the Quinn Law Firm, are all investigating the Chessmen and you, too. That means, as she so quaintly put it, they will start at 'the moment we all dropped out of our mothers' wombs.' Are you getting it now, Mr. Speaker?"

"So what? Who cares if she finds out I gave Billy Jensen a black eye when I was ten years old? Who cares if I showed some guys my penis when I was twelve years old? We were comparing sizes. All kids do that. So I was a bed wetter for a long time. That makes me human. I went to high school, had tons of girlfriends, kissed them all, but never had sex, did some heavy petting. So what, again?

"I worked after school at a grocery store. Yeah, sometimes I stole cookies or a soft drink. But when I did that, I always stayed a half hour longer to clean up to make up for it. I worked my way through college, waiting tables, tutoring other students, and I worked during summers as a camp counselor to help pay for college. That was where I met you guys. I thought I would have to work some more to put myself through law school, but then I met Livinia. She fell head over heels in love with me, and that was the end of having to work odd jobs and summers. She put me through law school, and she and her family helped me start out in politics. Who cares about stuff like that? As for you guys, who were born with silver spoons in your mouths, I doubt there is anything of interest there."

Maxwell Queen stirred himself and leaned over his desk. "Back that up to our last summer as camp counselors and the last-night party and bonfire before we all left to go home. The three of us were headed for Harvard Law the following week. You were returning for your senior year in college, even though you are a year older than we are. With all the work you had to do to get through college, it took you six years to finish. Did you forget about that, Buzz?"

Buzz flapped his arms again as he started to pace frantically.

"Stop! You two are going to ruin my carpet!" Maxwell shouted. "Well, did you forget, Buzz?"

"Of course not. That . . . What . . . You don't forget something like that. I tried because you said we needed to forget it. Just so you know, I never did. I don't care how much the three of you lie to yourselves, you didn't forget it, either. So don't lie to me and to each other now. Is that why Josh left? If he said he's not coming back, then he sure as hell is not coming back. If this gets out, I'll be ruined. I couldn't run for dog catcher in this town or anywhere else."

Buzz whirled around. "You said, Maxwell, that something like this could never happen. Where's the proof that it did happen? Where? If you're right, and there is no proof, then there is nothing for Lizzie Fox to find, is there? Or is there something you know that the rest of us don't know?"

"You really are stupid, Buzz. I'm getting sick and tired of pointing that out to all of you. Of course there is something. *The girl!* A woman by now. Where is she? How do we know Lizzie Fox won't find her? We don't know the answer to that. *We* sure as hell never tried to find her. For obvious reasons. She's out there just waiting to be found," Maxwell said.

"Twenty-seven years later! All of a sudden, she's going to come out and nail our asses to the wall, is that what you're saying?" Eli snorted in derision.

"If she hasn't come forward up to now, why would she suddenly do so? Even if she did, who would believe her? She doesn't know who we are. It wasn't like we told her our names. The statute of limitations is long past, so we cannot be prosecuted for what we did. And, anyway, it would be her word against ours.

"People would listen, though. It will be fodder for the media. They love anything salacious, and this would be as salacious as it gets. Twenty-seven years is a long time," Eli said.

"Maybe we should try to find her ourselves. There has to be a record somewhere of the people who lived in that hippie community. They had to pay taxes on the property. They must have held jobs. Surely, someone in the nearest town would know something," Buzz said.

"That will be like poking a hornet's nest," Maxwell said. "Those people are probably scattered to the four corners of the globe by now. If you think they've been sitting around all this time waiting to nail us, then you're crazy," Maxwell said.

"Then what is your suggestion?" Eli asked.

"I don't have a suggestion. Personally, I think that Lizzie Fox was blowing smoke. Why would she go to all that trouble, effort, and cost if we don't fight the divorce? If we toe the line the way she wants, and the divorce goes through, then everyone gets what he or she wants. She did say that if we played our cards right, we still had a chance to go to 1600 Pennsylvania Avenue on Buzz's coattails. That statement makes me think that she just wanted to rattle us. Let's face it, I don't think there have been people born yet who don't have a secret or two they don't want bandied about," Maxwell said, his voice and tone gathering more confidence as he went along.

"If you actually believe that, Maxwell, I have a bridge I can sell you cheap. That lady, Lizzie Fox, never says anything she doesn't mean. If she said she's taking us on, she's taking us on," Buzz insisted. "Tell me again why you sold all that property. You said that as long as you owned it, nothing could come back to haunt us. Now you're singing a different tune, and you're making me nervous."

"It was a good business deal at the time. Eli, Leo, and I paid twenty-two million for it four years . . . after . . . after the last summer we worked there, the year after we graduated from law school. You didn't have any money, Buzz, and Josh said he wanted no part of that deal. A year after we bought it, we tore everything down and let nature take over. Then, five years ago, some hedge-fund billionaire, Bradford Holiday, approached us to sell him the property.

"You might or might not know this, but this firm handled Holiday's divorce. We saved him ten times what he would have had to pay out to his wife as a settlement. We made all that go away for him, and he kept his money. Thanks to us. As you know, Buzz, in this business, one hand washes the other.

"Holiday came to us when he found out we owned the

property and said a group of investors was going to build some kind of resort for the rich and famous, as he put it. They paid us fifty million dollars. More than double what we paid for it. What kind of fool would turn that down? Since Eli, Leo, and I are far from being fools, we took the deal. But like I said, that was a drop in the bucket to what we saved him in his divorce. He was appreciative.

"But to this day, that acreage has not been developed. I don't know why. Investors, as a rule, are a temperamental lot. That land might never be developed, and they can all take a nice tax write-off, which I suspect was their intention all along. Can I prove that? No, I can't, but unless one of you comes up with a better answer, I'm going to stick with what I think."

"What are we going to do about Josh?" Eli asked.

"What *can* we do, Eli? The answer is nothing. We can't force him to come back to the firm if he's serious about leaving. He certainly is not dependent on his share of revenue from here. He has as much, if not more, money than the rest of us. The man is a frugal bastard. He won't turn on us, but he won't help us, either. He's going to take his wife and go to ground somewhere. That's his way, we all know that."

"All right, now, let me get this straight. We're doing nothing, is that right? We're just going to sit here and contemplate our belly buttons while Lizzie Fox drives us into the ground, and we spend the rest of our lives in prison. That's fine for the three of you—Josh, too, if you want to count him in. You all have money to burn. I do not. Livinia was the one with the money, not me," Buzz sputtered, his face mottled, his hands shaking.

"The statute of limitations has passed, Buzz, a long time ago. We cannot—let me repeat, *cannot*—be prosecuted for what happened that night. Not now, not tomorrow, not next year, not ever. You want to poke that hornet's nest, be my guest. The three of us are sitting tight, right, boys?"

Eli and Leo nodded reluctantly.

"So you're hanging me out to dry, is that it? Every man for himself is what I'm seeing here," Buzz Lambert said, with his face a pasty white.

"No one is hanging anyone out to dry, Mr. Speaker. It's business as usual, all the way. You go poking that hornet's nest, you're going to get stung. I think we all need to agree that we're going to do nothing. At least for now," Maxwell said.

"Business as usual, my ass. Josh saw the handwriting on the wall. He's gone. Maybe it's time for me to go, too. I can see if I can mend some fences where my son is concerned. Who knows? He might even offer me a job. Which even I know I do not deserve. I'm going to go home now and pretend I had a relapse and try to figure something out. You three do what you want. Just remember that word *preemptive* you threw around at that press conference you insisted on."

Wilson Lambert's shaky legs managed to get him to the door. He turned around for a last look at his "friends." He didn't say a word, just quietly closed the door behind him.

The three Chessmen looked at one another. "He's going to be a problem," Maxwell Queen said. "What do we do, gentlemen, when we encounter a problem?"

"We make it go away," Eli and Leo said at the same time.

"Exactly. Now, I know it's still a bit early, but let's head out to a nice lunch on the firm so we can discuss the best way to make this particular problem go away. But first we need to send out a letter to Fox and the Quinn Law Firm saying we are contesting nothing, and it's smooth sailing for Livinia Lambert. A nice touch, and a good way to end this rotten morning."

Chapter 18

Jack cracked an eyelid to look at the red numerals on the bedside clock. They were blurry, but it looked like it was 4:45. He groaned. Then he felt a warm breath on his neck and ear. "Aaaah." He liked the tickle and suddenly felt warm all over. He knew he needed to get with it, because Nikki was rarely, if ever, this frisky so early in the morning. He moved his leg and instead of feeling his wife's warm body heat, he felt the cold-sheet side of the bed. His eyes snapped open. Staring at him were two huge brown eyes and two pointed ears.

"Damn it, Cyrus, how many times do I have to tell you not to lick my ear! What's up with you? It's not even five o'clock yet!" The big shepherd let loose with a soft woof; then Jack heard the shower. He groaned. So much for early-morning gymnastics.

"Okay, okay, I get it. You want to go out. Go! You know how to open the door and turn on the light. And on your way, turn up the heat! I taught you how to do that. C'mon, don't make me get up and freeze my buns off. You've got all that hair to keep you warm. Give me a break here." Jack dived back under the covers Cyrus was intent on pulling off the bed. "And you'd better make your bed before Nikki gets out of the shower."

Cyrus backed up a step, then another, to take in the situation. It looked to him like he was on his own. Three orders all at one time. He pondered the situation, then straightened the covers on his bed at the foot of the master bed. He barked to show he could obey orders. He barked again when he got to the door. In the hallway, he let loose with a second volley of sound; heat turned up. A minute later, Jack heard the chime that meant the alarm was turned off, then another robotic voice announcing that the kitchen door was now open.

"That's the smartest damn dog in the whole universe," Jack mumbled to himself just as his wife stood poised in the doorway of the bathroom with nothing on but a huge yellow towel.

Jack groaned again. "What's going on? It's not even five o'clock, Nikki."

"I needed to get an early start. I want to stop by my new associate's place to drop off her handbag. I thought I could do it yesterday, but I ran out of time because I didn't get to the police station to pick up our bags till late. There was no way to get in touch with Amy, so I decided to do it early this morning.

"I'm surprised, though, that she didn't call me after she picked up a new phone. I think I'm worried, Jack. I do not have a good feeling about any of this, and on top of everything else, I think she suspects the mugging was a put-up job."

Nikki sat down on the edge of the bed. Jack looked at his wife and thought she was more beautiful than any movie star. He had no thoughts now of getting frisky. All he wanted to do right now was help her because he could tell she was in distress. Never mind that the towel was slipping or that Cyrus bounded into the room like a tornado and leapt on the bed. Playtime! Not.

"She should have called me, Jack. Why didn't she?"

"I don't know, Nik. Maybe she was traumatized. Maybe

she fell asleep and forgot. Hell, there could be a dozen reasons why she didn't call. I guess you'll find out when you
get there."

Cyrus barked just as Nikki's cell phone rang on her side
of the bed. Before she could move, Cyrus had it in his
mouth to hand over.

"It's Carol. Oh, God, something must be wrong for her
to be calling me this early. What?" she snapped into the
phone. The room was silent, and at Nikki's sharp tone of
voice, even Cyrus stopped pawing at the bedcovers.

"You are not going to believe this," Nikki said, ending
the call. "The super just called Carol to tell her the boiler
went out, and there's a flood in the basement. There's no
heat. Carol is on her way in and will call everyone to stay
home, and that includes me. She said it's forty-eight degrees
outside. It's going to take five days to get a new boiler installed. Just what I need, another glitch. They weren't kidding about Murphy's Law. I can't wait to see what happens
next."

"Next? You're kidding, right? You don't have to go into
the office. Carol is going to reschedule all of your appointments. So that means . . ." The yellow towel flew across
the room. Cyrus howled and hopped off the bed. "Shut
the door on your way out!" Jack ordered.

Cyrus shut the door—another trick his master taught
him that he had aced.

Nikki walked up the flagstone path at seven-thirty. She
huddled inside her long white coat, hating such cold
weather so early in the season. She made a mental note to
get in touch with the groundskeeper who maintained the
property to rake the leaves and debris from the ferocious
winds of the past few days. She could feel her stomach
start to churn when she realized that Amy's rickety old car
wasn't in the driveway. She knew in her gut that her new

associate had flown the coop. Her gut instincts had been on the money.

She fished out the spare key from her wallet and opened the door. She called out Amy's name as she walked through the rooms toward the staircase leading to the second floor. It was cold, so that had to mean Amy had turned down the heat or never bothered to set the thermostat last night. If she'd even slept here, which was now starting to look doubtful.

Last evening, when she got home, she'd checked the two cell phones in Amy's purse. During the five hours when they were out of her new associate's possession, calls had come through on the burner phone, four from her soon-to-be ex and three from her soon-to-be ex–mother-in-law. Her regular Verizon cell had given up one call, a message left from the Landover Realty Company saying a nine-hundred-square-foot apartment that fit her budget requirements had just come on the market, and to please call for an appointment to see it.

The safe house was small. It took only a few minutes to walk through the first and second floors to see that there was no trace of Amy Lambert left. The bed was neatly made and looked like the young lawyer had never slept in it. There were no wet towels in the bathroom, no smears on the mirror over the vanity sink. All neat and tidy.

Downstairs, Nikki headed to the kitchen, the heart of every home. She opened the refrigerator. It was empty but running. Not even a bottle of water. Nikki turned it off and left the door open. The stainless-steel sink didn't have so much as a drop of water on it. She turned around and looked at the breakfast nook, nestled under a three-sided bay window, along with a wraparound padded bench. That's when she saw the corporate credit card and a note written on a piece of yellow legal paper in the center of the table.

Dear Ms. Quinn,

If you're reading this, then you know I'm gone. I want to apologize to you for taking up your valuable time. I can only imagine what you must be thinking. Again, I am sorry. This check should cover your billable hours. If it's too much, apply the balance to someone who needs a little extra help. I did not charge anything on your corporate card.

By way of explanation, Ms. Quinn, sometimes life hands you some things to deal with that are simply beyond a person's control, and they act on impulse. That's what happened with me.

Thank you for hiring me. I feel I would have been an asset to your firm if things had worked out. I'm sorry it didn't work out for us. The key is under the mat by the front door.

Amy Lambert

Nikki read through the short note three times until she had it committed to memory. Then she sent off texts to Jack, Lizzie, and Carol.

Her chin cupped in both hands, Nikki stared out the bay window at the swirling autumn leaves, which appeared as frenzied as her thoughts. The check was double what was owed for work to date. No charge on the credit card. The explanation left her stone-cold, but it reinforced her trust in her gut instincts.

She saw rather than heard fat raindrops pepper the bay window. *Oh, great, just what I need, another crappy day to go with my rotten mood,* she thought. And yet she didn't move, but continued to stare out at the darkening morning. Her gaze turned dreamy as she tried to remember how many people had stayed here in this little safe house before she and the others, mainly Pearl Barnes and her underground railroad, could get them to safety. Hundreds. Maybe even a thousand or more, if you counted the children. Amy Lambert was the first casualty—if you could even call her that. Not because of anything she, the girls, or Pearl had done wrong. It was Amy Lambert who was wrong.

Which now opened up another can of worms. Amy knew about the safe house. She had to alert Myra and Annie, who would, in turn, alert Pearl that the safe house was out of bounds, at least for now. She sent off a quick text, adding a dozen exclamation points at the end of the brief sentence.

Nikki's sigh was so loud, it startled her that the sound had actually come out of her mouth. She gathered up her things and jammed them all into her shoulder bag. She couldn't leave Amy's purse here with her laptop. She slung it over her right shoulder. She looked around to make sure all the lights were out. She marched her way to the front door, turned for one more look, and opened the door. The key was just where Amy said it was. She picked it up, locked the door, then slid the key into her pocket. She wondered if Amy had even had a key made yesterday. Possible but doubtful. This was one place she would never come back to.

Nikki made a mad dash for her Jeep, climbed in, and turned the heater on full blast. What to do? Where to go? Maggie's house, of course. She could stop at the donut shop and get some of Maggie's favorites. Before she put the Jeep in gear, however, she sent off another text to Jack, telling him where she was going and when she thought she would be home. **Make something nice for lunch. Soup would be good,** she added as a PS.

Nikki made good time through town, even with her stop at the donut shop, and arrived at Maggie's just as Ted Robinson was about to pull away from the curb in the

Post van. She tapped her horn lightly for Ted to move ahead so she could take his parking spot. *Win-win this morning,* she thought sourly.

Ted pulled ahead and double-parked. He got out and walked back to where Nikki had her Jeep parked. She rolled down the window. "How's our girl this morning, Ted?"

"Scary good. Please don't ask me to elaborate on that. What are you doing here so early?"

Nikki told him. "That proves you were right all along. Always go with your gut feelings. I do. They never fail me. So what's your game plan?"

"I'm not sure I have a plan of any kind. For right now, I think it best if I stay under the radar. I haven't really gotten past Maggie and me eating these donuts and drinking a pot of coffee. No, that's not true. In the back of my mind, I was thinking of taking her out to the farm if she's good to go. Is she, Ted?"

"Yeah, the doctor gave her the green light two days ago. I just didn't tell her. If I had told her, she'd have gone outside to try to rake leaves. Are we going to have a meeting tonight, Nikki?"

"By the way, Ted, how did Dennis make out with that hedge-fund guy? Do you know?"

"I do know, and he bombed out. He couldn't get past the receptionist. He said he tried every trick in the book, and all he got for his efforts was the demand he leave the premises or the police would be called. So, yeah, nothing there. Listen, I gotta go. I have to pick up Espinosa. I'll see you tonight."

Nikki rolled up the window and turned off the engine. She grabbed her purse and the one belonging to Amy Lambert and slung them over her shoulder. With the donut bag in her hand, she sprinted for Maggie's front door. She rang the bell and waited. A smile as wide as the Grand Canyon rippled across Maggie's face. "Company! I'm excited, and are those donuts I see? Yes, they are donuts! I just made a pot of coffee. Well, Ted made it before he left. Did you see him?"

"I did. Boy, you are not going to believe this, Maggie," Nikki said as she followed the newly retired editor in chief through the house and out to the kitchen. Hero hissed his disapproval when neither woman paid any attention to him.

"Try me. Nothing, absolutely nothing, surprises me these days. Are you going to work, coming from work, what?"

"Can't go to work. No heat. The boiler blew up. So I went out to the safe house to drop off Amy's purse."

"And she took it on the lam, right?"

"How did you know?" Nikki gasped.

"I'm a reporter, that's how. Oh, those donuts look so scrumptious. Boston cream, my all-time favorite after chocolate-filled cream and orange Creamsicle, but I do love those blueberry ones, too. So what are you going to do about the boiler?"

Nikki explained about how long it would take to re-place it. "I thought I'd stop by here, see if you had made any headway, and take you out to the farm if you're up to it. Are you? We all need to be together to try to make some sense out of all of this."

"Nikki, I am so ready you would not believe. I have se-rious cabin fever. I am about to climb the walls. I don't care if it is raining, snowing, thundering, whatever, I just need to get out of here. Should I pack a bag? I can't do steps yet, so you'll have to do it."

"No problem. Just tell me where everything is."

"Just pack sweats, top drawer. Underwear, second drawer. Socks, drawer on the right. Ted brought the rest of my stuff down here. I can gather it up. I also have to call my cat sitter to come by in case Ted elects to stay out there, too. Don't tell him I said this, but the truth is, I don't know what I would have done without him and Espinosa."

"You should tell him that, Maggie. Everyone likes to be appreciated. He really loves you. He'd try to get you the moon if you asked him, and like the song goes, he'd climb the highest mountain. Look at me, Maggie. Ask yourself how you would feel if Ted suddenly wasn't in the picture. Ask yourself how you would feel if he walked out of here this morning and never came back, and what you would regret. I think about that every time Jack and I go at it. Brings me right down to earth in a heartbeat." Nikki pretended not to see Maggie's eyes fill with tears. "I'll just . . . just go upstairs and get your stuff."

"Why do you always have to be so right?" Maggie mumbled, but Nikki was already on her way up the stairs and didn't hear a word she said.

Twenty minutes later, Nikki had the Jeep headed toward Pinewood. She'd sent another text informing Myra that she was bringing Maggie, and would Myra, please, make up the spare room on the first floor for her, as Maggie would be staying over. She'd ended the text with a suggestion to call everyone for a meeting. Her postscript said it would be nice if Charles made something good for dinner. Hint. Hint.

Myra's response was **Done and done**. Just like the message Starry Knight had left for Annie last week. *Hmmm.*

With no traffic to speak of, Nikki was making excellent time, even with the now-heavy rain pouring down. "Crazy weather for this time of year, eh?" Nikki said, hoping to erase the miserable look on Maggie's face.

"Uh-huh. Listen, Nikki, it's not that I don't love Ted. I do. I . . . It's complicated. I don't think I could . . . could survive if something happened to him. Like Gus. When he died, I about lost it. And here's the kicker: I didn't love my husband the way I love Ted. So, if anything ever did happen to Ted, it would be worse. It would be the end of me. I know it.

"I'm working on it, I really am. Sometimes I think I'm more like Kathryn than I realize. She is never going to commit to Bert. It's just who Kathryn is. Will she regret it in later years? Probably, but then it will be too late, and she'll be all alone. I'm not saying she should marry Bert so she won't be alone. But if she doesn't love him the way she loved her husband, Alan, then what's the point?

"Then there's Lizzie. She thought she wanted to die. She couldn't go on without her fiancé. Jack saved her life that night in the freezing cold. She went on to find true, wonderful, magical love, and has a son who means the world to her. Everyone is different, Nikki. Like I said, it's complicated, but I am working on it. Just believe me when I tell you I do love Ted. I will always love Ted. And he knows it, too."

"Well, then, that takes care of that. I'm satisfied your head is screwed on straight," Nikki said lightly. "Hey, did I tell you Jack taught Cyrus how to turn the heat up in the morning? He's a whiz. He can turn the alarm off and on, and now he can even open the back door to let himself out in the morning. That dog should be in Ripley's Believe It or Not museum. Jack should go into it, too. He totally has the patience of a saint when it comes to teaching Cyrus, and that dog soaks it up like he is a sponge."

Maggie laughed, a genuine sound of mirth. Nikki relaxed at the sound. "Hero can't really do anything but purr. I'm okay with that, though."

The rest of the trip to Pinewood consisted of dog and cat tales, with both women laughing and giggling.

Life at that moment was good.

Chapter 19

Even though the dining room at Pinewood was the largest room in the house, with the table seating twelve, it was filled to capacity, with Charles and Fergus fetching the kitchen chairs for extra places. The sisters and their guys were meeting in the dining room because Maggie couldn't manage the narrow, moss-covered stone steps that led to the catacombs and the war room below the house.

Everyone was in attendance except for Kathryn, who was on the road. She'd called earlier and asked to be called once the meeting was under way; she had some information she needed to share.

Charles waved his arms in the air for silence. When he had everyone's attention, he said, "Let's recap here with our latest updates before we make the call to Kathryn. Feel free to correct me if I have anything wrong.

"For starters, Dennis was not fortunate enough to make contact with Bradford Holiday. It wasn't for lack of trying or expertise. Men like Bradford Holiday, whose fortunes run in the hundreds of millions and sometimes billions, simply do not talk to lowly reporters. There's no need. In his opinion, there is nothing Dennis could do for him. If he could have used Dennis in some way, he would have granted an interview. Mr. Bradford Holiday is on our shelf for now.

"Yesterday a messenger from the Chessmen delivered a letter to the Quinn Law Firm saying they were on board with the Speaker's divorce proceedings and that everything was being done expeditiously toward that end. That was just written confirmation of what Lizzie said we could expect. Is it suspicious? Absolutely. We will deal with that at the right time, if need be.

"Nikki's new associate, Amy, has disappeared. Nikki thinks she saw through the pretend mugging and realized that the handwriting was on the wall. At this moment, we do not know where she is. She did return the key to the safe house, Nikki's corporate credit card, and the money Nikki gave her. Nikki and Lizzie's instincts were right. It was all a setup. As of now, we don't know everything about the why of it, but we are pretty sure it has something to do with the Chessmen, since before applying for a job with Nikki's firm, she tried to get one at Queen, King, Bishop, and Rook.

"In time, we will figure the whole thing out. What we do know for certain is what we got off Amy's laptop. We have her background and now know that Bradford Holiday, who is sitting on our shelf for the moment, is Amy's adoptive father. We have those two ends tied together. And we also know that the Chessmen represented Bradford Holiday in the divorce action in which he took his ex-wife and adopted daughter, Emily/Amy, to the cleaners, so perhaps that is what ties Amy to the Chessmen. But for now, Amy is going on our shelf, right next to her adoptive father. Do any of you have any questions so far?" No one did.

"All right, then, Abner has a report he'd like to deliver."

"I'm going to be right up front here and tell you all that as good as I am, I was not able to hack into the Chessmen's files," said Abner. "No, no, don't look at me like that. I said *I* couldn't hack into them. . . . I didn't say it couldn't be done, because I enlisted the aid of a friend who was able to do it for me. I have here, in my hand, a flash drive that has everything we need to roast those guys." Abner's voice was so gleeful, the others got excited.

There was pure awe in Yoko's voice when she said, "You have all their client files! Like *all* of them?"

"Uh-huh. Plus a ledger-summary type of report on how they screwed over the spouses of the clients they represented." Abner laughed to show what he thought of that particular piece of stupidity. "I can't believe those guys didn't factor in people like me possibly hacking into their secrets. So smart on some things, dumb as dirt on others. Oh, I also have all their passwords now, and all their bank balances and brokerage accounts—not only those in this country, but those offshore as well. Avery helped tremendously, as did my . . . um . . . friend."

Annie held up her hand; her face was puzzled. "Am I having a senior moment here? If Emily/Amy walked off into the night, then we have no mission. I thought she was our mission. What are we left with here? Nothing, as far as I can see. So the girl changed her mind about working for Nikki's firm. Obviously, she changed her mind about the divorce papers she filed also. Isn't that the end of the story?"

"I agree with Annie," Myra said. "Why are we even here having this meeting? What is it we hope to accomplish? Whatever it is that you are all seeing is simply eluding me."

Jack Emery bit down on his tongue. He was tempted to say something, but when he saw the stubborn set of his wife's jaw, he kept quiet.

"What about the Speaker of the House's divorce? Did we decide whether that is tied into anything?" Isabelle asked.

"Somehow, someway, it is. I tried calling Livinia in Hawaii

all day today on both her regular cell phone and her burner phone. She did not answer either one. I also tried calling Amy's husband, Jeffrey, but he didn't answer, either. I must confess that I don't know what it means," Nikki said, "but I know damn well it means something."

"Dear, I really don't want to rain on your parade, but you've been saying that for over a week now, and other than the fact that the Chessmen are despicable lawyers with a penchant for chess, we have nothing. We need something a little more concrete," Myra said gently.

"Hold on, everyone. I'm in agreement with Nikki, and so is Ted. There's more here, we just haven't found it yet. Perhaps Kathryn has the answer. She did say she has news to share. Then again, the answer might lie on that flash drive Abner just turned over. Perhaps they're tied together. We won't know until we hear from Kathryn and check out the flash drive," Maggie said.

"Then let's do it! Call Kathryn. Where is she? Does anyone know?" Dennis asked as he tinkered with a gizmo in the middle of the table that would allow everyone in the room to hear what Kathryn was saying as soon as the call was made.

"She was in Minnesota earlier this afternoon when I spoke with her," Yoko said.

The room turned silent as Nikki placed the call. "We're all here, Kathryn. We have you on a speakerphone that Dennis set up. Talk away, we're all listening."

"Hey, all!" Kathryn said by way of a greeting. "This is a really good time for this call because I just pulled into a truck stop for gas and something to eat. I don't know if what I'm going to share with you is of any importance or not. For some reason, my gut is telling me it is.

"Every July, I head toward the Adirondacks and all the produce markets to deliver Georgia peaches and Bing cherries. Over the years, I've gotten to know a lot of the people I deliver to, like Bill and Mary Cunningham. They own over fifty markets and are one of my heaviest loads. They live somewhere close to Tupper Lake, where you said your new associate came from, Nikki. It's where that billionaire hedge-fund guy lives, her adoptive father. I got to thinking about that last night, so I called Mary and asked her what she knew, if anything. It was just one of those girly gut hunches. I ran with it.

"Mary said Holiday does not associate with the common people like herself. Back in the day, when he was still married to his wife, she would come in with the little girl around the holidays. Easter for the egg hunt they always put on, the Fourth of July for the sparklers, the pumpkins for Halloween, and, of course, the Christmas goodies they handed out, the candy canes and stuff. Mary said that in her opinion, the mother tried to keep the little girl as normal as she could.

"They only heard about the Holidays' divorce after it occurred and after the mother's death, years later. She did say Mrs. Holiday was too young to die. She was quick to tell me that little towns like those are hotbeds of gossip, and she heard it all, like the little girl was adopted from the commune, and the stories that went with it."

"What commune?" all the listeners asked at once.

"That's what I asked." Kathryn laughed. "Mary said the area's only claim to fame were the hedge-fund guy and this commune, Trinity. Not like back in the late sixties. She said it was a little community of maybe one hundred fifty or so people. Some young rich guy owned the property and set it up. Built cabins for the people and paid for everything. He had no other family, but he married someone named Pilar. Then he built a bunch of educational campsites for kids to go to in the summer. She said she distinctly remembers one site was a chess site and another a math-and-science site. Eight in all, she said. The counselors all came from big colleges.

"Then Mr. Pyne, that was the rich young guy's name, died and left it all to Pilar and her daughter, Layla, who had just been born. She said they were a mind-your-own-business group of people and never caused any problems. They used the doctors and dentists in town, shopped at their stores, always paid cash.

"There were only a few children in the community, and they were all home-schooled, but she doesn't know exactly why. She met Layla many times. Said she was fey in her opinion. Dreamy, and she said she seemed to float in the white gowns she wore when she walked. She had hair down to her waist and always wore a crown of flowers and leis, too. Even in the winter. They had a huge greenhouse that she tended just for flowers. A pretty girl, as she remembers.

"Then Pilar died. Mary couldn't remember when, but her husband, Bill, said at least twenty-five or twenty-six years ago. He likened it to the year they had some kind of bad storm. Mary agreed when he refreshed her memory. They have their own cemetery, she said.

"A year or so after Pilar's death, the young girl left the community. To Mary's knowledge, no one has seen or heard from her since. Then a few years after she left, the property was bought up by some holding company. The last remaining residents packed up and moved on. No one said where they went. Bill said the property sold for twenty-two million. That was boo-koo money back then, and it still is. Some lawyer from New York handled the sale was the rumor. All the cabins and the campsites were torn down as soon as the sale was finalized. The property now is just overgrown.

"This is the best part, so listen up. A while back, Bill thinks, maybe five years or so, the property was sold again, this time for fifty million dollars, to some land developers. The guy who headed the syndicate was Bradford Holiday. They were going to build some kind of tony resort, but a problem came up with the cemetery because it was right in the middle of the whole shebang. Nothing was ever done after that. That property is just forest now.

"Okay, folks, that's what I wanted to share with you. I gotta get back on the road after I take care of business. I'll check in with you all later when I stop for the night."

Nikki pumped her fist in the air. Maggie let out a whoop of excitement as Annie and Myra smiled, and all the others were grinning and laughing.

Ten minutes passed before Charles called a halt to the laughter. "Now that we have something to sink our teeth into, I think it's time we start to chew. Nikki, you're good at this. Take us through what we have and factor in Kathryn's news."

Abner held up his hand. "Hold on a minute. There's something I forgot to tell you all. My bad, but I was a little excited with the news I did have. I said we broke the passwords to all of the Chessmen's accounts, and that's true. What I forgot to mention was that the Chessmen have a deal with the banks and brokerage houses that no monies can be taken out or transferred until they call in to approve it. They have voice-recognition software, or something or other, in place. Once they call in, there is, for want of a better word, a secret word or phrase that will allow them to complete their transaction. These guys are smart. Before they end the call, they set up the next secret word or clue for the next secret-code transaction.

"The bottom line is that no one but the Chessmen know what that word or clue is. Even my . . . um . . . colleague cannot read minds. So just be aware that helping ourselves to their funds when the time comes will not be a slam dunk."

"How could you forget something so important?" Dennis demanded.

"I'm human, kid. That's how," Abner snapped. Properly chastised, Dennis hung his head in shame.

"Well, now we know, so let's move on here," Charles said.

Nikki looked down at the yellow legal pad in front of her. Anyone seeing her scribbles would think they were from a doctor writing out prescriptions. "As Jack likes to say, I didn't see this coming. We'll start at the beginning.

"And the beginning starts with my new associate, Amy Lambert. We now know that she had an agenda and that she used my firm to act on it. As much as I hate to admit this, I do not think she ever had any intention of working for us. On the other hand, if she was out to get revenge on the Chessmen, maybe I am wrong, and she was planning to stick around for a while.

"Nor do I think she ever intended to go through with the divorce she initiated. She brought her husband into the game. Is it merely a coincidence that he just happens to be the son of the Speaker of the House? I personally do not think there is any such thing as a coincidence.

"Enter Livinia Lambert, wife of the Speaker of the House and mother to Jeffrey and mother-in-law to Amy Lambert, who wants to file her own divorce action against the Speaker. She came to me under a false name and had a list of dos and don'ts. It was all a little fishy, but then most divorce cases tend to have secrets and problems, and, almost invariably, the lawyer gets blindsided by those secrets and problems.

"At the moment, Livinia says she is in Hawaii. We, or at least I, do not know for sure if that is true. It's what she said. For all I know, she could be around the corner in some hotel. She is not responding to my phone calls. Even allowing for the time difference, if she is in Hawaii, she should have picked up on my voice mails by now. She has not. That's all we know on Livinia.

"Next up is our bogus mugging and Amy's skipping out on us. I think she made the whole deal. We, and by *we*, I mean Avery Snowden, got us background on her we otherwise would never have gotten. We know where she came from, that she was adopted by Bradford and Pamela Holiday, a very wealthy couple who lived at the time in the Adirondacks. We also now know that the Holidays divorced and Mr. Holiday used the Chessmen to handle his divorce, which led to Mrs. Holiday's getting taken to the cleaners. Mrs. Holiday died the year Amy went off to college. Mr. Holiday paid out the bare minimum for mother and daughter to live on after the divorce. Amy was forced to work her way through college. Her adoptive father cut her loose and was heard to say she wasn't his blood—she was adopted—and therefore no longer his responsibility.

"A court of law would disagree, but Amy never went that route. Her real name is Emily Holiday. She changed her name legally when she went off to college.

"Amy/Emily met Jeffrey Lambert, and they got married. According to her file on the computer, they were true soul mates. Soul mates headed for the divorce court, but only after he sets up a trust fund for her that she claims she does not want. That was done for our benefit. At this moment, we do not know where Emily/Amy is. I still have her purse, her burner phone, her Verizon cell, and her laptop. We're at a dead end with Amy.

"We now know the area where Emily/Amy and her family lived. Kathryn's source told her that one of the area's claims to fame is/was Bradford Holiday. I guess because he is so rich. The other claim to fame, if fame it is, is the commune called Trinity. I'm calling it a commune, but the others refer to it as a little community of one hundred fifty or so people. A man named Pyne owned acres and acres of property, where it was all built by him. Not physically built, but he paid to have it done. He also built, we think, eight educational campsites for kids to learn in the summer. Mr. Pyne died a few days after his only child was born to his wife, Pilar. The name of that child was Layla. We know nothing of Layla or her mother, Pilar, other than that she passed away. The mother, that is. No one seems to know where Layla, the daughter, is.

"A few years later, according to Kathryn's source, the property was sold, and the community and campsites were torn down. Nature took over. It's doubtful anyone going there would ever know that a community of real people and the campsites ever existed. Years and years went by, and then, a few years ago, it was sold again, this time to Bradford Holiday and a group of investors who were going to build a high-end resort.

"The flaw in that plan was the community's cemetery. It is right in the middle of the property, and the town fathers said it could *not* be moved. The original selling price was twenty-two million dollars. That price went to fifty million when Holiday and the investors bought it. Nothing ever happened. The place is the same now as it was back then. We're thinking close to twenty-five years.

"We need to know who handled both sales," Nikki said. "We need to know where the money went. To whose account? And who and how did that particular attorney know where to find Layla Pyne. This is the part that I think is our mission. We need to find Layla Pyne. She is now the key to all of this, in my opinion. Do any of you see this differently?"

"Not me!" Maggie said. "Do any of you remember what Kathryn's source said?" Not bothering to wait for a response, she said, "Think, people! Who do we know who wears a crown of flowers in her hair, has hair down past her buttocks, and wears hippie garments? Think!"

"The owner of the Daisy Wheel!" Dennis shouted so loud that Myra clamped her hands over her ears.

"And remember Avery said when she bought the Daisy Wheel, she showed up with shopping bags full of cash. *Cash!* Think along the lines of no paper trail. What there is of a paper trail carries the name Starry Knight. *Not* Layla Pyne," Ted said.

The group's sudden outburst at Ted's words was louder than a bomb going off.

Maggie laughed the loudest. She held up her hand for silence. "Because I am a reporter with a very active imagination, I have a scenario I'd like to present to all of you. I see by the expression on Ted's face he is thinking the same thing I am. Anyone want to hear it? I grant you, it is a stretch, but in the end, it is the only thing that makes sense once you cross all the t's and dot all the i's."

"Of course we want to hear it, dear. Don't keep us in suspense," Myra said.

"Okay, here goes . . ."

Chapter 20

Charles once again held his hand up for silence. The others obeyed instantly, but there was still an electric current of excitement running through the room.

"Question, people. Do we have any sense of urgency here, or can we take our time mapping out a strategy? In other words, are we going to operate by the seat of our pants, which is something we've never done, or do we map out a foolproof plan? I need to know how you all want to play this," Charles said. All eyes turned to Nikki.

"This is how I see it. We've been operating in the dark from day one. If that's operating by the seat of our pants, so be it. It's working. I see no reason to switch up now. If we wait, plan and create a strategy, we might get left out in the cold. Everyone knows you can't trust the Chessmen. I vote to move quick and fast. Basically, we have just about all the information we need. At least suspect. We just have to nail it down.

"By that, I mean we have to find out if the Chessmen ever served as camp counselors at one of those education camps. I'm willing to bet they worked summers at the chess camp for kids. I'm also willing to bet that particular camp is a stone's throw from the Trinity community Kathryn's source told her about. But we need hard proof.

That means written proof. College yearbooks will probably give us our answer. If they did do something that last summer, they wouldn't put it on their résumés. They wouldn't want anyone to know that they were within a hundred miles of Trinity. In any of the write-ups that I've read, I never saw anything about their working. They were rich kids, no need to work. So why did they? Their love of chess would be my guess. Remember, that's how they all came together in college—because of their love of the game.

"We need to find Layla Pyne. I think we all know who she is, unless any of you know another hippie-like female who runs a restaurant and paid for the building that houses it in cash, carried in two shopping bags, to avoid a paper trail. We need to know for certain if Starry Knight is Layla Pyne. There might not be any birth records, since she was born in the community and, I presume, delivered by a midwife. I read somewhere that communes like Trinity kept ledgers and Bibles. Each commune had *one*—a master book with no copies. I don't know if that's true or not, but somewhere there has to be a record. We need to find it or who has charge of it. That's not something one would discard because it's a record of births and deaths. Or . . . we have Myra and Annie go to the Daisy Wheel to confront Starry Knight. She might—and I say, *might*—talk to them. I'm betting she will talk to them, once they tell her how much information we have.

"Abner said he has the Chessmen's files. All those cases where the women lost out. Like Pamela Holiday. We need to get in touch with all of them and invite them to our grand-slam event, especially if we tell them we're going to get them what they should have gotten in their divorce settlements.

"Which now brings me to the second part of all that. Abner, hack into those banking records. We, at the proper time, want all of the Chessmen's clients' money sent into one account, far, far away. This way, when we distribute it to the women, it can't be traced. Let's see how those fat cats like living on peanut butter and jelly or macaroni and cheese for months on end, like a lot of their wives had to do. Can you do that, Abner?"

"I can. Just tell me when you want it done." They all clapped their hands and smiled broadly.

"What fun this is going to be," Yoko giggled. Harry smiled. He was always happy when his little lotus flower giggled.

"Won't those men go to the authorities and file complaints? That's a federal offense. And it's illegal," Dennis said, his eyes wide at what he was hearing.

Jack Sparrow looked over at Dennis and raised one eyebrow. "And your point is . . ."

"Uh . . . I guess I just realized I don't have a point."

"All we have to do now is decide where we're going to bring this all to a close. Oh, and please, someone, send Kathryn a text telling her what we're doing. Any suggestions?" Charles asked. Isabelle volunteered and was typing out a text before Nikki could finish speaking.

Maggie raised her hand. "The racetrack would be my first suggestion. I forget which guy owns it, but there are bleachers that can accommodate a lot of people. I think it's Eli Rook. That's in case we want to invite all four hundred women to see the grand finale, which I happen to think is a good idea. I also have an idea about that. We'll need Abner's expertise again to hack into the reservation list for the weekend reserved for Eli Rook. That might take some doing, calling all of the names and canceling the reservations without Rook's knowing. We'll have to have people in place to take over the racetrack that weekend. His weekend is the last one in the month, right, Nikki?"

"Yes, that's right. How do we handle phone calls to

Rook or the firm? We can't have anyone getting in touch with Rook, or any of the others, before we make our move. Can we black out their phones somehow?" Nikki asked.

"Avery will handle all that," Charles said. "How long will it take you, Avery?"

"If I put all my operatives on it, two days at the most."

"Abner, how long for you to do all you have to do?"

"I'm just one guy. Two, three days. Depends if I run into trouble," Abner said.

"How should we go about notifying the wives of the people on the client list who got swindled in their divorces? That might take some time. People move away, don't leave forwarding addresses, that kind of thing," Charles said.

"That's where the client list comes in. We hack the husbands' records, and somewhere in their files will be the wives' addresses. They won't always be current, but we can use their Social Security numbers to track them," Avery said.

"We girls can do that," Annie said. "So we're talking a week here, give or take a day or so, right?"

The others agreed, which meant it was now carved in stone. One week of information gathering before the Chessmen were punished for their misogynistic, evil doings.

Jack laughed out loud. "They sure won't see this coming!"

"Clear something up for me, because I want to make sure I understand all of this," Espinosa said, speaking for the first time since they had all gathered. "Are we saying that Nikki's new associate, Amy Lambert, who is Bradford Holiday's adopted daughter, is also the birth daughter of Layla Pyne, also known as Starry Knight, who owns the Daisy Wheel? And both don't know, at this point in time, that they are mother and daughter, right?

"If that's what we're saying, that means the Chessmen as a group, or at least one of them, raped Layla Pyne twenty-seven years ago, and they have kept it a secret all these years. Right?"

"Yes," Charles said.

"What about the Speaker of the House? Was he involved?" Espinosa asked.

"We believe so," Charles said.

"Well, then, have you given any thought to how you are going to get him out to the racetrack at the end of the week? He doesn't usually attend those weekend retreats. At least I didn't see any mention of it in anything I read," Jack said.

"I think we can cover that with all the high-tech gurus we have working for us. He'll be sent a text from the Chessmen ordering him to join them that particular weekend. A command performance, so to speak," Annie said. "He won't dare be a no-show. When they say to jump, the Speaker says how high. I don't see a problem."

"I'm clear on it all now." Alexis squeezed Espinosa's hand to show she thought he was right to clear things up in his mind.

"So, are we pulling an all-nighter, like back in the old days, or are we calling it a night and picking up in the morning? If my opinion counts, I'm for the all-nighter," Maggie said, excitement ringing in her voice.

"I second that," Ted said, loving the eager smile he saw on Maggie's face.

"An all-nighter it is then," Charles said. "The boys and I will go down to the war room. You ladies can keep the dining room. I know you're all itching for us to leave so you can plan on how you're going to make those men pay for all their wrongdoing."

"Dear, you are so astute sometimes, you amaze me," Myra said sweetly as she kissed her husband's cheek. "Go, go, shoo! You boys do what you have to do, and we'll do what we do best."

"And that would be . . . ?" Charles called over his shoulder.

"You don't want to know, dear. Truly, you don't," Myra said softly.

Charles shuddered. His wife was right; he really did not want to know.

"What did Myra mean?" Dennis asked. His voice was so jittery, the parade to the war room stopped in midtrek.

"What did I tell you about asking questions like that, kid?" Harry said, eyeballing the young reporter.

Dennis squared his shoulders. "It's what I do, Harry. I'm a reporter. I ask questions. What's wrong with that?"

"Nothing is wrong with that when you ask the right questions. You asked the wrong one just now. From here on in, it's NTK. What that means is when the ladies want you to know, they will tell you. Give it up, kid."

Dennis grimaced when he saw the others glaring at him, especially Ted Robinson, his idol. "Okay, Harry." He might not ask any more questions, but one way or another, he was going to find out the answer to his question. The thing was, would he be able to handle the answer? Then he remembered the promise he had made to himself never to piss off Harry.

It was day three when Myra slipped into her coat to head to Annie's to pick her up. Their destination: the Daisy Wheel. She turned around and looked at Lady, who was staring mournfully at her. "I won't be gone long. We'll go for a nice long walk when I get back. Stay alert."

Lady barked softly to show she understood, then lay down on the carpet by the sink, which gave her a clear view of the back door and the TV monitor overhead.

Ten minutes later, Myra pulled her car to a stop at the foot of Annie's long drive, way surprised to see her friend waiting for her. Annie hated the cold.

"Took you long enough," Annie grumbled. "Do you have everything? Are you sure you didn't forget anything?"

"Annie, I have everything you said I needed, in that envelope, right there beside you. I'm not sure we're going to be making a case. We're simply going to tell her we know her secret and that that secret is safe with us. We're going to show her a picture of her daughter. To be honest, that's as far as I got in my thinking. We aren't even sure she won't kick us out and refuse to talk to us. Even though it's early, she doesn't start serving till four o'clock, and there are still going to be people there, the sous chefs, the food-prep people, and, of course, the waitstaff."

"We send them all packing and put a sign on the window that says it's closed. How hard is that to do?"

"Annie, we're not going there to start a war. We're going there to talk. *TALK*."

"See, Myra, that's where you're wrong. She has to know right from the git-go that this is the end of the road for her. The truth is, I think the poor soul will be relieved. If we're right on all of this, imagine carrying all that baggage all these years with no end in sight. I say we shut it down and hope she falls into line. I have my gun, so wipe that look off your face."

"Oh, good Lord. Please promise me you won't shoot up the place."

"Are you out of your mind, Myra? I would never promise something like that. If you keep arguing with me here, I'll end up shooting you."

Myra clamped her lips shut. The rest of the trip into town to the Daisy Wheel was made in silence as Myra paid attention to her driving, and Annie read through the contents of the manila envelope in her hands.

"Myra, how do you really feel about all of this?" Annie asked quietly.

"In the beginning, not so good, but the more we found out, the more my thinking changed. The things and the lengths people will go to for money boggle my mind. Lawyers are supposed to be held to a higher standard. Look at Nikki and Alexis, not to mention Jack and Lizzie. They care about the clients. Not about the money. They care about justice and what's fair. Do you have any idea how much pro bono work her firm does? Half of all her business. She never told me that, Jack did.

"Then you see those Chessmen and how they operate, and it sickens me. So, to answer your question, I am good with all we're doing. And doing what we're about to do might bring peace and closure to many who, otherwise, would never get it. For starters, Starry and Amy. Anything else? We're almost there. We beat the traffic, but it's going to be a bear going home."

"Think *kitty cat,* not *bear.* I'll be driving on the way home, Myra."

And that was the end of that.

Eight minutes later, Myra parked her car in the Daisy Wheel's oversized parking lot. She looked around and saw only seven cars. The staff's vehicles, she presumed. "I say we head to the kitchen entrance. The door will probably be open, so the workers can toss the trash when it piles up. You okay with that, Annie? No guns!"

"No guns, no pearls!" Annie did a pretend lunge to snatch at Myra's pearls, but Myra danced away in the nick of time.

"Okay, okay, but you only use it to threaten if it even comes to that."

"Whatever you say, Myra," Annie said sweetly. "All right . . . we're here. Do we knock or just barge in? I'm all for the element of surprise myself."

"Then let's do it!" Myra had to use all her weight to open the heavy steel door, but she managed. Annie brushed past her to the surprise of the staff at their workstations. "We need to see Starry. Like right *now*! Where is she?"

A tiny girl wearing an apron, which was six sizes too big for her, pointed to the meat locker.

"Fetch her, please," Myra said. The little girl scurried off to return with Starry, who was holding a box labeled FRESH SALMON CUTLETS. She set it down on one of the counters and wiped her hands on her apron.

"What are you doing here? Guests are not permitted in the kitchen. It's too early for dinner. We don't open till four. Even if we're friends, I cannot allow it, ladies."

"Starry, listen to me. You need to send all these people home. You need to put a sign on the door saying you're closed because of a family emergency. Please do not make this more difficult than it already is."

"I'll do no such thing. I don't understand. I thought we were friends. You can't come in here and tell me what to do. The answer is no."

"Now, Myra?" Annie asked.

"Not yet."

"Then let me put it to you another way, *Layla*. We need to talk, and the only way we can do that is if you do what I asked."

Starry Knight's face turned ashen. She wobbled on her feet as she struggled to remain erect. She nodded. "Donna, put a sign on the door. Make it look pretty. Say we're closed until further notice because of a family emergency. The rest of you, go on home. You will all be paid double time for tonight and for every day we remain closed. Plus a bonus. Don't worry about this, I'll clean it up, but, Steve, please take the salmon back to the meat locker. Make sure all the lights in the dining room are off. But leave the light on over the door so customers can read the sign. Connor, disconnect the phone at the desk. Hurry, please."

It took a full forty minutes before the Daisy Wheel was

on full lockdown and the last car driven out of the parking lot.

Myra fingered her pearls as she watched Starry trying to pull herself together. Annie was making coffee and having a hard time of it with the massive machine.

Myra was relieved when she saw the color coming back to Starry's cheeks.

"How did you find out?" Starry whispered.

"Through your daughter. By the way, she looks just like you, Starry. She's a beautiful young woman. She's a lawyer and is married to a very rich man, a man who made it on his own, and who just happens to be the son of the Speaker of the House." Myra felt herself start to choke up at what she was seeing on Starry's face. She was the dying woman in the desert who had suddenly found all the water in the world in the person of her daughter.

"You actually know my daughter? You've seen her?"

"No, Starry, not personally, but my adopted daughter is a lawyer, and your daughter applied for a job with her firm. Annie, please show Starry a picture of her daughter."

Annie opened the manila envelope and drew out a picture of Amy Lambert. She handed it over to Starry, who started to cry and couldn't stop. "She does look like me. She really does. I've looked and looked for her, but no one would tell me who they had given her to. I begged and pleaded, but they wouldn't tell me. I've been searching for her all these years. Where is she? I have to see her. Please, you have to help me."

"Starry, we don't know where she is right now. You need to sit down. Annie, please get us all some coffee while I explain about Amy to . . . to her mother." Starry went limp and almost fell off the chair she was sitting on at Myra's words.

"Tell me," Starry whispered. Myra told her everything she knew.

"Now it's your turn. Tell us everything, then we'll tell you what our game plan is," Annie said as she patted Starry on the back.

"You have most of it. I was raped by four guys, camp counselors, from one of the education camps. They were drunk. Actually, there were five of them, but one just turned tail and ran, even when I pleaded with him to help me. It was a nightmare, something no woman should ever have to go through. When it was over, I was so battered and bruised, I had to roll down to the pond and soak. I stayed in the water for hours.

"It was almost dawn when I made my way to the house, where my mother was dying. She knew, even in her condition, that something bad had happened to me. I told her everything, how they jibber-jabbered among themselves, laughing and hooting and hollering. She told me to write it all down, because I kept repeating it to myself, over and over, during the attack. I thought it was some kind of code that college boys used among themselves. I still don't know what it means.

"My mother died the next day, and we buried her in our cemetery. Just a wooden cross to mark her grave. Mama left everything to me. I didn't care about Trinity or the money. Then I realized I was pregnant. I wanted to kill myself, so the elders watched over me day and night. When I delivered the baby, it was taken away immediately, and the birth was never mentioned again. I never knew what they did with her. All I knew was I had a baby girl. I didn't recover as quickly as the elders thought I should. I was weak, anemic. It took a good seven months before I felt anywhere near human. I stayed on at Trinity for another six months before I made the decision to leave. I told the others, and they fought me, but they couldn't stop me. There was a lawyer in town whom Mama used to handle my father's estate. Mama said my father was very rich, and we would never have to worry about money. I asked the lawyer for some money to start off my new life. I made him promise not to tell anyone where I was, and because he was a lawyer and ethical, he kept the promise. Anytime I needed money, he would send it to me in care of general delivery, wherever I was.

"I just bummed around, from menial job to menial job, until I started to work at a restaurant and found out how much I liked cooking. Sometime during the second or third year, the lawyer got in touch with me and said he had an offer on my property. The sum was so staggering, I said yes. I knew I would never ever go back there. I told him to give the others whatever they needed to live out their lives, and he did that. The rest was mine to do whatever I wanted."

"Believe it or not, we are pretty sure that the boys who raped you are the ones who bought your property, Starry."

Starry nodded. "That makes sense, I guess. Lock up the scene of the crime. Years later, when I felt I was ready, I bought this building and had it renovated for the Daisy Wheel. The rest you know.

"That's it all in a nutshell. I was never able to find the boys who raped me, never able to find my daughter. I just resigned myself to this way of life. By the way, this getup I'm wearing, that's not me these days."

With a flourish, Starry whipped off the long-haired wig and tossed it across the kitchen, the crown of flowers losing their petals in the process. Myra and Annie watched in amazement as Starry ripped at the white gown she was wearing over khaki slacks and an Izod T-shirt. "That outfit was just a gimmick, and since it worked, I stuck with it. I always hated it because it reminded me of that night. I guess, for some crazy reason, I was punishing myself.

"From what you said, I guess you know who those four college boys were?"

Myra and Annie nodded.

"Tell me."

"I think you know, Starry. You just don't want to believe it or bring it out in the open. It was the Chessmen and the Speaker of the House. I don't know which one ran off, only you would be able to identify him. I'm going to go out on a limb here and say that the jibber-jabber, as you put it, which they were hooting and hollering about in their drunkenness, was chess moves. Show me or write down what you remember," Myra said.

Starry got up and ran over to her little desk in the corner for a pencil and paper. She wrote down the letters and numbers just as she remembered them: "qg4+qg6" and "bf7 bxf3."

Annie's eyes narrowed as she stared down at what Starry had written "You were right, Myra, chess moves. We've got them! We've, honest to God, got those bastards."

"Now you lock up here. First, though, we have to decide what to do with all this prepped food. Then you are coming with us. Can you call some shelter to come and pick it all up . . . like now? We'll help you pack it up. I think you should give it all away for now, all the meat in the locker and all that stuff in those six refrigerators. Do you agree?"

Starry nodded.

"Tell me, why the name Starry Knight?" Annie asked.

"The sky that night had a million stars winking down on me. I used to like to lie in the water and stare up at them and dream all kinds of dreams. Knight because it happened at night. I just did not want to ever forget. It's that simple."

Annie and Myra nodded. It really was that simple.

Chapter 21

Myra Rutledge frantically paced up and down the courtyard at Pinewood as the others looked on. "I don't understand, at least one of us should have remembered that tomorrow is Halloween. How did this happen?"

Everyone started to talk at once to defend their memories. The responses ranged from "We were rather busy, Myra" to "I was never big on Halloween" and then "It's not like we were planning on having a costume party tomorrow night."

Charles saved the day and lightened Myra's mood when he said, "We'll be back here no later than midnight. I'll spend the entire day tomorrow making pumpkin pies, carving pumpkins, and cooking a delicious dinner for all of you. Just to be clear on all of this, look over there under the sycamore tree. Do you not see eight very large pumpkins? Young Dennis dropped them off yesterday. Now, can we do one more run-through here to make sure we're all on the same page?"

"We have all our paperwork right here," Abner said, waving a thick, bright blue accordion-pleated envelope, which looked like it must weigh at least fifty pounds. "In here, I have all four hundred twelve divorce files from the Chessmen's firm. We were unable to locate nine of the wives, but we are not giving up. We will find them or their children. The checks to the women are already made out. The moment we get to the track, I will sweep the money out of the husbands' accounts and into the account the checks are drawn on. No point in giving the gentlemen even a tiny edge. We are good in that respect.

"I also have in this envelope checks from the Chessmen's accounts. I took the liberty of ordering them and picked them up yesterday. I was amazed at how easy that was. And they have no clue. We agreed at last night's meeting to give each wife and her family five million dollars. We also agreed to give each of them another five million dollars from the Chessmen.

"Once we get the Chessmen to tell us what the verbal passwords to their accounts are, we do the checks, move the funds, and are in control of all that glorious money to do whatever we want with it. Husbands and lawyers will be reduced to paupers. That's my end of things."

Jack spoke up next. "The nine buses carrying the wives just hit the highway. To make it easier on everyone, I had them all meet at a central location. It was a little tight scheduling so many people, but the wives were so excited, they made it work. If we leave in the next ten minutes, we'll get there at least an hour before they do."

Avery Snowden spoke. "My people are already at the track. By now, they have incapacitated the six rent-a-cops who take care of the track when nothing is going on. They will have all five race cars lined up at the starting point, gassed up and ready to go. The trophy car, Rook's prized possession, Mario Andretti's winning vehicle, is front and center.

"If the Chessmen run true to form, they should arrive at the track thirty minutes from now. They always travel in one car. As far as I know, Josh King will not be there. We're still searching for him. He's gone to ground, which leads me to think the man knew this day would come at some point and planned for it. His house is empty, and none of his neighbors know anything. He probably left under the veil of darkness. Bradford Holiday will also be attending and will drive himself there. I'm leaving now. If you need me, or if anything changes, call me on my cell."

"Starry is traveling with Maggie, Ted, and Espinosa. The guys are going in Dennis's van. We girls are taking the *Post* van. All cell phones and the landlines are jammed. That means no calls in or out of the track compound. Ours will still work. The customers who were scheduled for this week were all notified that the weekend was canceled. Myra and Annie sent out refund checks, along with a small bonus to make up for their canceled weekend. They said there was no blowback, so we're good there. We will, of course, reimburse both Annie and Myra, since they paid for the refunds out of their own money. Did I leave anything out?" Nikki asked.

"I don't think so, dear. We should leave now, unless there are questions." When no one spoke, Myra made a motion to the waiting vehicles. "We'll see you in two hours."

The *Post* van was the last to leave Pinewood, with Kathryn, who had returned to join the group two days ago, driving.

"I have to say that I am enjoying this adrenaline rush," Annie said. "I can't wait to see the expression on those weasels' faces."

"The best part will be that they are being taken down by a bunch of women," Myra said, then giggled almost uncontrollably. The others turned to look at her and the expression on her face. Myra threw her hands in the air and laughed out loud. "I just love it when we come out on top. When do we get to dress up?"

Yoko started to laugh and couldn't stop. Isabelle had to pound her on the back. "The minute everything is in place.

And you were worried about Halloween, Myra," Alexis chastised. The girls broke into laughter as they settled back for the two-hour ride to the racetrack. During the ride, they talked of everything and nothing to relieve the tension, and then the conversation turned to Livinia and Amy.

"I so wish that young woman was with us. She was the catalyst, the reason we're here right now having this conversation," Annie said.

"Avery's people will find her. If not today, then soon. As for Livinia, the next time I see her, I'm going to give her a good piece of my mind," Myra said.

"I think we should just shoot her and be done with it," Annie said.

"I know that in your other life, you were either Annie Oakley or a gunslinger. You want to shoot her and spend the rest of your life in prison, go for it," Myra snapped as she fingered the pearls on her neck.

"Like I would really go to prison! Seriously, Myra."

"Ladies, ladies, ladies, enough already. There will be no shooting, and no one is going to prison, but if that should happen, not to worry. We'll spring you, Annie, right, girls!" Nikki laughed.

"In a New York minute," Alexis said.

"We're coming up to the mile marker. We'll be there in another fifteen minutes. If you guys stretch your necks, you'll be able to see a line of yellow buses behind us. Stay alert, everyone," Kathryn said.

While everyone was craning their necks to see the line of buses, the Chessmen and the Speaker were getting out of their car. Directly behind the Chessmen was Bradford Holiday, driving a Maybach and looking like a thundercloud. There were a hundred different places he'd rather be right now, but the ominous tone of his lawyers warned him to do as they asked. He hated the desolation. He also hated car racing, chess, and the survival camps that his lawyers doted on. He only had one true love, and it was money. He climbed out of the Maybach, straightened the jacket of his ten-thousand-dollar suit, jerked at his tie, and walked over to the four men waiting for him.

"This had better be good, gentlemen. Every minute I'm here, I'm losing money. What's going on?"

"I was just going to ask you the same question. What are you doing here? You aren't on the reservation list for this weekend," Maxwell Queen said sourly as he looked around for his security staff, which always welcomed guests and carried their bags to the clubhouse.

"What do you mean, what am I doing here? You invited me. Actually, the message demanded I be here, so here I am. One more time, what's going on?"

"I didn't invite you," Queen said. He looked at the others, all of whom shook their heads. "Then I guess it was Josh who must have taken matters into his own hands. Well, you're here now, so let's go inside."

"Where are the security guys?" Rook asked. Queen shrugged, and an uneasy feeling began to settle between his shoulders.

"Hey, check out the track! Who moved my cars? What the hell!" Rook took off at a dead run toward the track and his prize possessions, which no one ever touched but him.

He bit down on his lip before he turned around to stare at his colleagues. Then he noticed the silence and the absence of the staff. He felt the first prickle of fear on the back of his neck. "Someone . . . call the guards!" he bellowed.

"Seriously, Eli, this is your track. The staff members are *your* employees. You call them," Leo Bishop snorted.

"My phone's not working. See if yours is working, Maxwell. Leo, is yours working?"

Both men shook their heads.

"Holiday, check yours."

"No, no bars. Don't you have a landline inside?"

Rook was already sprinting toward the lodge. He fumbled with the key, opened the door, and ran to the office; the others were right behind him. He saw them all at once, a group of men standing in his office, watching him and the others.

·"We thought you'd never get here, boys. Welcome! Sorry we didn't have time to get balloons and all those welcome signs you always see at parties. Well, we're a hospitable group, and we're your hosts for the day," Jack said. "Sit! Oh, sorry about that—no chairs. That leaves the floor. Don't make me tell you twice."

"Who the hell are you? What do you want? Are you planning on stealing my cars, is that it?" Rook roared. "This is my lodge, so don't tell me to sit down!"

"I did ask him nicely. Harry?"

"You men should do what he says, or Harry will pull your brains out through your noses," Dennis trilled.

"What the hell!"

"You already said that," Harry said, marching over to the five men. "Do you know who I am?"

"Actually, I do know who you are," Leo Bishop said quietly. "Sit down, Eli. The rest of you do what he says. This guy is the number one martial arts expert in the world." He sat down.

"Well, I'm the biggest hedge-fund manager in the world," Holiday blustered.

"I really don't care," Harry said as he tweaked Eli Rook under the nose and eased him to the floor. "You want to be next, Mr. Hedge Fund guy?"

"I'm not without influence . . . you . . . kickboxing lunatic. I'll see that you lose your title."

Harry threw his hands in the air, then turned to Jack. "Tell me this dude isn't serious."

"What can I tell you, Harry? Some guys . . . they just don't get it. Take him out!"

The others watched as Harry did a dazzling spiral, his foot lashing out and striking the hedge-fund guru in the neck. Bradford Holiday crumpled to the floor.

"I think we have their attention now, Jack. Mr. Hedge Fund can get caught up when he wakes up. Or not," Harry said in a singsong voice.

Charles moved to the center of the crowded room. "I think it's time we told you why we're here and what we expect of you. We're here to ruin you the way you ruined the lives of four hundred twelve women. We brought you here to make it right. And, of course, to punish you for what you did to them. That's the first offense we are judging you on.

"The second offense is the rape of a young girl some twenty-seven years ago. Her name, which you probably never even knew, was Layla Pyne. Young Layla bore a child from that rape. The child was adopted by Bradford and Pamela Holiday and given the name Emily Holiday. Mrs. Holiday died the year her adopted daughter entered college. She died from an overdose of alcohol and pills. Young Emily was left to fend for herself—thanks to all of you because your client said she was adopted, and he was done with her. Well, she isn't done with him. When he wakes up, I expect you will tell him so. By the way, Emily Holiday changed her name to Amy and is now married to your son, Mr. Speaker. No, she is not now, nor was she ever, a gold digger. Any questions so far? Oh, my, when has a group of lawyers ever been rendered speechless?" Charles smiled.

The door opened, and Avery poked his head in. "Your guests are here and are in the bleachers, waiting for the show to begin."

"Who is that man? What show? What do you think you're pulling here?" Maxwell Queen roared.

Harry advanced a step and waved his index finger. "If this finger goes up your nose, your brain will be in your lap."

"I told you! I told you!" Dennis shouted as he danced from one foot to the other.

"All right, all right! What do you want?"

"What I want is the verbal code so I can liberate your money. My colleague sitting at the desk with the computer is ready to dial the number right now. There is no upside for any of you not to tell me. So let's get on with it, boys," Harry said.

"When pigs fly," Queen snarled, spittle flying in all directions.

Maggie inched her way over to the door and opened it. She motioned with her hand, and Starry Knight walked into the room. She was wearing her long-haired hippie wig, the crown of flowers, and her long-flowing white robe. She walked over and stood in front of the four men who had raped her so many long years ago. "All of them," she said quietly. "The one I begged to help me is not here."

"That's a goddamn lie," Maxwell Queen roared, and the others seconded his response.

Starry smiled. "Educated men like yourselves should know about DNA. These nice, kind, wonderful people will be taking a sample shortly. I would be remiss if I didn't thank you for buying my property. The money got me to this point in time where I can stand in front of you and accuse you all of raping me. I still remember what you four were hooting and hollering about. Chess moves. I remember each and every one of them. It's my turn now."

"The statute of limitations has passed. Even with DNA, it won't matter," Leo Bishop blustered. His partners backed him up.

"You're right. It doesn't matter. Your life, as you know

it, is now over. My daughter and I will live out our days spending and giving away all your money. I hope you all rot in hell for what you did to me." With that, she turned on her heel and went back through the doorway.

"You did good in there," Maggie whispered to Starry, who was removing the wig and gown. "Are you okay?"

"I am. I feel like I can suddenly breathe, like a thousand pounds has gone from my shoulders. I know they're getting off, and that's not okay, but I can live with it. I'll be okay. I'm going to go out to the bleachers and talk to all those women. I want to tell them all my story."

"I'll see you later, Starry," Maggie said as she opened the door and walked back into the room.

"Any progress?" she whispered to Ted. Ted shook his head.

"Listen up, everyone, the temperature is dropping outside, and our guests are going to get cold. The girls want to see you all. They said all but Abner and me are to go out to the bleachers."

The exodus was silent. The minute the door closed, four men were on their feet. Bradford Holiday was struggling to come fully awake. They eyed Maggie and Abner warily as they headed for the door, but it opened before they reached it. Maggie clapped her hands over her mouth, so she wouldn't laugh out loud. Abner did the same thing as seven black-clad figures entered the room. The only things to be seen were the whites of their eyes.

"Ninjas!" Maggie squealed at the top of her lungs. The group of seven offered up sweeping bows. The men backed up one step, then another, as they stared in horror at the black-clad figures advancing on them.

"I think they're the Vigilantes!" Abner shouted. "They're women! Look how they move, all graceful and . . . and . . ."

"*Lethal,*" Maggie said.

"Do something, Maxwell!" Leo Bishop shouted. "If

they are the Vigilantes, then our hours are numbered. That woman is right—those women are lethal."

"What the hell do you want me to do? There is no chess move for a situation like this."

"Boo hoo, too bad, too sad," Isabelle said behind her mask.

Kathryn strode forward to stand directly in front of the five men. "Listen up, you degenerates. This is the way it's going to go down. You saw Mr. Rook's racing cars out there on the track, right? Well, we're going to chain you to the back and race you down the track at a hundred miles an hour. Stark naked. Your skin will flay off the minute I step on the gas. Three minutes later, your racetrack will be full of bloody bits of flesh, and your brains will be flying all over. Six minutes later, it will be a boneyard out there. Now, that was a promise. If you don't want that to happen, give up the verbal codes. We'll do it one by one. We ask only once. The minute you refuse, you will be stripped down and led out to the track to an audience of four hundred three women who are taking bets as to how long you last. Now close your eyes and visualize what I just told you."

"You're not going to get away with this! You're lunatics. I know important people! I'll have you crucified. You'll spend the rest of your life in a federal prison," Holiday sneered.

Kathryn laughed. "I know important people, too, and they're all right here in this room. The part you are not getting is that you will never return to your lives, as you knew them. You will never again see your wives. The fact of the matter is, you will never leave this property on your own.

"Oops, that's not quite true, shame on me. If we drag your sorry asses down that track, and there's nothing left of your persons, the morticians will have to scoop up your remains in a bucket. That's the only way you leave here."

Nikki stepped forward. "We, the Vigilantes, pride ourselves on righting all wrongs that come to our attention. Now, having said that, in the interests of full disclosure, we need to inform you that we will be stealing, confiscating, appropriating all your money, then giving it away. We are going to make restitution to those you wronged.

"Unfortunately, there is no way we can make restitution for the rape all of you, but one, are guilty of. Nor can we make up for what Mr. Holiday did when he cut off his adopted daughter, the daughter one of you perverts foisted on the young girl you raped.

"What we can do, and will do, is spare your lives, but you will live the most miserable existence you can imagine for the rest of your days. You will wear rags, be barefoot, fight for morsels of food, and, in the end, probably kill each other. That's the bad news. The good news is you'll be alive, even though you will probably wish you were dead.

"You, Rook, you're first. March yourself up to my colleague, he's the one with the computer, and tell him what he wants to know. If you're fool enough that you can't see your way to doing that, head for the door, and you will be taken out to the track.

"Oh, even in this office, I can hear the sounds of those powerful engines. And I can hear those four hundred three women cheering for you. In case you aren't getting it, they are really looking forward to seeing you tied to the back of those race cars. Vengeance, gentlemen, is a dish best served up cold, and tonight is the coldest night so far this month. So what do you say?"

Sadly, there were no fools in the group.

The three Chessmen stepped forward, gave up their

codes, and watched as their money moved laser fast around the world, then came to a stop. Abner looked around, his eyes glassy at what he'd just done. He took a deep breath and let it out slowly. Philonious was going to be so proud of him. Then he laughed; twice he could feel the big man's fingerprint while the blizzards of numbers moved around the world. He continued to laugh; that's what friends were for.

"Shoot, I was hoping to drive one of those babies out there," Kathryn grumbled.

"What's stopping you? Go for it!" Maggie laughed.

"Someone should call Avery. Our job here is done," Nikki said.

"Don't you just love it when things work out according to plan, Annie? And the cherry on the cake is you didn't have to shoot anyone."

"I'm going to really love it when we start to give all that money away, and when Starry gets to meet her daughter for the first time."

Outside, in the brisk October air, the sisters stood in a straight line and waved toward the bleachers, where Abner was handing out his second set of checks. The women were crying and shouting and shaking their fists. All from happiness.

Out of the corner of her eye, Myra saw Starry Knight run across the track as Avery was leading the Chessmen, the Speaker, and Bradford Holiday toward an eighteen-wheeler. She shouted to him to wait.

"Oh, God, what is she going to do?" Annie whispered.

"I have no idea," Myra whispered in return. "She's saying something. I wish I could read lips at this distance."

"Well, I can. I know exactly what she's saying."

"What?"

"Checkmate, boys!"

Epilogue

"It's going to be strange tomorrow not to have Thanksgiving here at the farm," Myra said as she looked around at the others, who appeared to feel like she did.

"Tell me again how this happened. We've always had Thanksgiving here. Each of us had our little jobs, which Charles assigned us. I'm going to miss peeling the potatoes," Nikki grumbled.

"I'd like to know whose idea this was, anyway. No one even asked us if we were okay with going to the Daisy Wheel for Thanksgiving dinner. Charles just said we're going. *Period.* I have a good mind not to show up," the ever-verbal Kathryn said angrily.

"If it will help even a little, Charles and Fergus are there at the Daisy Wheel right now, helping Starry prepare our dinner, so both he and Fergus will be hands-on. I don't know why I say this, but I think the two of them are up to something. I'm hoping it's a surprise of some kind that will make us all happy. Charles is very good at surprises, as you all know.

"Let's just look at dinner at the Daisy Wheel as almost the same thing in a different location. Starry wanted to do this as a way to thank all of us for helping her. We all need to remember that. Besides, there was just no way I could say no," Myra insisted.

"We know, we know," Maggie said. "It's just that . . . it's supposed to be here, just like Christmas is supposed to be here. It won't be the same is what we're all trying to say."

"It will be whatever we make it. Thanksgiving is about being together to give thanks. The place shouldn't matter," Annie said. "So now, let's move on."

"Hard to believe almost a whole month has gone by since we ended our last mission. Aside from parceling out the rest of the Chessmen's and Holiday's monies, we can put this one to bed," Nikki said.

"Yesterday, Lizzie sent me, by overnight mail, the closing papers on Starry's old property in the Adirondacks. She said when she approached Bradford Holiday's investment group about buying it, they jumped at the chance to unload it. So she bought it, using the Chessmen's monies, for five million. The group took a hit of forty-five million. Soon after they bought the property, but too late to do anything about it, they realized that it could never be developed because of the cemetery. That was quite a coup, if you ask my opinion," Jack said. "It reminded me of something I read a little while ago. Seems this Ponzi scheme swindler used a portion of his ill-gotten gains to buy property in the Adirondacks. But when he went to develop it, they found a pair of nesting bald eagles. And that was the end of that."

"Are we really giving the property back to Starry?" Ted asked.

"Yes. Lizzie said it was the right thing to do. Got all the paperwork, along with the deed, right here, and Lizzie even put a red ribbon on it. We're to give it to Starry tomorrow, after dinner. I think she's right," Jack said. The others nodded in agreement.

Myra fingered the pearls adorning her neck. "For some

reason, I expected more blowback after we closed the mission. There was barely a ripple. The media didn't run with it for days and weeks. Like I said, hardly a ripple. They barely devoted a day to the Speaker of the House's resignation, saying good old Buzz was going to try to woo his wife back because he realized he didn't want a divorce, and taking a run for 1600 Pennsylvania Avenue wasn't worth losing his family. A day, that's it. The six o'clock news, then the eleven o'clock news. The twenty-four-hour cable stations mentioned it at the top of the hour, and then the next day, they were on to something else."

Annie laughed out loud. "I did like the coverage they gave the demise of the Chessmen's law firm—Queen, King, Bishop, and Rook. One mention was all I saw, and it simply said the prestigious law firm was emptied out overnight, and a sign was on the door saying they were closed. Of course, there was an uproar from the associates and staff, but it fizzled out within hours. Before you can ask, I do not know what happened to the files or the furnishings or the clients."

"No one was interviewed, not even the clients. No one asked where the Chessmen went. I rather thought the media would run with foul play or something, but they didn't," Maggie tossed in, a bemused expression on her face.

"I think, and this is just a guess on my part, but I suspect that, as a whole, the District was really glad to see them go," Ted said, a big grin on his face. "I suspect that a lot of attorneys are breathing a sigh of relief knowing that they will never again have to go up against the Chessmen."

"While we are on the subject, Lizzie has the Chessmen's power of attorney and is seeking buyers for the racetrack, the race cars, the chess club, and that wilderness outfit. Those monies will go to Mrs. Queen, Mrs. King, and Mrs. Rook. They've been mum on the subject of their husbands, giving out no interviews.

"I can't be sure of this, but I think Avery paid them each a visit and clued them in about what their husbands have been doing all these years. I also think they've all moved on. And, no, there has been no word on Josh King or his wife. Avery said it's better to just let that be," Annie said.

"So we're all good here then?" Yoko asked.

"We are better than good. Charles told me when we meet up next week, he will have a complete file on all the monies. Abner is helping him. People, we deserve to pat ourselves on the back. All that money is going to be put to such good use. I don't think we missed even one charity.

"Lives will be richer and more rewarding, not only for people but for the animals cared for by all the animal-welfare organizations we are helping. We've added two new ones—Wings of Rescue, where these pilots who have old planes fly animals from shelters to other states, where they find what they call Forever Homes. We're buying them new planes and helping in any way we can. And we also added another new organization called Have a Heart, where they volunteer spay and neuter. We bought them several mobile traveling vans. It will all be in Charles's report next week," Nikki said happily.

"What ever happened to Livinia Lambert?" Alexis asked.

Nikki shrugged. "She's called the office many times. I did not return her calls."

"And Amy?" Myra asked.

Nikki shrugged again. "She went to ground. Her husband is saying nothing. I called him over a dozen times, and he does talk to me, but he says nothing. Avery and his people are trying to find Amy. How wonderful it would be if she showed up for dinner tomorrow. But I guess that's too much to hope for, or else it goes under the heading of miracles, because it isn't going to happen. It will at some point.

"And on that note, I think Jack and I are going to call it

a night. It's been a very long day. We'll see you all at the Daisy Wheel, tomorrow at three."

The good-byes were short and quick, after which they all headed out to their cars; then it was just Myra and Annie in the quiet kitchen.

"Want some tea, Annie?"

"I-do-not-want-tea! What I want is a triple shot of Kentucky's finest. Will you join me, Myra?"

"Yes," Myra said smartly. "Hold the ice!"

"You rock, Myra. You really do!"

The Daisy Wheel was alive with laughter, talk, and smells that, as Dennis said, were out of this world. The tables were decorated with autumn leaves and mini pumpkins in honor of the holiday. The blinds were closed on the plate-glass windows and door. A sign in colorful script read, CLOSED UNTIL FURTHER NOTICE.

"Any more news, Avery, on Amy?" Annie asked.

"We're following up on a substantial lead that just came in, but that's about all we have. Sooner or later, we're pretty sure, she'll head to her husband, since we are assuming that the divorce was a ruse to help her worm her way into Nikki's law firm. We're watching him around the clock, and since Livinia returned home, her too. We're also hacking their phones. Just be patient. I haven't failed you yet, have I?"

Annie smiled, and not because she believed the old spy implicitly. She wasn't exactly sure why, but something about the way he said what he did made her think that he had a trick up his sleeve. "We were all hoping for a big reunion for Starry today of all days. We're a patient group, as you well know."

As a whole, the group hooted their opinions. Everyone knew Annie didn't have a patient bone in her body, nor did they themselves.

"What is so funny?" Starry said as she entered the dining room. She was untying her apron, and had a scowl on her face.

"What's wrong, Starry?" Myra asked gently.

Starry tried for a smile, but failed. "For starters, those two pretend cooks in the kitchen banished me. They said they would finish up. Charles said there was no way I could carry the platter with that big bird without dropping it. He said that was a man's job! Ha! And that other one, the guy with the Scottish brogue, he kicked me out of my own kitchen. What's worse, I'm out here! Now I'm not even hungry.

"I'm sorry. I didn't mean to . . . It's just that . . ." Starry's eyes filled with tears. "I hoped . . . wished . . . wanted today to be perfect. And it is for all of you, and I'm happy that I could make that happen for you guys. It's just that nothing has gone my way since that . . . that awful time so long ago. When you all swooped in like avenging angels, I thought all my prayers would finally be answered. My knees have calluses on them from kneeling and praying for what I call my own personal miracle."

Starry burst into tears and sobbed so loud and hard, the women all ran to her. They cooed and whispered all the words that women from the beginning of time knew to give comfort and solace. The men simply stared, their eyes moist at what they were seeing, knowing instinctively that if it was possible to make this all right, the sisters were the ones to do it.

A bell tinkled from somewhere in the kitchen. They all stopped talking when Charles poked his head out the doorway and instructed everyone to take their seats so they could get the full effect of the magnificent turkey that Starry had spent all day cooking. "Drumroll, please, people!"

"We don't have a drum, Charles!" Dennis said.

"Okay, everyone clap and whistle." The gang obliged until Charles called a halt.

"It is now officially Thanksgiving, and here comes the bird!"

Charles held one side of the swinging doors, Fergus the other side, to allow a young woman dressed in a long white robe, with a crown of flowers, wheel the turkey into the room and push it to the head of the table, where Starry was sitting.

The silence in the room was so deafening, so thunderous, it was as though the heavens above had opened their golden doors to reveal the pearly gates.

"Mama, I'm Amy. Can I please, please, sit on your lap? All my life, all I ever wanted was a mother to hold me close and tell me everything will be all right. Will you do that? Will you say that?"

Starry Knight held out her arms, and Amy slid into them. As Yoko said later, it was a perfect fit.

"Oh, myyyyyyy God!" Annie whispered.

Myra and the others reached for the napkins at their plates to stem the flow of tears, with Dennis West crying the hardest.

"I think we need another chair," Jack said, breaking the moment as he hurried to the far end of the dining room to fetch it.

"How did you do that?" Nikki hissed to Avery.

"I just found her and told her what she needed to know. The rest was Amy's idea. I don't think I've ever seen two happier people in my life."

"All right, people, it's time to partake of this wondrous meal. Who wants to say grace?"

"I will," Dennis said.

Every head in the room bowed. The words were soft, gentle, and full of meaning.

Ted wheeled the serving cart to where Charles was seated and handed him the carving knife and fork. Charles bowed, waved his tools in the air, then proceeded to slice into the huge, golden bird. He was rewarded with shouts of pleasure, but once again held up his carving tools.

"Don't tell me you're going to give us a speech, dear. We're starving here," Myra said.

"Not really. I just want to thank you all for coming. I want it said right now that while Fergus and I helped, it was Starry who prepared this magnificent dinner. I am now ready to carve, and then we are going to devour this succulent bird. One other thing—we have already prepared trays for all the dogs, and they can be picked up on your way out."

An hour later, the only thing to be heard were groans and happy sighs as belt buckles were loosened all around the table.

"The best part of all this is that Starry has people coming in to clean up. We can just take our doggie bags and our leftovers and leave. How cool is that, boys and girls?" Charles twinkled.

"I don't have a dog, Charles, and I don't see any turkey left on that carcass, either. I was hoping to have another Thanksgiving dinner tomorrow. I love stuffing and gravy, and it's all gone," Dennis grumbled.

"That's true, but Starry, Fergus, and I anticipated this might happen, so we roasted another bird with all the trimmings. Your leftovers-to-go bag has your name on it in the kitchen. Trust me when I say you will be eating turkey throughout the weekend."

Dennis beamed. "Well, okay, then."

Dessert was served. Pumpkin pie, pecan pie, and, of course, apple pie with homemade ice cream on top. Coffee flowed by the gallon. More groans of pleasure were heard as belt buckles were loosened still another notch.

"A champagne toast to all of you," Starry said, standing up, her brand-new daughter at her side. She tapped her wineglass with a spoon. "I want to thank you all for coming today. I don't have the words to tell you how much I appreciate all you've done for me and my daughter, whom I have just met and plan to never let go. Although I will consent to share her with her husband, if that is her choice. I want you all to know that, and if and when I ever open up the Daisy Wheel again, you all have carte blanche. So here's a toast to the people who right wrongs. All of you!"

The toast made, Myra looked at Starry, and said, "*If* and *when* you open back up is what you said. Are you thinking of *not* reopening the Daisy Wheel?"

Starry looked up and down the long table at all her new friends. "I don't know. There's something I have to do. I suppose it will depend on how long it takes me. I guess my answer is perhaps."

"Can we help?" Nikki asked as she fished for whatever it was Starry had to do.

Starry laughed. "What I have to do is quite different from what all of you do in your war against evildoers. Tomorrow I am driving up to the Adirondacks. I am going to clear more than twenty years of forest from Trinity's cemetery. The people who bought the property can't develop it because of the cemetery. I don't think anyone knew that, least of all me. Once I left, I never had the courage to go back there. I need to do that now. It doesn't matter that strangers own the property. I doubt they'll mind if I clean up the cemetery, and if they do mind, then I'll hire a lawyer to deal with them. Amy is going to help with the cemetery."

"Well, hold on just a minute now," Annie said as she rummaged in her carryall under the table. "This is for you, Starry. We bought the property back from the investment group. A friend of ours out in Nevada handled the purchase. It's all yours again, so you can do whatever you want with it. Speaking strictly for myself, I'd be honored to go with you tomorrow and help clear the grave sites. Truly, I would, Starry."

And then everyone was on their feet volunteering their help as Starry sobbed with joy into a wadded-up napkin, her daughter's arms around her shoulders.

"Drive? I think we should fly! I can have the Welmed plane ready at noon tomorrow. What about tools? I can get those in the morning and have everything loaded on the plane, and we even get to take our leftovers with us," Dennis said, excitement ringing in his voice.

Harry clapped Dennis on the back. "Then, kid, that's exactly what we'll do."

"I think we should think of this as a sort of back-door mission," Annie said.

"That works for me, Annie," Myra said.

"It works for all of us!" Charles said.

"More pie, anyone?" Fergus chirped.

He had no takers.